About the author

Born in Essex in 1947, Denise has lived in north
Yorkshire and Leicestershire.
She is a mother to two daughters, but unfortunately
her third child, James, died at the tender age of
seven in 1988.
Denise remarried and is now living happily in
Cumbria with her husband Alistair.

Dedicated to Alistair for his love and support

Also to my wonderful daughters Nicola and Natalie

And in memory of my beautiful son James

Denise J. Grey

PROTECTED MODE: OFF

AUSTIN MACAULEY
PUBLISHERS LTD.

A CIP catalogue record for this title is available from the British Library.

ISBN 9781786126597 (Paperback)
ISBN 9781786126603 (Hardback)
ISBN 9781786126610 (eBook)

www.austinmacauley.com

First Published (2016)
Austin Macauley Publishers Ltd.
25 Canada Square
Canary Wharf
London
E14 5LQ

Chapter One

Planet Earth – 2999 AD. Red hot boulders rain down on the toughened glass. Everyone is looking up at the continuous onslaught. The noise is deafening. They wait to see whether it will be the next one that breaches their sanctuary. The one that heralds their death.

In the heart of the building a group of men and women dressed in white protective suits are watching nervously at five young teenagers in the adjoining room. They too can hear the attack of nature on their haven. However, the adults know that they have to stay focused, they must concentrate on the teenagers in front of them. The three boys and two girls are looking back at them. They were quite calm. Now they are getting restless.

I see the adults watching us. I turned to Adam, 'What's happening. Why the delay?'

'I don't know, Rose. Let's hold hands.'

'I'm frightened, Adam.'

'Everything will be fine. The Elders know what they are doing.'

It seems, however, that some of the Elders have doubts.

'Are we doing the right thing?'

'It's the only thing we can do.'

'But they're our children.'

'Which is precisely why it has to be them. Because they are our children they know the consequences of ignoring the inevitable. If we have any chance at all of succeeding in this mission we have to act now.'

'I'm frightened for them.'

'And you think we are not. We have to be realistic. In a few years we could all be dead and what is the legacy we have left them? If we want to give them a sound future to build on we cannot afford to wait any longer.'

'Why are you sending girls as well? Won't it be dangerous?'

'The girls will act as a calming influence on the boys, and, we hope, against any adversaries.'

'How do you know they will be safe?'

'We cannot give any guarantees. We do know, however, what will happen to them if they stay here. We are giving them the chance of a long life. They are wearing suitable clothes to blend in with others of their age. We have taught them how to survive in the strange environment that they will find themselves. We can do no more.'

'They are still young, fourteen and fifteen is no age to face such challenges and such responsibilities. Have they been told of their mission?'

'Yes, they have been told.'

'May God guide our disciples and keep them safe.'

At the departure point we are quietly waiting for our journey to begin, we are nervous but also excited. We know how important this mission is and we are determined to succeed. From now on we stand alone. The adults are behind screens, some silently praying, others with fingers crossed. All have tears in their eyes as they watch.

The moment has come, the senior Elder crosses over to the controls. In front of him is an array of knobs, buttons and switches. It is all very old-fashioned but they have to make do with the materials they have found. He pushes a series of buttons, slowly turns knobs and then finally flicks a big switch. There is silence and everyone holds their breath. Suddenly a flash of lightening blinds them. A strong wind builds to a crescendo, twisting and pulling at clothes, rattling every loose object and then just as suddenly subsides.

When they open their eyes the children have gone.

Chapter Two

Planet Earth – 2000AD. The large fireplace in the pub is empty of its usual roaring fire. It is spring and the grate is adorned with a selection of pine cones. However, the elements are about to give a reminder that there is no guarantee of warmer weather to come.

An old-fashioned hand-plough is mounted above the mantle, in memory of days gone by. The bar is decorated with scores of highly polished brasses of every shape and size. The tall stools around the bar are occupied by casually dressed men laughing and joking. They are intent in washing away a hard day's work with their pints of ale.

Sitting around the fireplace are three men with faces ruddier than any fire glow. They wear a type of uniform, baggy trousers, checked shirts, caps perched on their heads and whiskers sprouting everywhere. Each man has his own tankard. They would not dream of drinking their ale from a glass. Even a townie will recognize them as men of the soil. Farmers for generations and proud of it.

'Well what do you make of them, Alf?'

'They're definitely strange, but I can't fault their work. Work like dogs they do, for ten hours solid, six days a week, and all they ask is for £15 and a bit of food.' Alf takes a swig from his tankard, wipes his mouth on his sleeve and then continues, 'The lass helps Martha, she'll do the washing, feed the hens and muck out the pigs. Always

4

willing to learn, she's even asked Martha to teach her some cooking.'

'Aye, can't argue with that, but they are weird. It's a good job they learn quick cos they don't seem to know even the basics, but once told, they're off, working like good'uns and not a mistake anywhere.'

'You know they're living in that run down cottage by the beck. I've counted five of them altogether. Must be a mess in there. It's been empty for as long as I can remember.'

Harry, the oldest of the group shakes his head, 'Well I have to tell you two, I've been down there, took them some fresh eggs. They kindly invited me in for a cuppa, and I was dumbstruck.' Harry pauses for effect, 'Well, it's as clean as a new pin, it is. I'm telling you.'

Alf and Bert shake their heads in disbelief.

One of the men standing at the bar must have overheard some of the conversation and he approaches the farmers.

'Are you talking about the outsiders?'

'Aye, we are. Why do you know something?'

'I know they are good workers, students I think, came here to work through the summer. We have two of them at the hotel down the road, cleaning and general dog's body work.'

'Students, aye that will account for their strangeness. But why do they all look the same. Pale skin and pudding basin haircuts, and dressed the same. Even the girls.'

Alf joins in, 'So let me get this right. There's five of them, it seems three boys and two girls. I've got one boy and a girl. What about you?' he asks looking at the hotel worker.

'We've got one boy and a girl too.'

'So where is the other one then?' Bert questions as he lifts his hat and scratches his head.

The bar man shouts over from the counter, 'I can tell you that. I see him walking to town every day, real early and then walking back, real late.'

Chapter Three

We huddle around a wood fire which is making weird shadows that dance on the walls and ceiling.

The cottage is our protection from this unknown world and between us we have made it as comfortable as possible. Learning new skills enables us to improve on our living conditions, but life is hard and we now realize how pampered we had been in our world.

'It is so cold here, how can people live like this?' I ask Adam.

'They know no better, Rose, it seems they're waiting for summer. It is supposed to be warm. That's when all the trees and flowers blossom and the birds sing.'

'What, outside! I can't imagine that. Don't they have domes to protect them?'

'You must forget all that, Rose, this is our life now, we must adjust and quickly, we have been sent here to do something very important and that is our top priority.'

As I look at Adam, there are tears in my eyes, but I'm not going to let them think that I am the weakest just because I am the youngest. I shrug my shoulders.

Adam then looks around at all of us, he is the oldest of the group and we automatically turn to him for guidance. What we do not realize is that he is as scared as us.

We had arrived nearly four months previously, in the middle of winter; our introduction to this strange life has been hard but in that time four of us have found work. The type of work that is teaching us about the people and their lives. Daniel's job is to travel to a nearby town, he spends his days going through archives and integrating with people of our own age. Our high intelligence enables us to absorb information at an incredible rate; each day is bringing us hopefully closer to starting our mission.

Daisy came in from the kitchen carrying a tray of steaming mugs.

We have developed a liking for hot chocolate, not only does it taste good but it helps us sleep.

'Time for bed, everyone,' she said as she hands out the drinks 'we all have early starts in the morning.'

Daisy has become a mother figure, and just like Adam who suddenly found himself in a position of authority, it was not her choice to be a matriarch.

'Nine o'clock is a bit early,' moans Daniel, 'I bet the kids in town don't go to bed until much later.'

Adam looks at Daniel and sees that he is changing; he is definitely becoming more independent in his attitude. 'You're getting to be too much like them, Daniel, but you must remember that their intelligence is not as finely tuned as ours, so they won't need to charge up as much as we do.'

'I suppose,' replies Daniel as he turns to go to his room.

Mark is just a bit younger than Adam, but he takes everything very seriously he is concerned about how each of us are losing our original identities. He turns to Adam, 'Do you think it's a good idea to continue letting Daniel go into town, he seems to be easily led into disruptive ways.'

'I don't see it as a problem,' Adam answers, 'in fact it is a bonus, as it makes us seem more credible.'

It is time for us to all take to our bed. I find I cannot sleep. I am remembering how we arrived in this strange world. It coincided with the turn of the millennium. Hundreds of people all over the world were enjoying massive firework displays to welcome in the year 2000, but in a small place in England there was a different kind of display. After a couple of blinding flashes we five materialized from thin air. We had rubbed our eyes and tried to make sense of the blackness that enveloped us.

We were surrounded by trees and in the distant skies we had seen multi-coloured flashes and heard thunderous bangs. It had been very frightening but we controlled our fear. Our first priority had been to find shelter.

Without a word we had proceeded in single file out of the trees and across a field, five young adults with hoods over our heads. Silhouetted against the lightened sky we must have resembled a line of praying monks. Finally we arrived at our destination, a run-down cottage standing next to a beck. The Elders had sourced this cottage from ancient maps and had tried to coordinate our arrival point as close as possible.

The cottage was very basic but it was dry and with a little bit of work it soon became an ideal base. It had been a mild winter but we were still pleased to see an open grate where we could build a log fire to keep ourselves warm, cook food and dry our washing.

The skills that we had been taught are now proving a life saver, but at the time we thought we would never have to use such basic methods to survive. We were used to a more simple way of living; everything we ate, wore and generally needed was available at a touch of a button.

Our intense training had included a history of the people we were to join. We had to learn how to catch our own food and prepare it for eating, and what plants and fruits are safe to eat. We also had to blend in with everyone around us and try to find employment. Our main aim was to absorb as much knowledge as possible, without drawing too much attention to ourselves. Then we could find the right path to accomplish our task.

We were lucky to find casual work, people thought we were students and accepted us without much trouble. Adam and I were made welcome at a local farm and Mark and Daisy found work at a nearby hotel. We were willing to work long hours and for little pay. Daniel went into the town every day to access information.

The weather, however, is our biggest problem, in our world we were protected from the ravages of unpredictable weather patterns by the huge glass domes. Now we have no such protection.

In the last few months we had sheltered from gale force winds that had torn giant trees from the ground. We watched as the small beck near our cottage turned into a raging torrent being fed by unrelenting rain. It had continued for days, then weeks.

It is now the beginning of April and the air is getting very cold, people tell us that it is spring and soon the flowers will be opening to greet the arrival of summer. However, we sense that summer this year may take a bit longer to appear.

The next morning we wake up to a dazzling light. I rush to the window and I am amazed to see that absolutely everything is white.

'Where have all the colours gone?' I ask as I frantically try to scrape off the thick ice from the glass. 'And what's all this on the window, I can't see out properly.' Then I see a long icicle forming down from the broken gutter outside. 'What's that, it looks like glass?'

Adam puts his arm around me. 'So many questions, Rose, I'm at a loss as to which one I should answer first.'

We all tuck into a breakfast of oats and hot milk to insulate ourselves against the bitter cold. The farmers give us surplus food and the local pensioners have taken to knitting us warm clothes. Everyone is so kind. The people in the village cannot understand where we come from or why we suddenly appeared among their small community. They did know that we are dependable, hard-working and we always show complete respect and kindness to everyone we meet. That is good enough for the villagers, so everyone, without exception, watches out for us.

Although it has stopped snowing Daniel decides not to attempt the long slog into town, he plans to join Adam and I on the farm. He says that he can be more help to Alf and his wife today.

When three of us arrive at 7am, Alf is overwhelmed with our foresight, if ever he needed extra hands now is the time. I stay to help Martha with the cooking and cleaning while Adam and Daniel are assigned tasks all over the farm. There is so much to be done but the most urgent is to search for buried lambs and sheep.

It takes most of the morning to locate animals in distress; it is traumatic for Daniel when he uncovers his first dead lamb, only a few days ago the poor thing was among hundreds that he had stopped to watch as they jumped and chased each other through the fields.

Alf's sheep dogs herd the sheep and lambs across the fields, all the animals are finding it difficult as the snow is so deep, some fall into drifts but the boys and the farmer are forever vigilant and rush to rescue the casualties. The dead sheep and lambs are put in the corner of the field to be collected later. The lambs that are injured are carried on the back of a sledge pulled by Adam. It is bitterly cold and the knitted scarves and hats are a welcome insulation to their outdoor clothes.

The exhausted procession arrives back at the farm at midday, the injured and very young lambs are put in the barn. The rest are put in a small field close to the house where they can be watched.

Adam is amazed by the old man's stamina; Alf must be at least sixty but works like a twenty-year-old. In our world Alf would have been in the retired homes and waited on hand and foot, until his eventual demise.

Martha and I stand at the door of the farmhouse with steaming cups of Oxo.

'Dinner will be ready in half an hour.' Martha says in a way that means it is not a suggestion but an order. She knows how important it is to feed the workers, especially in this type of weather, Martha also knows that they will be straining at the bit to get out and do more before it gets too dark. There is a great deal to do and it is her duty to serve a good meal as quickly as possible so that they can eat and go back to work as fast as they can.

We all sit round the large wooden table and silently eat the steaming food in front of us. We are thinking about the work that still has to be done before nightfall. Adam and Daniel are feeling the drain on their bodies, they are still not used to battling against the elements, and the ferocity they are facing today frightens them. Being fit and able to cope with any task is no match to the driving wind and freezing snow. They find themselves fighting to keep up with the old man. He is becoming a hero to them.

As soon as Alf stands up and drags his coat off the back of his chair the boys are by his side. He smiles; he can see the weariness in their eyes.

'Come on then, my little disciples, let's get back to it and sort out those poor animals. They deserve a dry warm bed tonight and so will we by the time this day is done.'

Martha and I watch as the strange group trudge back into the fields. We start clearing up after the meal.

Meanwhile out in the fields the snow starts to fall again, at first it is just flurries tossed around in the strengthening wind, but it increases until it shortens their vision to a matter of yards. Their clothes are caked with snow, their eyelashes heavy with it. Daniel feels tears gather in his eyes, his hands are pulsating with pain, he is frightened his tears will freeze to his face. They work long and hard to save as many animals as they can before the night creeps across the fields.

Alf calls to them, 'That's it now; we can do no more tonight. God help any we have missed.' He whistles for his dogs to follow. Daniel breathes a sigh of relief. He is exhausted.

'Hey, wait a minute, where's Sam, he was here a minute ago?' Alf whistles again but the dog still does not appear. 'I can't go without Sam, he'll die out here. You go ahead I'll catch you up.'

The boys plough on through the driving snow with the other two dogs by their side, but Adam turns back, he knows it will be dangerous for the old man on his own.

'You go on, Daniel, I am going to help Alf. We will catch you up.'

Adam went back to Alf.

'Where did you last see Sam?'

'On top of that ridge, Adam, he was sniffing around as if he had caught the scent of a rabbit.'

Adam climbs the ridge but all he can see is a blanket of snow stretching endlessly in front of him. The wind is whistling through the trees but then he hears another noise, a yelp and then a whine.

'Up here, Alf, I'm sure I heard something.'

Alf scrambles up to join Adam. 'How can you hear anything over this wind?' Then he hears it too. 'You're right, lad, Sam must be down there somewhere. Now watch your step there's ditches down there full of frozen water.

Adam slowly descends the other side of the ridge, sinking up to his thighs in the frozen grasp of the snow. He cannot see anything, and then to his right he hears a weak whimper, Adam moves in that direction.

'Careful, lad,' Alf calls out to him, 'there's a ditch there.'

Too late, Adam's foot sinks quickly into the water, breaking the ice that camouflages the danger; he falls flat into the freezing water. The shock stuns him but the survival instinct kicks in; he turns and somehow manages to flail his way to firmer ground. He lies still with his eyes closed, when he opens them again Alf is standing beside him.

'Come on, you mustn't lie there you'll freeze solid, get up and move yourself. Keep the blood flowing.' Alf tugs at him until Adam gets up.

They both hear the whimper again; they turn and see Sam trying to drag a lamb out of the ditch.

'They must have frozen solid in there and when you fell in you broke the ice around them. It's a miracle they are alive.'

Adam and Alf pull the animals free of the ditch, Alf picks up his dog and Adam carries the lamb. They hope that what body heat is left will radiate between animal and human to help them all overcome the biting cold.

It takes half an hour to get back to the farmhouse, but it felt like hours, it is amazing the strength found in sheer determination.

Martha sits them by the blazing fire and gives them a tot of brandy to start warming them from the inside. Daniel and I take the dog and lamb to rub their coats until the wetness has disappeared and the blood is running through their bodies again.

'Alf, you and your animals will be the death of me, just look at the state of you both.'

'Never felt better, Martha, stop fussing. Adam, you go and have a hot bath, you can find a change of clothes in the wardrobe.'

An hour later Adam, Daniel and I leave the warmth of the farmhouse to trudge home to Daisy and Mark. It is hard going battling against the driving snow and sinking into drifts piled up in the road but finally we reach our destination.

'Where have you been?' Daisy demands, 'We have been really worried about you. Mark and I have been home for ages, the hotel let us go early and gave us some of the food from the kitchen to heat up.'

'That sounds great, just what we need after the day we have just had. Let us warm up a bit, and then after we've eaten we shall tell you all about it,' Adam says as he heads towards the open fire.

Later, when we are pleasantly full with hot food in our stomachs and sitting around a blazing fire, Adam relays the trials they had faced helping Alf on the farm.

'I really don't know how they survive in these conditions. We must seem really weak to them,' exclaims Mark.

The next few weeks bring sunshine and a welcome thaw; spring has at last arrived with summer following in its footsteps. We enjoy being out in the warm weather, watching the lambs and calves play in the green fields. Daisy and I pick beautifully perfumed flowers for our table, it is all so new to us. To actually be able to touch nature, in our world everything is immortalized in museums or on visual records. The freedom to enjoy such wonders almost makes us forget why we were sent here.

In other parts of Britain people are suffering from extreme flooding, earth tremors and in some places stifling heat waves. The weather patterns are in chaos; some people are blaming the greenhouse effect. They turn to the government to do something about the excess CO_2 that is being released into the atmosphere by unconcerned industries and careless monitoring. Others are saying that it is just the natural cycle of the Earth's development. It has changed dramatically many times in its millions of years of evolution and this is just another development.

However, we already know that it is a combination of natural progression and man's carelessness that has started this cycle of events. Neither of them on their own will have caused much damage, but together they are a lethal concoction. There is still time to limit the effects and this is our mission. We have been sent from the future to try to educate the people of the 21st century and to reveal the devastation that awaits them if they continue to ignore the signs.

Adam is sitting outside our cottage looking up at the cloudless blue sky, he can feel the warmth of the sun on his face and he finds it hard to believe that this will not continue for ever. Unfortunately he knows different. He watches us playing around in the beck and laying on the sweet smelling, soft grass. The birds in the trees are serenading us, while the bees buzz in and out of brightly coloured flowers.

'I know this is Sunday, our day of rest,' Adam shouts over to us, 'but we have to start our mission. We have all gathered information, made contacts, it is time to spread our message and offer our knowledge. It is our duty to try to prevent the holocaust that awaits these people.'

We all stop what we are doing and look at Adam.

'But, Adam, it's our day off and it so lovely here,' I whine. The others all mutter their agreement.

'Don't you understand, that is precisely why we have to do something now? Have you all forgotten what it was like in our world? We were confined in a glass cage watching the floods, storms and ravaging winds destroying what was left of the beauty that we can see now.'

We know Adam is right. We reluctantly return to the cottage and each one of us proceeds to write down information we will gather from our respective sources.

Adam and I ask Alf and Martha how the changes in weather patterns are affecting the running of the farm. Also the impact it is having on their animals and crops. We ask them what they think is causing the changes and are they worried about it all.

'My, you're asking a lot of questions, young Rose!' says a flustered Martha. 'What's got into you, girl, are you trying to do one of them assignment things or something?'

'Yes, that's right, Martha. It's about the greenhouse effect, and I thought as you are "of the soil", as such, you will be able to help me with a natural answer rather than all that scientific stuff.'

Martha puffs up with pride, to think she can give a better answer than one of them thick books.

'Well, if you put it like that, I'll be pleased to help you. Of course I read the seasons, the plants and trees. I watch the animals, birds and insects. You get more from all that than any book and if you've been on the land for as long as I have you will notice even the smallest change.'

So as Martha and I go about our daily chores we chat about everything under the sun.

'Don't you need to write this all down, girl?' Martha asks when we stop for a mid-morning break.

'No, I have a very good memory,' I smile.

'Better than my old brain,' Martha sighs.

'Not at all, Martha, you've told me loads without once having to look at a book or journal.'

'I have, haven't I? There's life in this old dog yet!'

We both laugh and go back to preparing dinner for the men.

Meanwhile Adam is helping Alf. The farm is mainly for livestock, although Alf grows hay for the animals to eat over winter, and some sugar beet. There is a great deal of manual work to do, mending fences and walls, making sure the drainage channels are working properly; flooded fields are a farmer's nightmare. All the gates have to be checked so that animals can't wander off and get hurt. There are dangerous trees to fell and hedgerows to check.

Alf will not admit to anyone, but secretly he thanks God for this strapping lad turning up out of the blue to help him. He knows that soon he will have to employ permanent help. Shame that children didn't come their way, Martha would have loved children and they could have helped them, when they got older, on the farm. Alf realizes that it is no good regretting though, things are as they are, and you have to make the best of it.

'Why have you got walls round some of your fields and hedgerows round others, Alf?' asks Adam as he fits another stone into a broken section of wall.

'Well, you see, I find that walls are better to keep the sheep and lambs in, and in some places hedgerows don't grow so good. But cows and calves usually manage better with hedgerows, if they have walls they go up to them and scratch themselves on the hard stones. Those cows are always scratching, then they knock the walls down cos they're so big and clumsy.'

Adam is getting quite good at dry stone walling, Alf is proud of his progress, he will make a good farmer one day.

'So what are the benefits of the hedgerows?'

'It's the natural habitat for smaller animals like birds, field mice and the like. If they don't have the hedges for protection from weather and foe they will soon disappear.'

'Why do you leave trees in the middle of fields, wouldn't it be easier to mow without them?'

'You're asking lots of questions lately. What am I, your teacher or something?'

Adam grins. 'Yes, Alf, you are, and a very good one at that.'

Alf takes off his hat and scratches his head, 'What am I going to do with you? Come on, we've got work to do.'

That night, back at the cottage, it is time to go over the information we have managed to accumulate during the day. There is a sizeable portfolio on people's attitude towards the greenhouse effect, the suggested causes and remedies.

'There's a couple of scientists staying at the hotel,' Daisy tells us, 'I'm not sure why they're staying there, but I get the idea they are doing some research for future plans in the area.'

'Now that could be interesting,' answers Adam, 'Mark, you must help Daisy to find out more about their plans. There is a nuclear power station down the coast and I've heard talk of giant wind turbines too. It could be about either of them or maybe something new.'

'I've heard the kids in town talking about increased security round a site just north of here, maybe it's got something to do with that.'

'You will have to do some detective work in town tomorrow, Daniel, to find out more.'

There is no shortage of information concerning the extreme weather conditions; there are two schools of thought depending who is doing the talking. An organization called the Green Party puts the blame squarely on to the misuse of natural resources and allowing poisonous gases into the atmosphere. The politicians prefer to think that only a small percentage is manmade, and the majority of changes are caused by the natural cycle of weather patterns.

The next day Daniel goes into town again and visits the library to study the news items in the archives; however, he finds even more conflicting reports which are again dependant on who is doing the reporting. After a few hours glued to the computer screen his head is buzzing. He looks up and notices the sun streaming through the window. Enough is enough he thinks, closes down the screen and wanders out into the street to enjoy the fresh air. As he strolls through the nearby park he almost forgets the problems facing everyone, but his conscience brings him back with a bang.

A summer thunderstorm decides to wet his spirits even more, so Daniel runs to the nearest refuge which happens to be a café at the end of the road.

It proves to be a good omen as it is full of kids of his own age and they are friendly as well. He orders a hot drink and sits at a vacant table in the corner where he can observe without being too obvious. It seems that most of them are college students, varying from the smartly dressed to the artistic types. They are chatting, laughing and generally enjoying themselves. Some are even debating important issues and the café owner is joining in with them.

Daniel smiles to himself. It isn't long before he is drawn into the discussion and he spends the next few hours mentally gathering information.

The café owner used to be a tutor at the college but opted out when his radical ideas were found unacceptable to the strict regime. Students frequent his café for lively debates and to be with other free spirited colleagues.

The atmosphere is brilliant and Daniel thinks it would make a perfect base to start their campaign; the people here are open-minded and knowledgeable.

Daniel looks at the clock, it is nearly four and he should really go back to the library. As he gets up to leave the café owner approaches him, he puts out his hand and says, 'Leaving already, that's a shame, my name is Jim, you're welcome here any time. So hope to see you soon.'

Daniel shakes his hand. 'Thank you, Jim, I'm Daniel. I'm sure you will see me again.' Just before he leaves he turns round and asks Jim, 'By the way do you know why there is increased security just north of here?'

'They must be testing the ground. They are trying to find a new site to bury the radiation waste from the nuclear power station. They won't want anyone disturbing them as it is a very controversial issue; they think we are so thick that we don't know what they are doing.'

Daniel smiles and waves to all his new friends and leaves. He can't wait to tell Adam that he has at last found an ideal location to start their quest. He makes his way back to the library to do some further research.

When Daniel finally leaves the library he steps out to be met by a beautiful evening. On the two-hour walk back to the cottage he sees the setting sun casting a golden mantle over the treetops. The river sparkles with hundreds of diamonds only broken occasionally when a fish jumps to catch an errant fly. The birds are singing their evening song, the cows and sheep are munching on succulent grass and all is peaceful. Daniel is deep in thought, he is remembering the world that he came from and how different it was from the paradise he sees around him. It is hard to imagine that it is the same planet.

That evening Daniel tells us about Jim, the café and the people he has met there. We all agree that it definitely sounds like a place we should visit and it could possibly become a base for us to get our assignment moving.

Daniel also tells us about the information he has uncovered in the reference library, it seems that the Green Party is a group of like-minded people. They seem pretty strong and have quite a large following; some of the members have even been elected to Parliament.

We realize that we still have a number of hurdles to overcome, the biggest being our ages. In our world we were considered intelligent adults; in this world, however, it will be hard to be seen as voices to be heard. The café will prove a useful stepping stone.

We are all relieved that the plight of the world has at least been recognized by some sections of the population, so we will not always be talking to the uninformed.

Chapter Four

Life is good for us but we know we have to move on. Adam calls us to a meeting. He feels it is up to him to keep us all on track and he knows we will not like what he is going to suggest.

'Is this another lecture, Adam?' The question comes from Daisy, she is known as the rebel of the group, she is very fiery in her manner and tends to disagree with almost everything. Her green eyes would blaze as she continuously shook her long, curly red hair in disagreement. We have changed dramatically from the teenagers that first arrived from the future; we are no longer carbon copies of each other. We have all developed our own personality and image.

'Not a lecture, Daisy, but a fact,' replies Adam smiling, his thick black hair is neatly tied in a short pony tail and his dark-brown eyes command authority. He has, however, the patience of a saint. Adam works on the principle that arguing is counterproductive and that every problem has a solution.

When Mark, Daniel and I join them Adam starts to reiterate the things we have all documented.

The unusual torrential storms which cause rivers to burst their banks allowing uncontrollable floods to cover areas, first in the South and then in the North, leaving a wake of death and destruction. Strong winds ripping ancient trees from the ground by their massive roots. Temperatures soar to record levels and people finding that sunburn is an additional hazard, causing an increase in skin cancer. Earthquakes and tornadoes measuring higher than ever recorded in this country.

Even the countries that are used to such extreme weather conditions are being battered by the wild and dangerous natural forces. Tsunamis of gigantic proportions racing in from the seas to flood islands, flattening buildings and vegetation, and killing every living thing in its path.

The polar caps are melting, letting loose giant icebergs which float into the main shipping channels. The level of the sea is starting to rise causing even more flooding.

The information is endless and also frightening when we see the chaos that is being unleashed.

'We know all this, Adam, but I feel that you are reminding us for a reason, so come on lets have the bottom line.' Mark is known for his straightforward manner and when he asks a question he expects a truthful answer.

Adam looks at his friends. He takes a deep breath and replies.

'The years we have spent in the cottage have hardened us to this strange world, but we all know the time will come for us to move on and speed up our campaign.'

I am dismayed and frightened; I feel uneasy about the way the conversation is going. 'But we don't all have to go, Adam, do we?'

'I'm sorry, Rose, but we do. It is time to say goodbye to the villagers, the hotel and to Martha and Alf on the farm. We will keep in touch and visit when we can. The kindness shown to us will never be forgotten.'

Our exit from the cottage and the village is met by sadness, but with understanding. The worst parting is between Martha and I; we shed torrents of tears through which we both promise to meet regularly. Alf is not the kind of person to show his feelings, that would not be manly, but inside his world has been turned upside down. He thinks of Rose as the daughter they never had and Adam as the son.

Daniel, Mark and Adam accept the offer of care-taking a house in the town; it belongs to a man in the village, inherited from his late mother. He has no wish to live there because he prefers the peace of the countryside. Daisy and I are able to rent a flat with some of the money we have saved.

The next milestone will be to find jobs. We are lucky in this because it is near to Christmas and there are many temporary vacancies advertised to cover extra work over the busy period.

However, even in this happy time of the year the underlying terrors still continues; the war in the Middle East where people are being blown up by suicide bombers and shot by snipers never seems to stop. The millions of people starving to death will continue their nightmare. The tsunamis and earthquakes, floods and hurricanes have no respect for Christmas.

Despite all this terror we are not immune to the festive excitement around us; we enjoy taking on the traditions of a twenty-first century Christmas and are whisked along in the hustle and bustle. Negative thoughts are overwhelmed by feelings of happiness.

The last week before Christmas is cold and wet but it doesn't dampen our spirits. Daisy and I join the lads in their house for the normal Sunday get together. We take it in turns to cook a traditional Sunday dinner and today Daisy and Adam are in the steamy kitchen preparing a meal for us.

'I can't believe how we managed on our tasteless nourishment at home,' Daisy recollects, 'we were just eating to survive, but now even the preparing of a meal is just as good as eating it.'

'We knew no better. What I can't believe is how easily this generation allows the rot to set in,' Adam replies angrily. A thought that haunts all of us continuously.

'Don't get angry, Adam, I really enjoy living as we do, but I cannot see how we can change things. People here are so set in their ways, so intent on being the richest nation, being the cleverest and racing through technology and science that they do not realise the damage they are doing.'

'I know what you are saying, Daisy, but we must never forget why we are here. We have witnessed the destructive forces; we know how bad it will become. It is our duty to use the knowledge we have to show them how they are affecting future generations. How we are going to get the people to listen to us is going to be our biggest problem.'

In the large dining room a completely different argument is being debated. There has been an unwritten rule between us that no romantic liaison will be allowed between ourselves and outsiders. However, Mark has met a girl at work and he has developed strong feelings for her.

'Can't you see how dangerous it can be,' Daniel reasons, 'our make-up is far advanced than these people, besides, the fact is we are here for one purpose only and we cannot afford to get distracted. We have friends and family back home depending on us.'

Mark is hurt, he had not gone out purposely to look for Mary, and the feelings he has for her are alien to his nature, but he did know that now he has met her he wants her to be with him always.

'How do you know they are still there, we have been away for years? How do you know that even if we do manage to persuade these idiots that they are destroying everything, and they change in time to protect what they have, that our world will evolve?' Mark's frustration is on a roller coaster. 'And another thing, none of us has ever voiced the fact that we have no way of going back home, but we all know we can't. So does that mean we have to live the rest of our lives like the so-called scholars in our time, locked away in a tall tower trying to find the answer for a balanced civilisation?'

We are shocked by what Mark has said, but know the truth in his words.

I feel tears gathering in my eyes.

Daniel comes over to me and put his arms around my shoulders. 'Don't cry, Rose, we are all in this together and we will always support each other. There is no need to be frightened.'

'But what he is saying is true, isn't it? We can never go home, we are stuck here forever.'

Daniel sighs, what can he say, he knew this moment had to come but not like this, he has to diffuse the situation until Adam and Daisy joins them.

'We have come to a very important crossroad in our mission. It is not something we can take lightly. So I suggest we take a step back for now, enjoy what is always a fantastic dinner and then sit down with a clear mind and go through our fears and wishes systematically.'

The room is silent, we know Daniel is talking sense, we arrived with logic and discipline, and we cannot let our time with a weaker generation taint our thinking.

'Great idea, Daniel, why spoil a good meal with the troubles of the world,' laughs Daisy as she comes in from the kitchen with a steaming plate of food, 'plenty of time for that afterwards.'

The mood lightens; for now.

Daniel goes towards the kitchen, thankful that we are all sensible enough to see that any issue can be solved, but at the right time.

'Wow, that smells great, the table's laid, do you need help to bring anything else through?'

'Everything in here is under control, Daniel, what about in there?' Adam questions, 'I thought I heard raised voices.'

'There are things to be discussed; but dinner first.'

As we sit at the table, we bow our heads, giving thanks for our good fortune and remembering friends and family no longer with us.

The next hour is spent tucking into a delicious meal, during which we gossip about events of the week. This time is for enjoyment.

After dinner we get down to business, Adam realises that whatever decisions we make this afternoon will not only affect the five people in this room, but the people outside, wherever they might be, and also the friends and family we have left from our own time.

Finally we all settle down and we look expectantly at Adam.

'I think we have done extremely well so far, integrating with people of this time, continually learning new tasks, even getting employment.' Adam then continues, 'However, we must have known that eventually we will have to take the bull by the horns and give it a good shake, otherwise we will be as guilty as those we need to educate.

'I don't know where to begin, but I do know that we have all got to be unanimous on any decisions that we make. So shall we just go round the room and hear everyone's comments and requests, and we can then put necessary items to the vote. You first, Mark.'

'Quite simple really, I want to form a relationship with a girl I have met. We have kissed but have not been more intimate. I know that physical relationships had been phased out where we come from, but we are all built the same and when I am with this girl I can feel the natural changes in my body.'

I blush at Mark's revelations. Daniel nods knowingly, he too has experienced the feelings of arousal but has been too embarrassed to say anything.

'Thank you, Mark, for being honest. It is quite evident by our reactions that we have all noticed that our bodies have adapted to the time we are in now, even after years of abstention. What we have to realise is that if we form close relationships outside of our group those partners will have to be told who we are and why we are here. Therefore we will have to be careful, they must understand our mission and support our aims. We cannot afford to be separated or to be made to choose between partner and colleague. Does everyone agree?' Adam looks around; some of us are looking down at the floor while others seem shocked.

'Well,' states Daisy, 'that's an opener, if ever there is one. I think if we are all honest we will admit to some kind of light relationship over the years, but we have been halted by the knowledge that we are not like them and we have too many secrets. However, I feel the time has come to carefully branch out into society as it is here, before the five of us are labelled as weirdos. It has been noticed how close we are with each other and when I am questioned I always explain that some of us are siblings and some cousins.'

We all nod in agreement.

'That seems fair enough, so everyone agrees with Daisy as to how to explain away our closeness. Now how about Mark and Mary?'

'I can't see it being a problem.' Daniel adds, 'I think Mark should bring Mary here to meet us. I have already met her, and she seems to be a really nice and genuine person, but I hadn't realised how close they had become. However, even though we might agree for us to have partners I do not see it as a licence to bring just anyone into our lives. We must be very, very careful.'

'Is that how you all feel?' Adam looks around the room as we all nod. 'Fair enough, motion agreed, we look forward to meeting Mary. Just one more word though, I cannot stress more strongly that caution must be observed.'

Adam turns to look for me; he is worried about my reactions to everything that is being said. It is obvious that I am finding the realities of our situation hard to digest.

I wanted time on my own so I had quietly left the room.

'I think that is enough for now, we don't want to spoil our perfect Sunday by too much truth and consequence do we?' says Adam, and then asks, 'Does anyone know where Rose has gone?'

'She went into the kitchen,' Daisy replies.

Adam finds me in darkness, leaning on the sink, looking out of the window; my blond hair is covering my pale face, so he can't see that I have been crying.

'What are you looking for, Rose?'

'I'm looking at the stars. Do you think they are the same stars we can see at home?'

'I'm not sure, but they could be I suppose. Rose, I know you are finding this hard, but you must start seeing this as our home now. You are not a fool, you must have realised that technology here is not advanced enough to be able to duplicate the procedure to return us back to the future.'

'In the back of my mind I know, and when I was on the farm surrounded by the beautiful countryside it didn't seem to matter. But here it does matter. I'm finding things harder than everyone else and my emotions are all over the place. I actually cry myself to sleep every night. I don't know how much longer I can go on like this and I'm scared,'

Adam puts his arm around me. 'You are not alone, we are all scared. The responsibility that has been given to us is vast, but we can only do our best. The first few years we were here was an adventure, but now we have to really get down to business.' Adam pauses; his thoughts are going through the seemingly impossible task that lay ahead of us. 'But I promise you, Rose, I have said it before and I will keep saying it until you can believe me, we will always be together helping each other through every step of the journey. You must never feel that you are alone.'

I turn to face him, tears are now streaming down my face, I know that I am the weakest of us all, and that frightens me. If only I hadn't been chosen. If only I could have stayed on the farm with Alf and Martha. 'Thank you, Adam, I will try to remember that,' I reply as I wipe the tears away and give Adam a weak smile.

We return to the dining room where everyone is laughing at a comedy film on the television.

Adam makes a mental note to ask Daisy to keep a close eye on me. He does not think that the problem has been solved.

Chapter Five

Christmas Day dawns, definitely bright and crisp, but no snow yet. Daisy and I have slept over at the boys' house so that we can all be together from the off. We have manufactured our own tradition for this special holiday. There is always a real six-foot Christmas tree absolutely covered in white lights, loads of sparkly decorations and each one of us has chosen our own special ornament which we hang on the tree ourselves. On top of the tree is a large gold star to represent all we have left behind.

I am the first to stir, I go into the sitting room which resembles a fairy grotto. The windows are steamy with the heat from the kitchen. The huge turkey has been cooking all night and the smell permeates through the house. The atmosphere is full of electric anticipation. However, I can only feel unbearable sadness, I look at the pile of brightly-coloured gifts under the tree and try to work up some positive emotions. I can't because I feel I am slowly dying from the inside, it is as if someone is trying to blow out my candle of life.

'Caught you!'

I jump and then force a laugh. 'Merry Christmas, Daniel.'

'Were you going to peep at the presents?'

'No, not me, I am going to check on the turkey.'

'Yeah right!' Daniel smiles as he kisses me on the cheek. 'Merry Christmas, sis.'

'What's going on here?'

I turn and see Mark coming out of the bedroom.

'You're up early, and dressed already. Where are you going?'

'Don't you remember, Rose, Mary is joining us today. I'm just off to get her. Do you want to come with me?'

'Can I?'

'Of course you can. It's a lovely day outside; the sun is turning the frost into thousands of glittering diamonds, just as it did in the countryside.' Mark knows that I need every bit of positive feedback they can give me. I look so weak and unhappy all the time, even my hair is hanging lankly around my face and my blue eyes have dulled. They are all worried about me. It is a lucky coincidence that Mary is a ward sister in the local hospital, she might be able to give advice on how to help.

Mary lives the other side of town so it will take at least half an hour to get there. I am quiet for a while, once again in my own thoughts. I must snap out of it so I ask Mark how he had met Mary.

'One of my colleagues at work fell and hurt himself quite badly and I took him to the hospital. We were waiting in out-patients when I saw Mary caring for an old man; she was so kind and patient with him. I was watching her and she looked up. There was like an immediate recognition between us and it all started from there.'

'Doesn't she want to spend Christmas with her own family?'

'Mary is an only child and her parents died in a road accident a few years ago. Her grandparents are also dead. So she is all alone.'

'That's sad.'

'Yes, it is, but out of sadness comes joy of a different kind. You must remember that, Rose.'

'Very philosophical, Mark,' I reply with just a trace of a smile on my face.

They pull up outside a tall Victorian house, the door opens and an attractive girl with long dark hair comes out to meet them.

'Merry Christmas, Mark. I'll just go and collect my things.'

'She's very pretty,' I said as I climb into the back seat. 'She won't mind me being here, will she?'

'Of course not. Mary can't wait to meet everyone.'

Mary bundles all her parcels into the boot of the car and joins Mark in the front seat. She leans over and kisses him. I blush to see such an open display of emotion.

'So who is this vision of beauty sitting in the car with us?'

I blush even deeper.

'I'm Rose,' I stammer.

'What a perfect name for you. I'm Mary, and I'm looking forward to getting to know you and your friends. Mark has told me so much about you all.'

By the time we arrive back at the house we are chatting as if we have known each other for years. Mark lets out a silent sigh of relief. It's going to be all right he thought.

The door of the house opens and Daisy runs down the path to meet Mary, she is very excited to get another woman in their midst, the balance of boys to girls is at last going to even out. She ushers a bewildered Mary into the warm house.

'What about my bags?'

'Don't worry; the boys will bring them in.' Daisy says, as she clears a chair for Mary, 'It is so great to meet you at last, we have hundreds of questions to ask you.'

'Leave the poor girl alone, she looks terrified.' Laughs Adam.

'Sorry about Daisy. We don't usually have visitors. I'm Adam, can I get you something warm to drink, tea, coffee or a glass of Christmas sherry?'

Mary smiles. She is frantically trying to adjust to her surroundings and the overwhelming attention. Mark has told her that we are different and we tend to keep ourselves private from outsiders.

'A glass of sherry will be great. Thank you.'

Mary looks around the room; the Christmas tree is decorated unusually but beautifully. There are no photos or pictures on the walls, but plenty of plants and floral decorations everywhere. It is quite evident that our one love is nature.

Mark comes to her and sits on the arm of her chair. 'I told you we are different, just go with the flow. All will be revealed later, but for now let's concentrate on the presents under the tree.'

'That's the best suggestion we've heard today,' shouts a group of people behind him.

Adam steps forward. 'Before we start the festivities let's raise our glasses to friends and family no longer with us, and also to guidance in our lives.'

We raise our glasses to the toast, and then Daniel and I take our positions by the tree while everyone settles down ready for the distribution of the presents.

The next hour sees brightly-coloured paper being thrown everywhere and the sound of laughter echoes through the house. Mary is finding it hard to believe that so many people can live so closely together and still get on so well. It is true that in many ways her new friends are very much alike. In fact she would say that it is quite eerie, the similarities between them.

The Christmas dinner is the highlight of the day, crackers are pulled and mottoes read out for everyone's enjoyment.

Mary loves the attention everyone is offering her. Our questions seem strange sometimes, especially as she senses our high intelligence. However, the time has come for her to learn the truth about us.

'Well, Mark, I think Mary must be tired of us asking her questions. We must now be as open with her about ourselves.'

Mary feels a shiver run through her. Has she been lured into a strange sect? What are they going to do to her? Mark takes her hand and smiles comfortingly.

'I suppose you're right, Adam,' Mark agrees, as he nervously runs his fingers through his curly brown hair. He is so afraid he will lose Mary when she knows the truth.

The room goes deathly quiet. Mark starts to explain. Who we are, where we have come from and our given mission.

Mary listens. She looks at each of us one by one. Then she looks at Mark, he is still holding her hand. There are tears in his soft blue eyes. We are all quiet, but there is a strange atmosphere in the room. Mary didn't know what to do. She has just been told something that is so surreal. It can't possibly be true.

'Say something, Mary, please.'

'I don't know what to say. I suppose this isn't a joke, is it?'

'I'm afraid not. Every word is true.'

'But that means you are all over a thousand years old!'

'If you look at it like that, I suppose we are.'

'Can I have another drink, please?' Mary asks as she frantically tries to digest all the information that has been given to her about her new found friends.

'Do you think you can still feel the same about me?' Mark has his fingers crossed. Mary has gone very pale. Was it right to tell her or should he have waited?

'I don't know. In fact I don't know about anything anymore.'

Adam is the first to speak. 'Mary, we had to tell you because we know how important you are to Mark. In fact now that we have met you we can see you are a special person. Our previous life is gone from us; we have no way of returning. So our lives are with this time and our mission still stands.' Adam pauses and then continues, 'We don't know whether we can make a difference to the people we left behind, we don't even know whether they are still surviving in that constricted world. We are, however, going to try our utmost to improve your future and your children's future. We have the use of our superior knowledge but we must find a way of utilising it to the appropriate affect for this time in history.'

'So what do we do next? It is Christmas day you know. So I suggest we continue celebrating unless Mary would like to ask some questions.'

'I think not, Daisy,' Mary answers, with a shy smile, 'I do have hundreds of questions, but not now, not today. Let Christmas continue.' She gets closer to Mark and squeezes his hand. Mary knows she loves Mark so she will take everything else one step at a time, hoping that eventually she will be able to accept the incredible story she has just been told. The atmosphere in the room lightens.

Christmas evening is relaxed; the log fire burns brightly as stories are swapped. There is peace in the house.

Snow arrives with Boxing Day morning. Arrangements are made to walk in the nearest fields where the inevitable snowball fight ensues. We arrive back to the house cold and wet but happy. I go to the kitchen to make hot chocolate for everyone and Mark helps Daniel to get the log fire raging again.

Mary feels like one of the family, she feels good; better than she has done for years. She sits in the chair smiling, watching everyone rushing about doing their own things.

'You must let me prepare lunch,' she calls over all the noise.

'We can't let you do that, you're our guest,' Mark answers.

'I feel a bit more than that after what you told me last night, so you must let me do my share,' replies Mary. 'How hard will it be, turkey and chutney sandwiches all round. Right?'

'Sounds great.' We all agree.

Mary is due to go on night duty later, but before she leaves she turns to her hosts and says, 'I have one question before I go?'

We look at her apprehensively.

'What's that, Mary?' Adam asks cautiously.

'How can I help?'

We all laugh. Mark throws his arms around Mary. 'A thousand ways, Mary. In fact I think you have already started.' He kisses her tenderly on the cheek.

Chapter Six

No one could have guessed that the first two weeks in the New Year will change hundreds of people's lives. The town where we live and work is on the coast and it is divided by a river that flows from the mountains above the town. In these mountains are a number of beautiful lakes and at least one of these lakes is used by a larger town further south as a reservoir for their water supply.

It has rained persistently for days and the ground is sodden. There are a few days of sun but it makes no impression. The last straw is twenty-four hours of a relentless downpour; over ten inches of rain fell in that time. The river swells to unbelievable heights; it bursts its banks and spreads across the fields. Emergency services are called out to move people from threatened homes, but the worst is yet to come.

The town in the south being supplied by the reservoir say they can't take any more water, so the dam is breached to let the water out. It comes down the valley like a tidal wave hitting a beautiful tourist town, then on to the next smaller town. The water floods the main street to the height of ten feet, homes and businesses are swept away with bridges, livestock and pets.

Still it went on following the ground downwards towards the sea. The raging torrent continues relentlessly until it hits the last town and there it tears down two bridges and seriously damages a third, devastating everything on a low level. Finally it comes to the sea where a spring tide is reaching its highest at ten metres, but the force of the flood water will not allow the tide to advance, this causes a massive whirlpool. In this whirlpool is evidence of things that have been carried down the mountains including cattle and sheep which are being endlessly swirled round and round in a macabre dance of death.

'Did you hear that the main road bridge has been swept away?' Mark says in amazement.

'And the footbridge into town,' Daniel adds.

'The last bridge has been condemned as dangerous; they think it will go at any time!'

I whisper, 'Is it starting, is this how it all starts? Are we too late to stop it? I am so frightened.'

'Rose, don't cry. It is terrible but people will bounce back, you see.'

Mark and Adam want to be of some help but are at a loss as to which way is best. 'Why don't you join me at the café?' Daniel suggests. 'I'm sure we can do with extra hands. We will have all the rescuers and emergency services coming in to warm themselves up.'

'Good idea, we need to do something useful and it will be nice to meet Jim again. I bet he will have a few things to say,' Mark replies.

The café is heaving with people. There is a group of men in hi-vis jackets, all of them dirty and wet, cradling steaming mugs in their hands. Another collection of people who must have been emergency service personnel are chatting quietly in a corner. The usual students are sitting round a table nursing mugs of coffee. But in the corner is a woman with a baby in her arms and two children clinging to her coat. The woman is sobbing softly; her short dark hair is matted and as it clings to her head streaks of mud run down from it on to her face. Daniel has never seen anyone look so desolate. His heart is breaking just watching her.

Adam and Mark are heading for the counter to help Jim. 'Are you coming, Daniel?'

'I'll be with you in a minute, Adam.'

Daniel approaches the forlorn mother. 'Can I help?' he asks politely.

'No one can, not anymore,' the woman answers quietly.

Daniel sits down next to her. 'I know it seems bad now, but it will get better, I promise you.'

'I had a visit this morning. It was the military. They told me my husband has been killed in Afghanistan. Now tonight, my whole life has been washed away. All my memories, my belongings. Everything.'

'You have your children, and they need you.'

'What good am I to them? I have nothing left to give them.'

'You have your love, and that will be enough until you are able to give them more.'

'Those are kind words, but this time words are not going to make things better. I do not have the strength anymore.'

'Have you eaten?'

The woman shakes her head.

'I'll get you and your children something warm.'

'No, you can't. I haven't any money.'

'You can pay me back later.'

Daniel goes to join Adam. He explains about the plight of the young mother and her children.

'I fear that it will be no good telling you not to get too involved.'

'Correct,' Daniel answers and smiles. 'Now, have we three plates of steaming soup, bread and some warm milk going spare?'

Daniel returns to the woman and puts the food down on the table. The two lads grin and tuck into their soup.

'Manners, Tom, Charlie. What do you say to the kind man?'

'Thanks, mister.' They chorus and then continue to fill their stomachs.

'I'm sorry about that. They are normally polite.'

'Don't worry; it has been a strange day for them. Now what about the baby? I've got some warm milk here, will she drink it?'

'Yes, thank you, I've got her bottle.'

'Let me feed her and then you can eat your soup.'

'Well, I don't know. Jenny's a bit shy.'

'Let's give it a try, shall we?'

Daniel takes the baby and puts the bottle to her lips. Jenny takes it greedily; she must have been desperate for the comfort.

'That's settled then. Now you eat your soup before it gets cold.'

The woman smiles gratefully.

'So, we have Tom and Charlie and this little one is Jenny. I am Daniel. What do I call you?'

'Rebecca. Becky, everyone calls me Becky.'

'Have you any relatives nearby, Becky?'

'No, I am an orphan and my husband's parents have died. We have only been in the area a few months so I don't know anyone that well.'

42

'Well, you know me now. And I know of a four-bedroom flat that only has two girls in it. So there is room to spare. I'm sure they will be delighted to have you and your children stay.'

'I couldn't impose on strangers, it wouldn't be right.'

'It wouldn't be right for me to leave the four of you to chance your luck outside on a night like this. I will just give them a call to let them know we are on our way.'

Daniel left them eating and went to phone the girls.

'Hello, Daisy, is that you?'

'Of course it's me, you fool, what's up, Daniel?'

Daniel explains about Becky and her children. He also mentions the death of Becky's husband.

'The poor girl. She must be at her wits end. We will get her room ready; give us an hour to get sorted.'

'Thanks, Daisy, see you later.'

Daniel tells Becky that everything has been arranged and then he goes to get them a drink each.

'What's happening then?' Adam asks.

'The girls have offered to put them up.'

'I hope you know what you are doing, Daniel.'

'All I know is that it feels right and that will do for now.'

At our flat Daisy and I are running around like maniacs. We are so excited to have another woman sharing with us, and children as well. We know it will be awkward for everyone, but Becky's terrible day makes us feel so fortunate in our lives and we want to share it with her and her children. I feel useful again and it is a joy to get the spare room ready for our visitors.

The knock at the door startles us. Daisy opens the door.

Standing in front of her is a young woman with a baby in her arms and two young lads holding on to her coat whilst trying to hide behind it. Standing at the back is a beaming Daniel.

'Come in, come in. You must all be freezing. What a terrible night.'

Daisy guides them into the sitting room where I am waiting for them.

I stand forward and offer my hand in welcome to the woman. 'You must be Becky, I'm Rose. We are so pleased to meet you.'

'You are all so kind to offer a stranger such generosity. I hope that I will be able to repay you one day.'

Daniel steps forward, 'We are only doing what anyone else would do, so stop feeling guilty. Let's show the children your rooms.'

We had gone round to some of the neighbours to beg for some games and cuddly toys for the children and now we can hear the cries of surprise and joy as the boys enter their room.

'Thanks to you both, you've done me proud. I have to go back and help Adam and Mark for a while at the café but I will be back later.'

During the evening Mark and Adam have heard of terrible trouble in a small hamlet to the north of the town. The river has roared across the fields and hit there first before devastating the town. They decide to go there and help where they can. The scene that greets them is mayhem. The RNLI boat is rescuing an old woman and her dog from a bedroom window, the river is just below the second floor. Some people have clambered up onto their roofs and are shouting for help. Another house has completely lost its kitchen and conservatory, smashed like a box of matches; they actually see the river stealthily take it, like a thief with its swag.

There is no wind and hardly any light as the electricity is slowly shutting down. The only noise is the roar of the river and the pitiful cries for help. Cats and dogs that are unlucky enough to be caught outside as the swollen river creeps on are fighting against the onslaught. Most of them manage to get to safety.

As the lifeboat approaches them Mark shouts, 'What can we do to help?'

'Take this lady to safe ground, there are taxis waiting to take the rescued to community halls.'

Mark and Adam help the woman and her dog out of the boat and take her to a waiting taxi. She is sobbing and they try to reassure her, but what can they say. Her whole life is floating down to the sea.

The night is long and hard, helicopters appear and airlift people from their roofs. The lifeboat is searching for marooned people and animals. Everyone tries to do as much as they can to help the victims.

The damage caused by the onslaught of water and debris is fast. It is over within a couple of hours, but the devastation in its wake will take years to repair. There is only one fatality, a policeman. He was on the main road bridge that straddles the town, it is reported that he had felt it shudder. The policeman stopped all the traffic, saving an early bus, lorries and cars but he was not quick enough to save himself. The bridge gave an ear-splitting groan and then collapsed into the raging torrent below taking the heroic policeman with it. It left a thirty-foot gap in the road and all that is left is electricity and phone cables swinging in the wind and a fractured gas pipe spewing gas out into the air.

When dawn breaks the carnage opens out to them like a scene from hell. Ironically the day is bright and sunny.

Many people come out to see exactly what has been happening. The river is still high, everywhere is crawling with police, rescue services and the army. Helicopters buzz above from international and national news TV channels. Then the people on the north of the river suddenly realise the extent of the damage, two bridges down, one condemned. They are cut off from the town. Instead of a ten-minute walk they now face a ninety-mile diversion to go shopping.

Chapter Seven

Becky and her children settle in well with us, she does the housework and prepares meals. We tell her she doesn't have to do all that work but she says it is to repay our kindness and to keep her mind from dwelling on the awful things that she has to face. Tom and Charlie go back to school and they seem to cope better with their situation now that they have a sense of normality back in their lives. Daniel comes to visit every day. He brings books for the boys and cuddly toys for Jenny. Daisy notices that Becky's eyes light up when Daniel arrives. She can understand her wanting comfort but she is a bit worried that Daniel might think it is more than that.

'Hello again, Daniel, you are a frequent visitor these days!'

'Hello, Daisy. Well, I can't just dump my poor refugees onto you and let you get on with it, can I?'

'Too right,' Daisy replies jovially. 'While I remember, can I have a word with you before you leave?'

'Of course. There's nothing wrong is there?'

'No, nothing is wrong, I just want to ask you something.'

When Daniel goes into the living room Tom and Charlie throw themselves at him, talking twenty to the dozen.

Daniel laughs, 'Slow down, I can't understand a word you are saying.'

'We've been to see the soldiers; they're building an army bridge across the river so that people can walk into town again,' Explains Tom.

'Yes, and they have army tents and lorries and things,' adds Charlie.

'Wow, that must have been exciting, I will have to go and have a look myself.'

'My dad wasn't there though,' Charlie whispers.

Daniel ruffles Charlie's hair and looks over at Becky, she just shrugs her shoulders.

'Come on then, let's see what I've got in my bag.'

The awkward moment dissolves as the lads try to get into Daniels carrier bag.

When Daniel goes to leave Daisy sees him to the door.

'So, what's on your mind, Daisy?'

'I'm just worried about Becky.'

'Why, there's nothing wrong is there?'

'She is very vulnerable at the moment and I see how she looks at you. I feel she is looking for someone to put her life back on track, and at the moment that is you.'

'Everyone deserves friends and I don't mind helping her as much as I can. Becky is a lovely woman with adorable children and I will be there for her as long as she needs me.'

'What about you. How far are you hoping your friendship will go?'

'I know what you are getting at, Daisy, but I'm just taking it one step at a time. I know the risks and the problems so don't get too worried about me. I really appreciate you helping; it can't be easy having another woman in the house let alone children.'

'You've got to be kidding, Daniel, Becky does all the housework and cooking. We are living like royalty here!'

Daniel smiles, 'Thanks anyway, I'll see you tomorrow.'

On the way home Daniel thinks about the things Daisy has said and he knows she is right. He also has to admit that he has got feelings for Becky but he knows that he will have to tread very carefully.

Snow and ice follows the floods which makes the recovery even harder; the only silver lining is that each week brings us nearer to spring.

It is quite obvious that nothing will be the same again, the town and its historical setting has changed forever, and the new bridges will be single span and probably made of steel. The beauty of multi-arched stone bridges will never adorn the river again.

Life falls back into a kind of normality and I fall into another negative period. I love having Becky and the children staying with us but now the novelty is wearing off. I can feel my mood changing again and I do my best to combat the downward trend.

Daisy has noticed that I am not eating properly and I am growing visibly thinner as well as getting paler. I know that Daisy is telling Adam and I am aware that the others are worried about me, but I don't know what to do.

The Sunday tradition continues and is now a literal party because of our extra guests. Becky's children love the weekly get togethers as there are so many more people to play with them. If it is a dry day Daniel and Mark play football with them and if it is wet they play on the computer games inside.

Mary and Becky get on well together and take their turns in making Sunday dinner, while Daisy looks after little Jenny.

'How are you coping, Becky?'

'Day by day, Mary. But I don't know how I would have managed without the girls' help and of course the lads. I have to admit they are a strange bunch of people; I have never met anyone quite like them. They are all so kind and patient. They are like angels put on this earth to smooth troubled waters.'

'That is a very apt description,' Mary replies pensively.

They continue quietly preparing roast beef and Yorkshire puddings. Both lost in their own private thoughts.

Dinner is heralded as an overwhelming success and everyone sits down to watch a children's comedy film afterwards. Everyone that is except Daisy and Mary. They excuse themselves and go into the kitchen to clear away the dinner things.

'What's all the secrecy, Daisy?'

'It's Rose, we are a bit worried about her.'

'I did notice she is not eating and she does look rather pale.'

'She has been like this before,' Daisy explains, 'she is the youngest of us and she finds it very hard to accept our true position here.'

'I can understand that but I can't help feeling that there is something a little more physically wrong.'

'What makes you say that, Mary?'

'Well, you are all very advanced and have adapted well to our rather crude way of doing things. Maybe Rose's body is not adjusting in the same way. Our food could be too rich or maybe the extreme weather conditions are affecting her.'

'We thought it might have been because she is too young to experience our journey back through time.'

'It can be that as well.' Mary pauses and then continues, 'I really don't want to use modern medication on Rose. Goodness knows what the chemicals could do to her. However, I can get some natural remedies and see whether they will help her.'

'I'd rather it is something she does not know about just in case it makes her even more anxious.'

'Of course, Daisy, I understand. It will only be something that can go into her drinks to make her calmer. Or even a soothing bath oil. Sometimes it is stress that can bring on the most severe ailments. Combat the stress and the battle is won.'

'That sounds good, Mary. Thank you.'

'No problem,' Mary replies, 'let's go join the others now. It sounds like we are missing a great film judging by all that laughter.'

Over the next few weeks Daisy starts introducing the natural remedies into my diet, they think I am not aware of their intervention. I will try anything though if it makes me feel more normal. I know they watch me intently for improvement in my moods and my appetite, but nothing changes. In fact I seem to be losing weight even faster and Daisy has caught me crying a couple of times.

'What can we do, Daisy?'

'I don't know, Adam. Do you think we have given it long enough to work?'

'We will have to talk to Mary again.'

'You're right, Adam, we can ask Mary on Sunday. I'm sure she will say we are worrying unnecessarily.'

Meanwhile I am in my room, crying yet again. I feel so unhappy all the time and I do not know why. It is getting to be such a strain pretending to everyone that there is nothing wrong.

I know I cannot return to the life I had in the future but I cannot continue feeling so alien among the people that surround me now. I make a decision and I will tell everyone next Sunday. There is only one place I can go and feel happy again and that is back to Alf and Martha on the farm. Its amazes me that now I have made a positive decision I feel much better. I also realise that I am letting the others down as I will not be helping with their given task, but I honestly do not think I will be much help if I continue to be ill all the time.

I can hear Becky playing with little Jenny and go to join her.

'Hello, Becky, it's a lovely day outside, shall we take Jenny for a walk in the park?'

'I'm waiting for the boys to come home for dinner but you can take her if you want, she loves to see the ducks.'

'On my own, are you sure that's all right?'

'Of course, I can't think of a safer pair of hands.'

It felt good to be so trusted. I dress Jenny in her outdoor clothes and was soon pushing the pushchair through the park.

The sun is shining and the birds are singing. Spring is definitely in the air, early bulbs are pushing through the earth and some trees are showing buds ready to explode into young leaves.

I sit on a bench near the pond surrounded by a noisy group of ducks demanding food from Jenny and I. Little Jenny giggles and claps her hands as I start to throw bread on the ground. The ducks' need for food seem endless so soon there is no bread left and we watch them waddle back to the pond complaining loudly.

I push Jenny back home, by the time I arrive the boys are home and Becky is preparing dinner.

'You look like you enjoyed that, Rose,' Becky remarks as she takes Jenny out of the pushchair. 'Your cheeks are rosy and your eyes are sparkling. Fresh air obviously does you good.'

'I do prefer being out in the open. Where we come from we had to stay inside. It is so much better being able to breath fresh air.'

Becky looks at me quizzically. She is not sure what I mean. I realise that I have spoken out of turn, but the moment goes by without any awkward questions.

When Adam arrives that night I took him aside to confess my slip of the tongue.

'Don't worry, Rose. We have agreed to tell Becky on Sunday.

'Is that wise?' I question. 'Becky has got a lot to come to terms with already.'

'You must have noticed that Daniel has feelings for Becky and her children,' Adam replies. 'So we are going to see whether she will like to join us on a more permanent basis.'

'Well,' I exclaimed, 'I know it's spring and all that but we seem to be multiplying at an alarming rate.'

We both laugh. Adam is pleased to see me in such an upbeat mood at last.

Sunday arrives and, as usual, the dinner puts us all in a good mood. However, there are two of us who are waiting nervously for the time when important things are to be discussed. We are both wondering if we are doing the right thing and whether everyone will understand our reasons.

Mary and Mark know that Daniel is going to explain to Becky about our task and where we come from, so they suggest that they take Tom, Charlie and Jenny for a nice long walk after dinner.

The time has come. Becky realises that something is amiss and she is frightened that we are going to tell her she has to leave.

Everyone is sitting quietly drinking coffee. Daniel goes to sit next to Becky. She starts to cry.

'Don't cry, Becky,' Daniel says as he puts his arm round her shoulders. 'What's the matter?'

'You're going to tell me I have to go. I have been so happy here with you and I have nowhere to go.'

'You silly thing. Of course we are not going to make you go. But I do have something very important to tell you and there is a chance that you might not want to stay when you hear what it is.'

'That sounds even more ominous.'

Daniel starts by telling Becky how important she and her children have become to him, and then he tells her who we really are and where we have come from.

Becky does not say a word. To her it all sounds unbelievable, but continues to listen.

When Daniel has finished Becky looks at him and says, 'You're having a joke with me.'

'I wish I was. However, every word is true. We come from the year 2999, we were sent by our Elders to see whether we can help change the course of the eventual destruction of our world.'

'But that is terrible how could they send children back into the unknown with such a burden on their shoulders? Now I know what Rose was saying the other day about having to stay inside where she came from.'

Daniel explains that in our time children mature mentally far faster than now. He also tells her that many of the adults were against the project but they had reached a point of no choice.

'We, well especially me, would like you to join us. What do you say; do you think you can accept us and the task we have to try to achieve?'

We all look at Becky expectantly. We are surprised she has taken the information so calmly.

'What do you think? Nothing can shock me anymore in this crazy world. My life has been a catalogue of pain, you have all helped me and my children to pick up the pieces and start living again. I will always have a black space in my heart where my husband should be, but I will do everything I can to help you make a better life for our generations to come.'

We clap at her response. We are so relieved and surprised by Becky's easy acceptance of everything.

Daniel gives a huge sigh of relief.

When Mary and Mark return with the children they are taken back by the party atmosphere but realise that everything has gone perfectly so they join in with the celebrations.

I know the time has come to tell everyone of my decision, I hope they accept it as well as Becky has accepted our revelations.

'I have something to say.'

They all turn to look at me. It is very unusual for me to speak up in front of everyone, so I immediately have their undivided attention.

'What's up, Rose?' Adam asks kindly.

'I have decided that I want to leave the town and go back to live with Alf and Martha. I've spoken to them and they seem really pleased. I am not happy here; I don't seem to be able to settle. I will miss you all very much but I am no use to you, I can't cope the way you all can. Can you forgive me?'

My decision has not come as a shock, everyone knows how unhappy I've been. They were all frightened it was something worse, maybe a fatal illness.

Adam speaks for everyone, 'We all know that you are unhappy and if this makes you smile again then it's what you must do. However, you must keep in touch and visit us often. We will, of course, come and see you as often as we can.'

I am so relieved. 'You're not angry with me?'

'Of course not, you silly thing. But you won't get rid of us that quickly we will be coming to see you all the time. All we ask is that you keep smiling.'

It is a tearful farewell when Mark and Mary drive me to Alf and Martha's farm, but they can all see it is for the best. Alf and Martha welcome me as if I was their long lost daughter and once again I have a sparkle in my eyes. Something that has been missing for a long time. Mark feels positive for the youngest disciple as he drives away from the farm with Mary.

Chapter Eight

Things once again begin to fall back into a frustrating routine. We know that we are not moving forward with our mission. Our extended family is fitting in with remarkable ease, but even the newcomers are waiting for some kind of action.

It is Daniel who starts the ball rolling again.

'You'll never guess what I'm going to do!' Daniel shouts as he bursts through the door.

'Good grief, Daniel, you nearly gave me a heart attack,' Mark exclaims as he turns to face Daniel. 'What's all the noise about?'

'Well, first I have a confession to make. I've told Jim about us.' He pauses to wait for the backlash, but it didn't come.

Adam smiles, 'We know you have. Jim contacted us to confirm what you told him. In his words he said, '"I just wanted to make sure I didn't have some kind of nutcase working with me". So he has given us his support whenever needed.'

'Oh! Cheek of the man,' laughs Daniel, 'anyway there is a local election coming up and Jim suggested I went in it as a candidate. How do you like the sound of "The Future Party", the Party who looks out for you and your children through the coming years of global change?'

'Sounds good, but you will have to have a manifesto so that you are ready to answer any questions, and how do you register as a new candidate?'

'That's all sorted; Jim has done this before so he knows the procedures. He has even said he would be my campaign manager.' Daniel is so excited about the prospect of being able to make a difference he has to take a deep breath and collect his thoughts before continuing. 'Jim asked if we ever needed extra space can we use this house. We have so many students and customers at the café that want to help; it will mean this place becoming very busy at times. Would you mind?'

Adam has to smile at Daniel's overwhelming enthusiasm. 'I can't see a problem; in fact I think we are all grateful for the opportunity to have an outlet for our work. Well done, Daniel.'

We all agree and congratulate Daniel on his idea. We are relieved that finally we can really start setting the foundations for our given task.

The next few weeks are a maze of activity. Jim is true to his word, he helps to register Daniel into the forthcoming elections, leaflets and banners are made, local media are informed of the party's aims and promises. Public meetings are arranged.

At the first public meeting the hall is packed. Daniel cannot believe it but Jim says it is because people are so fed up with the same battling parties in the government they are looking for a fresh approach. Especially one that has the state of our planet as a priority.

Daniel has not prepared a speech, he has decided to speak from the heart for thirty minutes and then answer questions. He steps on the stage and almost steps off again. His heart is beating so fast, there are so many people looking at him waiting for him to say something positive and intelligent. Then he sees his colleagues, we start to applaud to give him our support. People turn to look at us, bewildered, and then the rest of the audience start to clap.

The applause dies down and Daniel thanks them for their warm welcome. He turns and points to the pale blue banner suspended above him with the words 'The Future Party' printed out in white.

'I'm here to talk about this. Our future, our children's future and most important our planet's future. Because, of course, without our planet nothing has a future. We live on a marvellous creation, the fuel it gives to us has taken millions of years to create but we are using it at an incredible rate. When we started to use fossil fuels hundreds of years ago there were fewer people and less industrial use. But the population has increased dramatically and our technology has soared. We all enjoy and take for granted a higher standard of living, which is great, but we are now experiencing the cost to our environment.

This is not a local problem, it is a global problem and that is the way it must be tackled. Not each country doing their little bit or blaming others for the consequences of greenhouse gases, rising seas, melting polar caps, extinction of animals, earthquakes, tsunamis and floods.

The blame goes on each one of us and the natural cycle of our planet. We need to work together, and with the planet, to come to a compromise, so that we can all live safely and together.

I haven't come here to lecture; because I know that everyone is fully aware what natural changes are taking place. I would, however, like to have the opportunity to represent each and every one of you, to keep you fully informed and to help you save our world for generations to come. If we don't do something now in a thousand years the whole world will probably be inhabited by a few people in glass domes like the Eden Project. They will be too frightened to go out because the air will be contaminated and the weather will be unpredictably wild. They will spend their days eating processed food and trying to work out how they can reverse the damage mankind has done over the centuries. Do we really want to wait until that happens? The process might be inevitable, but we can help slow it down instead of accelerating the changes by our greed for progress and our ignorance to the consequences.' Daniel pauses and then asks.

'Has anyone got any questions?'

A wave of hands go up and a sea of cameras flash. Daniel has not realised the press have attended the meeting.

Daniel points to an elderly man at the rear of the hall. 'Yes, sir, what is your question?'

The man stands up. 'My name is Sam Butler and I am a farmer. I want to know how you intend to get all the governments in the world to come to some kind of unilateral agreement. That is the only way we can stop the degeneration.'

'Thank you, Sam. A very valid point. I am not going to say it will be easy, but everyone knows that something has to be agreed. Sooner rather than later. In the last three decades the so-called freak weather patterns are noticeably more frequent. At such an extent that they are casually being accepted as normal. It will be one of my prime concerns to stop this casual acceptance and to get officials to agree that we need to take firm steps to protect the environment. But I cannot do it alone; I need the backing of the people. People like everyone in this hall tonight. You have all come here because of your own personal concern. I want to deal with each one of your concerns until we can see improvements.'

Sam Butler sits down, and Daniel hopes he has given him what he wants to hear.

The next question is from a local newspaper.

'What makes you think you can succeed where many others have failed?'

Daniel thinks carefully. He wishes he can tell them that he knows what the consequences of apathy are, because he used to live in the remains of such a world, but he can't.

'I cannot guarantee that I can go as far as I want to, but you can be sure I will die trying. I know what the alternative will be and it will not be nice. I will take on the challenge one step at a time. The first step is to get a seat in the local election, and then I want to enter into parliament. Once I am there my aim will be to shout so loud the whole world will hear me. It is up to the people here to help me take that first step and I will promise everyone that they will never regret it. My life's work will be to make a better future for every living being on this planet.'

'That's a bold statement,' the reporter shouts, 'how do we know you won't get side-tracked like all the other elected members and end up being a nodding donkey so that you do not lose all your perks?'

'Because I have only one purpose in life, and that is to help my fellow man. I have no interests in self-gratification, I love just living and I want to make sure that we all have the opportunity to continue enjoying the benefits of our beautiful world for thousands of years to come.'

There are many more questions and Daniel tries to answer them as honestly as possible. After about an hour people start to drift away so Daniel closes the meeting.

Many of the press want quotes and pictures but finally Daniel is able to leave the building, he is absolutely exhausted and is glad when Jim offers to drive him home.

It is the first time Jim has been to the disciples' house and he is curious to see their set up.

'Well done, Daniel, you certainly got their interest,' Adam says as he pats him on the back.

'We will see by tomorrow's newspapers if they really take it seriously. I hope they do because it is our biggest push yet to try and change future events and we need all the support we can get.'

Jim is hovering in the background not wanting to impose on Daniel's glory.

'Come in, Jim, you are one of the family now and we are pleased to have you on side. There is so much you can educate us on procedures and red tape. You have already helped us enormously and we are very grateful.' Adam is beaming; he is so pleased that we are finally getting down to serious work. 'I'm not sure whether you know everyone; we have an extended family now, let me introduce you.'

Jim leaves later, his head is buzzing with all the information he has been given about the strange group and their promise to their families from over 900 years in the future. It is an incredible story but he believes them. He also believes in their dedication to help the human race prevent a global catastrophe.

Chapter Nine

I am enjoying myself with Alf and Martha, the fresh air and simple life are just what I need to bring the colour back to my cheeks and a positive attitude to my thoughts.

The farm is becoming hard work for Alf, he is in his late seventies and the years are taking their toll on his stamina.

'Rose, I don't know what to do about that stubborn old man,' Martha despairs, 'he just won't admit he needs help. He'll drive himself into an early grave. Mark my words he will.'

'Don't fret, Martha. I'm sure there are plenty of young men that will jump at the chance to work on such a lovely farm. Just leave it to me. I'll make Alf think it is his idea to employ a helper.'

Martha chuckles as she watches Rose knead the dough to make some bread. Rose is such a treasure, 'sent from heaven' is how Martha sees her and she knows that Rose can wrap Alf round her little finger.

Alf comes in, 'What you laughing at, woman. Up to no good I bet. Women! Bah.'

He disappears into the next room and both women smile at each other, bound by their shared secret.

Alf comes out a few minutes later, 'I'm going down the Dog and Gun to have a few jars before tea. So I will leave you two to your scheming.' With that he goes.

Bert and Harry are already drinking when Alf arrives at the pub. 'You're late, Alf; we wondered where you'd got to.'

'There's so much to do on the farm I just don't seem to have the time to do it all.'

'You should get some help Alf. None of us are getting any younger.'

'That's what Martha says, but I don't want some whipper-snapper mucking everything up!'

'You're a stubborn man, Alf. Here, drink your ale before I do.'

The three men continue to bait each other and after a couple of pints they all disperse to their separate homes and waiting women. Hopefully with a substantial meal.

Martha and I have fed the dogs and chickens and now we sit at the table which is already set for the meal waiting on the stove.

The door opens, 'Well, where's my dinner then!'

We smile and dish Alf's food on to the plate. He always pretends to be angry, but secretly he feels blessed to have two lovely women in the house. Alf knows he is well looked after and Martha hasn't looked happier for years, Rose fits in to their lives like a pea in a pod.

After the meal has been eaten and everything is cleared away, Alf reads his newspaper and Martha continues to show Rose how to knit. She is knitting a long multi-coloured scarf using all the leftover pieces of wool.

Alf looks over the top of his paper. 'What you knitting there, girl, it looks like a rainbow.'

'It's a scarf, Alf.'

'Well, it has better not be for me. I'd look a right Jesse with all those colours.'

The women laugh and tell him it's for Rose.

'Thank gawd for that.'

'Hey, look at this. Your mate is in the paper. Standing for election at the locals.'

'What's that, Alf?'

'Young Daniel is standing for the elections. The Future Party it says here. Well, I'll be blowed. Good for him I say, let's hope he can bring some common sense into the government. Someone has to start the ball rolling.'

'Can I read it after you, Alf?' I asked, I felt so pleased that positive steps are being made. It makes me feel less guilty for opting out.

'Here, lass, you can have it now, I'm finished with it. How about another cup of tea, Martha? I'm parched.'

It is quite a big piece about the meeting. It seems a lot of people attended and Daniel was able to come across acceptably. There are a few adverse comments but the remainder of the article is positive. It says it is a pleasant change to have someone with a firm belief that he is there to help the people and not that the people are there to promote his success. There is also a nice photograph of Daniel smiling. I will cut that out and put it on my wall.

I love living on the farm but I do miss the others. I decide that I will have to go and see them all.

'Martha, will you mind if I go away for a couple of days to see my friends?'

'Of course not, Rose, I know they will love to see you.'

I go to bed and lay there smiling I am so lucky to have such lovely friends. It takes me a while to get to sleep. My head is buzzing with plans and excitement.

I arrive at the house on Sunday morning, Tom and Charlie run to meet me.

'Rose, you've come back, are you going to stay?'

'Have you come back to play with us? Where have you been?'

'What a lot of questions.' I bend down to hug the boys. 'Who's going to take my bag in for me?'

They struggle for a while and then decide to share the pleasure. I follow behind them, laughing at their obvious difficulty.

'Nice to see you again, Rose. You look well; the country life is definitely good for you.'

'Thanks, Mark. Where is everyone?'

'They have gone to buy a special dinner for the return of the prodigal sister. We are going to eat well today.'

I notice Jim sitting on the sofa.

'Hello, Jim. What a surprise seeing you here.'

'Hello, Rose, how have you been?'

'Very well, thank you. Are you staying for dinner?'

'I hope so. I'm helping to cook it,' Jim replies smiling. 'I've been made an honorary member of your group and I have pledged to help as much as I can.'

'That's really great, Jim; we need more people like you if we are ever going to make a difference.'

During the next hour the house becomes full again and the kitchen is a hive of noisy activity.

They do me proud, dinner is fantastic. The conversation is lively, Daniel talks about the campaign and I fill everyone in on the gossip from the farm.

During the afternoon Becky takes her children to the park so that we can discuss business in peace.

'I can take leaflets and posters for the village. Everyone is talking about you, Daniel. I think you will get a lot of support there.'

'Thanks, Rose, that will definitely help. I have another meeting planned in one of the local schools and I have a feeling it's going to be a tough one.'

'What about you, Rose, are you coming back home soon?'

I lower my head. 'I'm sorry, but the answer's no. I'm needed on the farm. Martha and Alf are getting a bit fragile and they need an extra pair of hands. Although Alf will never admit he needs help!'

'We understand, Rose,' Adam replies. 'And even though you are sorely missed the country air is obviously good for you. You look healthier than any of us!'

I thoroughly enjoy the next few days catching up with gossip but then I start to miss my home, so after a tearful goodbye and promises to visit again soon I return to the farm.

When I get off the bus Alf is waiting for me.

'Nice to have you home, girl,' he says as he takes her bag, 'Martha is cooking our meal so we had better not keep her waiting.'

As they neared the farmyard Martha comes running out of the house, her big white apron blowing in the wind and the sheepdogs hot on her heels barking madly.

'It is so nice to have you home again, Rose. I was frightened you might have wanted to stay in town.'

'No, Martha, this is my home now.'

After a delicious meal I go to sit outside on the porch. Although it is dark it is still relatively mild. I think about my life now and of my previous life. The dogs sleep soundly at my feet. I look up at the velvet night sky and hundreds of stars are twinkling down at me. I wonder if they still look the same in 2999, but no one will ever know because there was no sky then, just an orange fog of pollution covering the planet. Then there were the giant forks of lightening spasmodically dotting the foggy atmosphere crackling downwards from an unknown source. They would hit the ground with a force strong enough to make the earth tremble.

I listen to the farm animals calling and the night birds warning the little creatures that they are on the prowl. Moths fly around the lanterns and mice and shrews run for cover in the hay barn. How beautiful everything is but how easily it can all disappear. It is hard knowing the future, but it is even harder trying to show people what they are doing to their planet. Everyone seems so complacent, as far as they are concerned it is all scaremongering, and even if there is some truth in it, it will not affect them or their children. Then again if there is a slight cause of concern what can they do about it?

The evening air starts to cool so I go inside. Alf has gone to bed and Martha is making a hot drink for herself and me.

'It's getting a bit sharp out there, Martha.'

'It does that and without warning too. Alf's in bed, he gets so tired lately.'

'I've been thinking about trying to find someone to help on the farm. It's market day tomorrow so I'll go and ask around.'

'That will be good, Rose. I've heard that there is a boy staying over the post office. He is slightly older than you and is a quiet lad. He went to agricultural college in the city, drawn there by the bright lights and that, however, he found out it was not for him and he has come back looking for work.'

'Sounds about right, Martha. Do you know his name?'

'His name is Johnny. Most people know him. He's a tall one, with a mop of blond hair and he is as brown as berry.'

The following morning I walk into the village. It isn't hard to spot Johnny; he is sitting in the market square under the old chestnut tree. He is talking with some local farmers as they admire the stock up for sale in the pens. Luckily I know one of the farmers so I go to say hello to him.

'How are you, Harry? What a beautiful day for the market.'

'Sure is, Rose. Did you enjoy your stay in town?'

'Yes, it was lovely to see my friends but I missed Alf and Martha, so I'm pleased to be home again. Alf is getting so tired now I wish I can be more help on the farm but it needs a man. I'm not strong enough,' I admit, hoping that someone will pick up on her silent plea.

'Here's the man you need. Young, fit and looking for work.'

I blush; Johnny is really quite good-looking. As he turns to face her his unruly blond hair falls over his sparkling hazel eyes. He seems shy but with a hint of humour under the surface.

'Hi, my name's Johnny. So where's this work?' he asks. His voice is warm and comforting.

'Hello, I'm Rose, I live with Alf and Martha on their farm. Alf is finding it hard work on his own but he is too proud to admit it.'

'I know the farm, but I haven't met Alf yet. I can come by tomorrow, early, and offer my services and see how it goes from there.'

'That will be great.'

'How about you and I go and get something to eat and you can fill me in as to what needs doing on the farm.'

I accept the invitation and soon we are chatting like life time friends. We have a lot in common, especially our love for the countryside and the simple life. We both have sampled towns and found them claustrophobic.

By the time I start off home I am in a very good mood, with a smile on my face and a spring in my step.

Martha asks me about my day and I tell her all that I can remember about Johnny.

'Is he a nice boy?'

I want to say he is dreamy but say instead, 'Yes, he seems very sensible. He is coming here early tomorrow morning so we will have to make sure Alf is around.'

Martha makes Alf his favourite tea, and I ask how the work is going on the farm.

'I'm getting a lot of special treatment tonight. What are you two up to?'

'Nothing, Alf. We're just interested in your work.'

'Are you now? Well, I've been trying to mend the dry stone walling on the far field but its heavy work and it takes such a long time. I have to put all the other jobs on hold until I've done it. Which means I'm running a bit behind with sorting out the lambs for market.'

'Oh, Alf, can I help?'

'Thanks lass, but it's not women's work. I'll see whether Bert or Harry can come over for a day or two, but they may be up to their eyes in it too.'

We sit and eat our meal in silence. Alf is thinking that he may have to swallow his pride and hire someone. Although he doesn't know how he can find the money to pay them. I am thinking of Johnny, and Martha is thinking how tired her husband looks.

The next day is sunny and bright but with a keen wind blowing from the north. As we are finishing our breakfast there is a soft knock at the door.

'Who can that be at this time of the morning?' Alf grumbles.

Martha opens the door to see Johnny with his head down and shuffling his feet.

'Hello, young man, what can we do for you?'

'I was wondering if you have any work I can do?'

'You'd better come in and ask the man of the house.'

'Who's this then, Martha?'

'It's someone asking if we have any work for him, Alf.'

Johnny looks rather nervous.

'So what's your name, lad?'

'Johnny, sir.'

'And you want some farm work do you?'

'Yes, please. I don't need wages, just a roof over my head and food in my stomach.'

'Have you done farm work before then?'

'I was brought up on a farm and I went to agricultural college.'

'Did you now?'

'Let the lad sit down, Alf.' Martha turns to the young man, 'Have you had any breakfast? I have some bacon left over I can do you a sandwich and a cup of tea.'

Johnny smiles a prize winning smile. 'That will be lovely, thank you.'

I give him his drink and sandwich while Alf cross-examines him a bit more.

'Can you do dry stone walling?'

'Yes, it's one of my specialities.'

Alf nods. 'Right you are then, you can help me today and we'll see how it goes.'

'Thank you, sir, you won't regret it.'

'I will if you keep calling me, sir. My name's Alf and this is my wife Martha and the lass is Rose. Now come on drink up we have work to do.'

As soon as the men had gone Martha and I join hands and had a little dance around the kitchen.

'Well, that was easier than I thought it would be. My, what a nice lad he is, and he's got an eye for you, Rose.'

'Don't be daft, Martha; he wouldn't look twice at me.'

'He already has, my girl. Now we've got a lot to do, but first we better clear up the mess in here. Then we'll go over to the small barn, there's a nice little room above it that will be an ideal spare bedroom. It will need a clean though.'

I am surprised to see that there is already a bed in the room. Martha tells me they had used it for people who had got stranded because of bad weather or if anyone came to do some work on the farm.

We spend most of the morning cleaning and making up the bed, by the time we have finished it looked a right little palace.

When the men come back for lunch they find food on the table waiting for them.

'What have you two been up to?' Alf asks. 'You both look a bit flushed.'

'Working hard, Alf. You don't seem to realise how much there is for us to do here.'

'It's a good job you've got Rose to help you then, isn't it? And now I've got Johnny here to help me. So you two had better get the spare room ready for him.'

Martha and I look at each other and laugh, we didn't dare tell Alf that we have already done it.

'Right you are. Consider it done. Welcome to our home, Johnny,' Martha replies, as she and I break into another fit of giggles.

'Come on, lad, goodness knows what's got into those women. Let's leave them to it.'

Johnny gives Rose another of his smiles as he followed Alf through the door.

'There, what did I tell you, Rose? He's got an eye for you.'

I feel embarrassed but pleased.

Chapter Ten

Back in town Daniel is getting ready to embark on a new adventure. Jim quite rightly points out that although we have already grown accustom to many things that had disappeared in their time, we still have a lot to learn.

So far we have experienced road vehicles, grown used to nature buzzing round them and animals roaming everywhere. However, we had yet to face the big cities and the railway network that linked them.

Daniel has attended his last meeting with his normal enthusiastic insight to the problems that are unfolding through ecological misuse. He is, unfortunately, confounded by some wider issues that are raised and the media has jumped on his obvious inexperience in these areas.

Jim decides that it is about time that Daniel confronts the metropolis, they are going to spend a few days in London, and they are going to travel by train.

They arrive at the main line station in good time, Jim takes the opportunity to explain about buying tickets and the working of the destination board. Daniel is in awe of the large machines that roar in and out of the station pulling lines of coaches full of eager travellers.

'Wow, how do people know which train to get and whether it's going to stop where they want to get off?'

'That's what the destination board is for; it tells the final destination of the train and lists all the stops. It also shows what platform the train is leaving from and what time it departs.'

'That's really clever. But say you want to go somewhere that's not shown?'

'Then when you buy your ticket they will tell you where to get off and change trains to one that will go to your destination. Unfortunately you might have to change trains a few times.'

'That sounds scary. Don't lose me, Jim. I might never be seen again!' Daniel says laughing.

Jim realises that his friend may be of high intelligence but he still has a lot to learn and Jim feels proud that he can teach him.

They eventually board their train and are soon speeding through the countryside. Their journey is going to take a few hours so Daniel is able to take in the forever changing scenery. He is amazed at the number of large towns they go through and keeps asking Jim if they are London.

'No, not yet, you'll know when we get to London. It is big, really big.'

Daniel cannot envisage anywhere bigger than the multitude of towns that they have already passed. He always knows when a town is near because the fields slowly disappear and houses get closer together. Then there always seems to be a string of scrapyards piled high with crashed and rusted vehicles, followed by buildings in the middle of demolition. Then the station appears.

Eventually they hit the London suburbs, Daniel sees buildings that reach for the sky and Jim tells him they are flats, homes in the air. In the city centre the buildings are taller but they are mainly offices.

'You are telling me that people live up there in the sky?' It must take them a long time to get to the ground; there must be at least thirty floors.'

'At least,' replies Jim, 'but they have lifts, unfortunately they don't always work.'

Daniel thinks about being cooped up in a large building with hundreds of other people. Just like bees in a hive. At least in the home where he had come from there was space to stroll even if they were enclosed. He finds it hard to imagine so many people living in one city. He realises that millions of people must have perished when the Earth had finally dished out its revenge against centuries of neglect.

The train starts to slow down and it is swallowed by a towering Victorian building with a high cavernous roof supported by ornate iron framework and pillars.

When they leave the train Daniel stays close to Jim. It is rather frightening to see policemen with guns and dogs patrolling the departure hall. There are thousands of people milling around, but crouched up in corners are the homeless, tramps, drug addicts and alcoholics.

'Good grief, Jim,' exclaims Daniel, 'it looks like a scene from Dante's Inferno but without the fire. There are so many people; they look like lost souls trying to find their way out.'

'You're not far wrong, Daniel. Many of these people are probably visitors like us. There will not be many true Londoners here at this hour. Railway stations can be dangerous places for the uninitiated. There are many opportunists waiting in the wings ready to pounce on an innocent victim.'

'Let's get out of here.'

Jim smiles and turns to hail a cab. 'In you get, Daniel; we'll soon be at our hotel.'

The hotel is situated near the main line Victoria rail station, another grand structure that had been erected when steam rail travel was new and exciting. Daniel is awe struck by the buildings, the throngs of people rushing past in every direction, the mass of red buses and the black taxi cabs. He just stands and watches, he never imagined that anywhere could be so crowded, noisy and busy.

'Come on, Daniel, let's get booked in and get rid of our luggage. Then we will go out on the town. I will show you things that you will never have read in your archives at home.' Jim winks at Daniel and pushes him up the steps and through the doors.

That night Jim takes Daniel to Leicester Square. There must be a premier film showing at the Odeon because there is a red carpet leading to the door and hundreds of people clambering to see who gets out of each limousine. Cameras are flashing repeatedly.

Daniel laughs, 'Now I've seen everything. Why all the fuss, they are only ordinary people like us?'

'You know that and so do I, but to the majority they are heroes, as if the characters they play on screen are real.'

They move on to Piccadilly Circus with its flashing advertisements lighting up the buildings surrounding the square, and in the middle stands Eros pointing his arrow to the lovelorn of the city. The traffic is endless and the noise deafening.

The next stop is a small Italian restaurant for their evening meal.

'I don't think I've ever eaten an Italian meal before. I don't know what to choose.'

'That's all right, Daniel, play safe and have a bolognese or a lasagne.'

Daniel thoroughly enjoys the meal, which they wash down with a delicious Italian red wine.

'Not bad, eh?' Jim says as they leave the restaurant, 'Tomorrow we will try Chinese!'

Daniel is ready to try anything, 'What's next?'

'How about Trafalgar Square, that's where Lord Nelson stands on a high column looking over the City and below there are four giant lions protecting him. There are some beautiful fountains as well.'

'Wow, lead me to it. But we have several days here yet. We don't have to see everything today.'

'You must be joking. Even if we stay for six months we still wouldn't have the time to see everything that London has to offer.'

Trafalgar Square is flood lit, some of the lights are shining on the fountains making the water glisten. Lights shine on Lord Nelson at the top of his tall column and others are illuminating the fantastic columns of a Roman styled building standing at the top of a wide flight of stone steps. The Square is full of people, sitting talking, listening to music, taking photographs or feeding the hundreds of pigeons.

'What's through that big arch, Jim? It looks very important.'

'That's the Mall. It leads to Buckingham Palace, where the royal family live.'

'Can we go and see it?'

'Of course, that's our next point of call. It's on our way back to the hotel.'

They leave the hustle and bustle of Trafalgar Square and walk down the Mall.

'It's a very wide road and the buildings are very grand. What are all those poles for?'

'They're the flag posts. On ceremonial occasions flags will fly from them, sometimes the Union Jack or the Royal Standard, depending on the occasion. That large statue in the middle of the road is Queen Victoria, our Queen's grandmother.'

Daniel and Jim stood outside the railings of Buckingham Palace, the building is also floodlit, but Daniel is fascinated with the sentries and the unique sentry boxes they stand in front of.

'What are they wearing on their heads?'

'Bearskins. They are supposed to be very heavy, and look at their red jackets and gold buttons. They are the Grenadier Guards, the elite; they have a very high standard to maintain. However, they still defend the country when called upon.'

'They don't go to war wearing all that do they?'

'No,' laughs Jim, 'mind you I would like to see the enemy's faces if they did. They have combat uniforms they use for other duties.'

'So who is the reigning monarch now?'

'It's Queen Elizabeth II, but mainly in name only; she is getting very frail now. The majority of her duties are performed by her grandson Prince William.'

'Does she not have a son to step into line?'

'There are three princes and a princess, but the eldest prince has not always been too popular with the people, so the next in succession could be his son Prince William. Everyone likes him; I think he will be a good King.'

They turn left and go through St James's Park, it is dark now and as they go over the bridge that spans the lake they can see the Parliament buildings and Big Ben bathed in even more floodlights. Just behind these buildings is the massive London Eye wheel turning slowly, carrying some late tourists high above the Thames on the last sightseeing spin of the day.

Jim and Daniel sit in the bar at the hotel having a night cap before retiring.

'It is so weird, Jim. I have actually seen things that have been listed in our archives at home. No words or pictures can possibly capture the reality. Our world is just a place purely for survival. You couldn't call it a life, because it wasn't. It was just an existence, waiting for the inevitable to happen.'

'I can't even begin to envisage the life you came from. It is so sad to think that everything that has been developed over hundreds of years will be wiped out so easily.'

After a good night's sleep, aided by several nightcaps, the men are ready to explore some more.

'So what would you like to see today? There's the Natural History Museum, the Tower and Tower Bridge, St Paul's Cathedral and, of course, Parliament.'

'Let's follow history in the right order; we'll go to the Natural History Museum first.'

They go down to the underground station at Victoria and catch the District line to South Kensington. Daniel is relieved it is only a couple of stops, it is going to take some time for him to get used to travelling underground, and he hates the escalators, he always panics getting on and off. The handrail seems to go faster than the moving stairs.

They emerge from the station to blinding sunlight, but once they have grown accustomed to the glare they see the museum just across the road.

The two friends walk up the time worn steps with many other sightseers and into the main entrance hall. Daniel stops in amazement; there in front of him is the biggest skeleton he has ever seen.

'Wow, what is that?' He is completely transfixed.

'That, Daniel, is the bona fide skeleton of one of the biggest creatures ever to walk the Earth. Meet Diplodocus or Dippy for short.'

'We have pictures in our archives, but to actually see something like this is mind-blowing. I cannot believe that after carefully preserving such a wonderful specimen it will disappear off the face of the Earth yet again.'

'It is sad, and it is unfortunate that you cannot show what the consequences are going to be caused by mankind's ignorance.'

Daniel and Jim spend a few hours wandering through the museum. Every exhibit shows what the world has lost when nature tips the balance against all living creatures.

'It is regrettable, Jim, that in our time the birds and animals are locked away in our glass pods, we have tried to duplicate nature but it is not the same as having the freedom to roam. Underneath all the façade is nothing except the dogged perseverance to survive, an archive of microfilms and maybe a few, a very few precious books.'

Jim can tell that his friend is getting melancholy. 'I think it's time we moved on, Daniel. Let's go to the Tower of London and Tower Bridge. We can catch a bus this time so that we can see more.'

Daniel much prefers the bus. He still can't believe how busy the city is, people are scurrying around like ants. They see the large dome of St Paul's Cathedral on their left and the River Thames on their right. Then Tower Bridge comes into sight and next to it is the majestic Tower of London.

Daniel is astounded by the work that has gone into building the bridge. As they stand admiring the intricate design a tall ship appears and then the road section slowly starts to rise and separate so that the ship can sail underneath the structure.

'How about seeing the crown jewels, Daniel, and of course, the Bloody Tower.'

'Why is it called that, or should I not ask?'

'The Tower has a gory history. The Bloody Tower is where two young princes were put to death. They were only boys but were considered a threat to the monarchy. A large number of people ended their days rather horribly in the Tower. There is even a gate leading to the dungeons straight from the river. It is called Traitors Gate.'

'They're fancy uniforms,' remarks Daniel pointing to the guards standing at the entry to the Tower.

'They are officially known as Yeoman Wardens, but are also called Beef-eaters,'

'Why? Is that all they eat then?'

'Do you know, Daniel; I've never really thought about it. I suppose it is so easy to take things for granted. That's one of the biggest problems we have nowadays. Taking things for granted and then moaning when they disappear.'

Jim and Daniel are herded into the Jewel House with a party of Japanese visitors. It is a darkish room with large glass cabinets, lit by strong lights. The Crown Jewels take everyone's breath away. It is hard to comprehend that these marvellous pieces of jewellery are hundreds of years old, the craftsmanship is fantastic. The precious stones are so finely cut that every facet catches and throws back the light. The engravings in the gold are intricate, detailing every figure, leaf or flower to perfection.

Outside in the sunshine again Daniel notices the large black birds.

'I've never seen birds quite like them before, what are they?'

'They're ravens. It has been said that as long as they stay at the Tower of London, England will stay free. It might be just a legend but I'm told that they are encouraged to stay here. They probably think it is better to be safe than sorry.'

Daniel leans against the wall and looks down at the Thames.

'Fancy a trip on a boat, Daniel?'

Daniels eyes light up like a child's. 'Can we?'

Jim laughs, 'Of course we can. A boat will take us down to Westminster Bridge and we can see Parliament, Big Ben and Number 10 Downing Street where the Prime Minister lives.'

The river boat takes about half an hour to reach Westminster Bridge and Daniel listens avidly to the captain who talks about each point of interest, first on one bank and then the other. Daniel's head is turning left and right trying to pick out each monument or building mentioned. He sees the Shakespeare Globe theatre that was originally built in the 1500s and partly owned by Shakespeare himself, Cleopatra's Needle, St Paul's Cathedral, The Royal Festival Hall and many more. He feels quite exhausted when they finally leave the boat.

'That must be Big Ben and there is the Houses of Parliament. Jim, you will never know how much this means to me.'

'That church over the road is Westminster Abbey, most of the royalty get married there and have done for centuries, it is a beautiful building, don't you think?'

'It really is well looked after, especially with the fumes and dirt from the traffic bombarding the stone façade continuously. Can we go into Parliament?'

'We should be able to; I think the Government is in recession so we will be able to have a good look round.'

They enter the grand entrance hall, Daniel looks up to see the ceiling far above him and the tall, intricately carved wooden doors. By some miracle they are able to join a school group and they are ushered through the House of Commons with the green leather seats and then through to the House of Lords which sport the red leather seats. Even Jim is amazed how big the whole building is; it seems they have walked for miles through cloisters and corridors until finally they are out in the sunshine again.

'Well, that was an experience. How do you fancy working there, Daniel. That's some office?'

'You're not kidding. I don't think I would ever find my office if I worked there.'

They decide to have some refreshment before they walk to Downing Street, buying themselves overpriced hot dogs and a bottle of water each. They sit on the wall of Westminster Bridge and watch the people go by, count the red London buses and watch the antics of the black taxi cab drivers. The noise and hustle and bustle is mesmerising.

'Everyone is in so much hurry. Even the tourists don't seem to want to stop and savour the atmosphere. They just take their photographs and move on to the next attraction.'

'That's how it is nowadays, Daniel. No one actually stops and stares. All this history surrounding them and they couldn't give a damn. The only time they notice anything is usually when it upsets their routine. And then, oh boy, do they voice their opinions!'

'There are more people here than the number of people left in the whole world in my time,' Daniel says pensively.

When they finally reach the famous Number 10 they find that tall railings and double gates restrain them from actually standing outside the Prime Minister's residence. Jim explains that security demands protection from terrorists etc., but years ago his mother actually stood next to the ever present police guard on the steps and had her photograph taken with him.

'Times change, but not always for the better. The basic rule of Yin and Yang seems to have disappeared and I can't understand why. It is such an obvious concept, everything has to balance, from the workings of the human body to the man-made via the natural forces. It is so simple but overrun by technology and progress.' Jim sighs.

It is Daniel's turn to try to lift their moods, 'Come on, Jim, we're going home tomorrow. I have learned so much, I have a much clearer idea in the direction I need to take, so our excursion has been successful. I will be pleased to return to our little haven in the north, people are much friendlier there, but for the rest of today let's just allow London to show us what it can offer.'

Jim smiles at Daniel's continual enthusiasm. 'Right I know where I would like to go and I'm sure you will enjoy it too.'

'Not the underground again, Jim,' complains Daniel as Jim pushes him towards Westminster station.

'Afraid so, Daniel, but it will be worth it, we are going to wide open spaces with wild animals as well.'

Daniel is confused, how could there be wide open spaces in London, it is so full of high buildings, roads, traffic and people.

They leave the underground at Regent's Park and when they arrive at the top of the escalators they can see the sunshine welcoming them again. Across the road are trees and gardens, and of course, hundreds of people. It will take a long time for Daniel to get used to being surrounded by so many people.

They go through the turnstile into London Zoo and Daniel can't believe his eyes.

'Wow, look at all those animals, look at those elephants, they are so big and look at their trunks, and the giraffes, their necks are so long and so are their legs and so thin as well. They look like they may break at any minute, but the animals walk so elegantly.'

Jim is enjoying watching Daniel's reactions; it is like taking a young child out for the day.

Daniel and Jim spend an enjoyable afternoon visiting the reptile house, then watching the antics of the monkeys and gorillas. Marvelling at the penguins and polar bears and being wowed by the big cats, the lions, tigers, leopards, cheetahs and panthers and many more. The birds of prey are majestic, eagles, falcons, vultures and the wise old owls. Matched only by the beauty of the exotic birds from all over the world, birds of paradise, parrots and water birds in a multitude of colours. Their final stop is the large sea mammals: whales, sharks, seals, porpoises and the endearing dolphins.

By the time the Zoo is preparing to close Jim and Daniel are near to collapsing.

'I think it's time we sample the ale at a good old English pub,' remarks Jim, 'and I think I can see just the place.'

Daniel looks to where Jim is pointing and he sees a lovely old building surrounded by gardens.

They have a typical English meal washed down with the best real ale. As they sit and enjoy their surroundings someone starts to play the piano and soon the whole pub is singing along to a melody of old favourite songs. It is quite late when they return to the hotel that night; they are tired but full of good cheer.

In the morning they spoil themselves with a full English breakfast because it is going to be a long journey home.

Chapter Eleven

Johnny settles in at the farm really well. Martha is glad that Alf now has the help he needs and I am delighted to have the opportunity to spend so much time with Johnny, although I am still very secretive about my feelings for him.

'Our men will be home soon for their dinner, Rose, I think we should bake them a cake. Do you realise Johnny has been here for a whole month now?'

'Is it that long already, we will have to have a celebration. Have we any home brew left?'

'You go and draw some off into a flagon and I will rustle up a nice Victoria sponge.'

By the time the men return from the fields we have put a spread fit for royalty on the table.

Alf comes in first, he and Johnny are laughing about something that has happened during the day.

'Well, look at this, I think these women are expecting company, Johnny.'

'Don't be daft, Alf, it's for you two. Now go and get cleaned up and I will start serving.'

I have put on my best dress; I really want Johnny to notice me tonight.

'You going out, Rose?' asks Alf.

'No, I just feel like wearing something different.'

'And very nice you look too,' remarks Johnny.

I lower my head as I feels my face redden.

While we are settling down to a relaxing evening Johnny suddenly jumps up, startling everyone.

'I completely forgot. I found something really strange in the woods above the cottage where you used to live, Rose. I'll go and get it and see whether you know what it is.'

He comes back with a metallic sphere cupped in his hands.

'I have never seen anything like it before and I have no idea what type of metal it is made from.'

I look up; I feel the colour drain from my face. I take a deep breath.

'What is the matter, Rose; you've gone as white as a sheet?' Martha says as she gets up from her chair and puts her arm around me.

I pull myself together, 'Nothing honestly, I am just surprised to see it again. It belongs to Adam, he is very fond of it. I think it belonged to one of his parents before they died. It really is nothing special but I'm sure he will be pleased to have it back.'

Johnny is curious at Rose's reaction but he says nothing.

'Well, my girl, if it's that precious to Adam you had better take it to him. It's Saturday tomorrow, why don't you take the bus into town, it will be a good opportunity to see your friends again.'

'I think I will, Martha,' I examine the object in my hands. I know what it is but never expected to see anything like it again. My hands are shaking. 'I think I will go and pack so that I'm ready for the first bus.'

When I left the room Johnny looks quizzically at Martha.

'There are a lot of questions unanswered concerning Rose and her friends Johnny;' Martha tries to explain, 'the five of them suddenly appeared on millennium eve. They all looked the same and continually wore hoods. We were very cautious but they turned out to be extremely polite, clever and hardworking. The whole village helped them, but we never pried, we felt if they wanted to tell us where they came from then they would. They were a boost to our little community and we were all very sad to see them leave for the town.'

'But Rose came back?'

'Yes, she did not feel comfortable in the town and was sickly, but she has thrived again here. We feel blessed that she returned to us.'

'Do you think I should suggest going with her?'

'Not this time, Johnny. They have a very close-knit relationship, but in time I'm sure Rose will want to introduce you to her friends. Just be patient.'

Johnny nods. He likes Rose a great deal but he will play it at her pace.

I arrive at the boys' house before breakfast and tentatively knock at the door. Mark looking decidedly tousled opens it.

'Rose, what a lovely surprise, but why so early? We are all still in bed.'

'Sorry, Mark, but this is important.'

'Well, don't just stand there, come in. We had a late night, Daniel has just come back from a trip to London and he was telling us about everything he saw and had done.'

I go into the kitchen to make myself a drink while Mark wakes everyone else. Adam is the first to appear.

'What's the mystery, Rose?'

'Something has been found near where we arrived. We need everyone else here, but no outsiders for now.'

'Now I am intrigued. Leave it to me, I will get Daisy over here and then you can explain to all of us at the same time.'

'Thanks, Adam.'

A few hours later we are sitting together. I am nervous as I am still not used to being the centre of attention, the others look at me expectantly.

'Johnny, our new farm hand came in with this last night,' I reach into my bag and bring out the metallic orb. Everyone gasps.

Mark breaks the silence, 'Talk about a blast from the past, or should I say future.'

Adam takes the object from me and fondly turns it in his hands. 'It's a document device. They must have found a way to send us information.'

'Come on then, Adam, let's see what it says.'

'I think it might be prudent if we record the message, some of these devices only activate once and then the message is gone. Go and get the recorder, Mark.'

Once they are set up, Adam starts to turn the object around in his hands until he finds what he is looking for. There is a small pinprick of light shining from the orb; it is almost invisible to the human eye. Adam gently rubs it and the whole thing starts to glow with a pulsating light. We hold our breath. Then suddenly the orb splits in half. There is a strange whooshing noise followed by the voice of one of the Elders.

'We don't know whether you will ever get this message. We don't even know if you are all still together. We wish you well whatever you are doing and wherever you are. You are all missed continuously and are in our prayers and

our thoughts. Nothing has altered here; we are still trying to find the answer to help us improve our environment and our settlements. We have heard that some pockets of civilisation have started to burrow underground to try to join our scattered villages together.

There is an important reason that we took this risk to reach you. We now know that the destruction of life on Earth was not only caused by man's disrespect towards the balance of nature, or the increase in the number of violent earthquakes. Each of them tilting our planet's axis a bit further and altering the weather patterns. The final blow came from a large meteorite that hit the Earth violently in 2603. This meteorite was drawn in through holes in Earth's magnetic field that had been gradually exposed by our shifting poles. The solar winds from the sun had found these weak areas in our magnetic fields a hundred years earlier. Continually bombarding our planet with heat strong enough to vaporize much of the oceans and rivers turning large areas of the Earth's surface into deserts. That was our Armageddon.

We hope this helps you in your task.

May God be with you all.'

There is silence in the room, a few tears flow. The severity of our task is brought back to us.

A knock at the door brings us back to the present.

'I'll go,' Daisy says as she heads for the door.

When she returns she has a smile on her face.

'Who is it, Daisy?'

'It was a young lad wanting a 'bob a job' for his scouts group. I nearly told him we had a job for him, but I didn't. I just gave him some money. Poor mite, do you realise he could be the next World leader.'

We all laugh, glad that the tension of the last half hour has been broken.

Mark remarks, 'I can't believe this document device was found. I wonder how long it had been there.'

Adam turns the metal sphere in his hand. He is deep in thought.

'Penny for them.'

'Sorry, Mark, I was miles away then, or should I say years away. What are your thoughts?'

'I think it's time we start to form a campaign of action. We all hear and see the changes that are taking place and the devastation that it causes. It now seems evident that man is hastening the ecological cycle of our planet.'

Mark pauses and then continues, 'No one can alter the cycle but there is a chance it can be delayed long enough for mankind to prepare for the inevitable.'

Adam nods and then turns to Daniel, 'You're our ace card, Daniel. When you are elected we will have a foothold towards the parliamentary system. I hope you noticed I said when and not if. We all have to concentrate our energy into making sure Daniel is successful at the election. I'm open to ideas, so let's have them.'

'We can run a story in the local paper. I'm sure the editor would go for it if I led in with a bit of sensationalism.'

'Good, that will definitely help, Mark.'

'We can deliver leaflets. A carefully worded leaflet might raise interest to the townspeople,' Daniel offers.

I also offered to deliver leaflets to the villages and farms in my area.

Daisy says she will speak at women's institutions, WRVS and local church groups.

Adam smiles, he can't ask for better support.

Mark says, 'I'm sure I can help in composing and producing the leaflets.'

'Wow, that's what I call a backing team,' Daniel says, smiling, 'I just hope I can live up to everyone's expectations.'

'There are three weeks left until the elections so we have to put our heads down and come up with a message that will leave the voters in no doubt that Daniel is the man to vote for. Who's with us then?' shouts Adam.

'We are,' we answer.

When Becky and Mary arrive with the children they are faced with a hive of industry.

'What is going on here? We leave you for a while and return to what is increasingly resembling a paper mountain.'

'Hello, Mary,' Mark says as he helps her off with her coat, 'we have decided we must make a conservative effort to help Daniel get elected. We are trying to come up with a leaflet that is concise, packs a punch and informative. But it's not that easy, as you can see.' He laughs as he sweeps his arm round the room to indicate the ever increasing pile of screwed up paper.

Becky's children start running through the discarded paper. This encourages a paper ball fight and ends up with everyone joining in, then collapsing on the chairs.

'I think it's time for dinner,' Becky shouts, 'so clear up this mess and lay the table.'

'Yes, Mum,' Daniel says grinning.

We decide to have a more focused effort later, but as it is Saturday and the sun is shining, we all want to make the most of the weather and go out after dinner.

I leave to go back to the farm. I have not told anyone about my growing feelings for Johnny; I have decided that can wait for a while.

On the return journey I feel my spirits soar, I love the countryside and my life with Alf and Martha, but mainly I love being close to Johnny. It is great being with my friends again but there is a part of me that feels empty when I am away from him.

When I arrive at the village I take a deep breath of the country air.

'That's better.'

'Talking to yourself is the first sign of old age.'

I turn round and see Johnny behind me.

'What are you doing here?'

'I thought I would come and meet you so that I can accompany you home,' Johnny answers as he leans forward and kisses her on the cheek. 'Welcome home.'

I am so embarrassed, 'I've only been gone a few hours.'

'But it feels like months to me.'

'You're daft.'

'That's me, daft about you. Come on, let's get you home.'

I take his offered hand and smile as we walk down the country lane back to the farm.

Martha is standing at the door of the farmhouse when we arrive. She is wringing her hands in worry and there are tears in her eyes.

I run up to her, 'What's the matter, Martha, why are you crying?'

'It's that stubborn man of mine, he won't listen to me and now he's collapsed on the floor and I can't wake him and he is too heavy for me to move.'

Johnny rushes into the house while I put a comforting arm round Martha and guide her through the door.

Alf is laying by the hearth, he is deathly white.

'We had better not move him in case he has hurt himself when he fell. Rose, can you make Martha a cup of tea while I phone for an ambulance?'

Martha just sits in her chair quietly crying, tears fall down her cheeks on to her spotless apron.

The ambulance comes quickly and the medics lift Alf onto the stretcher while talking calmly to Martha. She wants to accompany her husband to hospital so Johnny and I say we will follow in a borrowed car.

When we arrive at the hospital Martha has calmed down a little and is sitting outside the treatment room. She gets up as soon as she sees us.

'I'm so glad you are here. Alf has come round a bit but he is covered with wires joined up to television screens that keep bleeping and buzzing.'

'Don't worry about them, Martha, they are called monitors and they help the nursing staff and doctors to see what is going on with Alf.'

'I am so scared, Rose, I don't know what I would have done if he had gone and left me.'

'It is just nature's way of telling Alf to slow down a bit.'

'I keep telling him that, but he won't listen to me. Stubborn old man. He insisted on shifting those bales of hay in the barn. I told him to wait until you got back Johnny, but no, he had to do it himself.'

'Now don't you get worked up again, Martha. We are here with you and Alf is in safe hands,' Johnny says as he puts his arm around her.

The doctor comes out of the treatment room and approaches Martha.

'Are you Alf's wife?

'Yes. Is he going to be all right?'

'Well, he will have to stay with us for a while, just so that we can keep an eye on him. He has had a mild stroke, so he will have to scale down his work otherwise he might not be so lucky next time. You can go and see him now. He has been asking for you.'

Martha hurries into the room, she is so pleased to see that Alf is now sitting up a bit, but he still looks extremely pale.

'You stubborn old man. Now maybe you'll listen to me in future.'

Alf gives a half smile.

'Do you know how much I love you, Martha?'

'It's made you go soft in the head!' she replies, but inwardly she swells with pride. 'They say you've got to stay here for a while. They don't trust you either.'

Johnny and I assure Alf that we will help Martha look after the farm. We reluctantly leave him to the experienced care of the hospital, promising to return first thing in the morning.

It is a hard night for us. The farmhouse seems empty without Alf. I make supper. Martha and Johnny then go to their separate beds, one exhausted with emotion, the other to prepare himself for an early start in the morning.

I clear the dishes and go outside to sit for a while.

It is a mild clear night, the moon has not yet risen but the velvet sky is decorated again with thousands of stars.

My mind wanders back and forth through the centuries. I feel like a speck of dust landing for a while then being blown onwards to another destination. That's all we are, I think, just a speck of dust in a gigantic galaxy. We have the power to accelerate changes, we can ruin the lives of every living thing, but in the end we have to bow down to extreme forces bigger than we can ever imagine.

Alf is discharged after a week of rest and told that he will have to have regular checks. During the time he has been in hospital Johnny, Martha and I have augmented a new routine that will still include Alf so that he does not feel useless. It will allow for everything to run smoothly if he or anyone else finds he is tempting fate again.

Chapter Twelve

I keep everyone in town informed of Alf's progress and they are relieved when they hear that things are back on track at the farm. Now they can concentrate on the forthcoming elections. Most of the printing has been completed and talks have already taken place at church halls, schools and clubs.

The media have been diverted away from the elections by the horrific killings of twelve local people and many more people wounded by a local man who went on the rampage with a gun. The police chased him for over four hours, but the gunman ended the siege by turning the gun on to himself. He is reported to have been acting out of character and many suggestions are coming forward, including an unexplained brainstorm.

The main consensus, after all the facts are brought out into the open which included terrible financial problems, family problems and a feeling of low esteem, that bad as all these were the gunman was dealing with them. So an outside force seemed to have temporarily kicked off the brainstorm. By the time he had reached an isolated wooded area he had come to his senses again and realised the full horror of the things he had done in the last four hours. He then turned the gun onto himself.

There is a theory that CO_2 was catapulted through our protective zone which allowed the over activity of sunspots to penetrate our atmosphere for a short time. This could have reacted on vulnerable people causing them to act out of character. It is a possibility that is being researched.

Scientists are realising that as our planet evolves there are going to be many unexplained phenomenons that will need to be addressed, aggravated by the damage being inflicted on our atmosphere.

Two months previously a volcano in Iceland had erupted and dust belched in to the sky at an alarming rate. This dust was blown over the United Kingdom and Europe, grounding all aircrafts. The disruption lasted for about two weeks leaving people stranded at airports.

Daniel is getting nervous, he knows he has a very important role and everything depends on him being elected. He also knows that he has a brilliant team of people helping him. He has one more conference to do and it will be his most important, because what he says will be remembered on Election Day.

It is twenty-four hours before the elections commence; Daniel and his friends have arrived at the local town hall for the conference. There are a lot of people milling around, of which many are reporters and photographers. Reports of a new type of candidate with a fresh approach have circulated among the media and they are all curious to see whether he is another crank or someone who really ought to be listened to. Either way they know they are sure of a good story.

The conference will allow each of the candidates to state their case and concerns for the people. After everyone has spoken the meeting will be thrown open for questions. As the town is a key seat to parliamentary parties the conference is being televised live.

'Have you seen all the people out there?' Daniel whispers nervously.

'You won't be the only one who feels vulnerable; the rest of the candidates will not be used to so much attention either,' Jim assures him.

'Speak from the heart,' Adam advises Daniel, 'you will be the only one out there that really knows what is going to happen if greed, stupidity and ignorance is allowed to rule heads.'

'You're right, Adam. I think I'm ready.'

Daniel walks onto the stage and takes his seat with the other candidates.

It is a long night and Daniel is the last to speak. He hopes everyone hasn't switched off before he gets his turn.

He speaks of his concern in respect of the changing weather patterns; he also mentions that he is fearful of the effects of the rate of progress and the consequences of this progress on future generations.

Bigger is not always better if it is just a quick fix and is completed without truly knowing how it will change the way we perceive our planet. Vast areas are being altered to cater for mankind's greed in possessing the newest, the best and the quickest way to riches.

No thought is being given to how future civilisation will cope with loss of imperative factors needed to maintain the cycle of life on this planet.

Daniel is aware that he might be talking in riddles to many people so he decides to simplify his arguments.

'If you think of a bucket of water left in the garden. It will stay full if it is left undisturbed. The sun's heat will evaporate some of it, birds and animals will make use of it, but then the rain will come and restore it back to its level and some might even overflow to the ground to water the plants. However, if you throw pebbles into the water you will not only make ripples but you will lessen the volume of water. If you throw rocks in the bucket the water will splash out until all that is left is a bucket of rocks and the natural resource has gone.

'Every time we change the way we live we are throwing pebbles into the natural cycle of our planet. Everything we use has to eventually be disposed of, if it will not break down naturally, we bury it. Sometimes we use innovative devices to improve our lives, but we do not realise the consequences of their use on future generations. They can emit the wrong type of gases during production or cause a problem at the end of its life because it will be buried with all the other rogue materials'

Daniel is aware that the hall is unnervingly quiet and he is hoping that it is because people are listening and that they have not fallen asleep. He decides to round of his arguments with poignant facts.

'You will realise by now that I feel very strongly about our future, but I haven't forgotten our present. It is my aim to improve everyone's way of living and that will ultimately improve our future. We need to be enlightened in the way we all can help to make a better a world, from the people at the so-called top, right down to us. We can't stop the natural evolution, but we can stop us hastening it. Thank you for listening.'

The hall resounds with applause, cameras flash and people cheer. Daniel's colleagues at the side of the stage start dancing around like children. It has gone well.

'Calm down, you lot, we've got to get through the questions yet,' Adam whispers, 'that is going to be the hardest for Daniel.'

The questions are fired fast and furious to all of the candidates and they all did their best to give a better answer than their rivals. After a gruelling hour the meeting is drawing to a close, but then the television cameras turn to a frail old woman at the back of the hall and the presenter agrees to allow one more question.

The woman stands with the help of her cane. 'I have one question for the young man in the Future Party. Do you think you can change the world single-handedly?'

Daniel replies from the heart, 'No, I think we have all done that together and that's the problem. What I propose is that we all work together to put our world back on an even keel.'

The old lady sits down with a smile and the hall gives Daniel a standing ovation.

At last it is over and it seems to have gone well, now all they have to do is to wait for the morning papers.

In the safety and relative peaceful surroundings of the boys' house they go through the events of the evening. Becky is watching television.

'Hey, look at this,' she calls, 'Daniel's on television.'

We all crowd round the screen and listen to the commentary.

'Who is this strange Daniel and where does he come from? It seems he suddenly arrives with four friends on Millennium Eve but there is no trace of any of them before then.'

'Oops,' says Daisy. 'Well, it had to happen, so we need to think up a plausible and untraceable story fast.'

'You're right, Daisy. The only people I can think of that are hard to trace are travellers, the people who used to be hippies in the sixties. They lived in communes and cut themselves off from the outside world. They are also well-known for participating in free love and hallucinogenic drugs.'

'They sound interesting, Mark, but will they have still been around in the time that people believe we were born?' questions Adam.

'I would think so, probably not as many as there were in the sixties, but still pockets of them dotted about.'

'So, all right, we're the children of hippies. Why did we leave and why five of us together?'

'I think we can all be closely related, considering all that free love. Maybe the commune were disenchanted with England and decided to move abroad. It is quite plausible that we would be allowed to set out on our own, because they also believed in free speech.'

'That's not bad, Mark.'

They run their story to the three outsiders, Mary, Becky and Jim; they want to know whether such a tale will be adequately accepted.

Jim is the first to speak, 'It's a bit flimsy but it can work. It is unfortunate that when someone gets in to the spotlight the media have great fun digging around looking for dirt. I think with a bit of polishing we can get away with it, and these hippies are well-known for their back to nature theories and living off the land without spoiling the environment. They are also quite well-educated but shun modern development so, yes, you lot will fit in to that category nicely.'

The time travellers do not know whether to be flattered or upset by Jim's observations, so they just laugh.

Adam speaks up, 'I feel it will be prudent to get our story over to the public before the voting starts, just in case people are hesitant after that news broadcast. So what about phoning the TV channel and ask if we can reply to their doubts.'

Jim offers to phone the TV Company who practically bit of his hand for an opportunity to be the first to get the low-down on the mysterious strangers. They offer a prime slot at midday with a repeat in the early evening.

The rest of the evening was spent going through what Daniel is going to say and then they have a dry run to throw up any awkward questions they can think of that he may be asked. It is midnight before they go to bed but they know they have done everything possible to strengthen Daniel's campaign, now it is in the lap of the Gods.

Daniel has to be at the local television studio at ten o'clock, he has not realised that the local and national newspapers have also been invited, but he takes it in his stride. He knows that there will only be one chance to get this right and his friends have done everything they can to help him.

After going through the tedious task of make-up he finally finds himself sitting in the studio listening to the countdown for the live programme to commence. His interviewer is well-known for his briskness in firing questions with a fair amount of sarcasm thrown in. However, Daniel is ready for almost anything, he looks in the wings and sees Jim giving him the thumbs-up. The rest of the family are going to watch at home.

'Good afternoon, everyone, and welcome to 'You Heard It Here First.' My name is John and it is my privilege to have with me Daniel who is standing for The Future Party in the forthcoming election.'

Daniel responds by looking directly into the camera, smiling and saying, 'Hello everyone.'

The interviewer comes straight to the point without giving Daniel any warm up time.

'Well, Daniel, we are all eagerly waiting to find out where you and your four friends materialised from, and it seems you appeared on millennium eve. Did you land in a spaceship or were you sent from above to guide us out of our corrupt ways?'

Daniel smiles again. 'It's not as dramatic as that I'm afraid.' He goes on to explain, as rehearsed, about the commune and the travellers and why the five of them decide to break away from their peers.

'But you are all highly educated, in fact, may I say, above and beyond other people your age, even of those that have been university educated. How do you explain that?'

'Again, it is not a mystery. Many great inventors and scientist are well-known for their eccentricity. The people in our commune came from all walks of life; they dropped out of conventional living for many reasons. The majority were extremely clever people and they were the ones who delighted in teaching the youngest of our group everything they knew. They also encouraged us to question every aspect of our lives, we were fed curiosity and what they could not answer we went to find the answers ourselves. This led to a strange but very intense education.'

'So are we to believe that you come from a commune that originated in the sixties, with all that flower power, free love and drugs. How come we have never heard or seen any of you before?'

'People only see what they want, we were always there but we did not fit neatly into any category. As we did not cause any trouble or interfere with day-to-day life people preferred to be blind to us. That suited us as well as them.'

The interviewer scratches his head, this man is not going to be drawn into an argument or even lose his temper. He is answering all the questions logically and with politeness.

Daniel looks in the wings and saw Jim smiling. So far so good.

'Now we know where you've come from, tell us why we should vote for you in the election.'

'I cannot make people vote for me, all I want is for people to question what is going on around them in every aspect of their lives. Everyone is in charge of their own destiny and that of future generations. No one person, company or country is too big or too powerful to have total control without being challenged by the people that their actions affect. I want to be in a position where I listen to the people and then challenge as directed by them.' Daniel pauses to collect his thoughts.

'But you call your party the Future Party; surely that is what every politician believes they are standing for.'

'True, but I want to project further than the next few years. I want to show how the consequences of our actions today will affect the life we lead in the next decade and beyond. There will come a time when being rich or poor will be the least of our worries.'

'What do you mean by that exactly?'

'We all know that our ecological situation is becoming precarious. We have seen things happening at home and abroad that have taken us by surprise. There has been devastation and death caused by what we call, 'unnatural weather patterns.' Our Earth is evolving which is natural, but things have started to speed up. We are causing that acceleration and we must address the problem or face the consequences.'

'Are you not being a bit of an alarmist?'

'I am not saying that Armageddon is just round the corner. What I am saying is that we need to look at our lives. The rate technology is advancing, and the pollution it is leaving in its wake. For every new invention tons of pollution follows and that has to be disposed of. It is our duty to future generations not to leave our rubbish to fester and ruin their lives.'

'Thank you, Daniel, it is very obvious that you are completely dedicated to your cause, but how is that going to help the man in the street?'

Daniel knows that he has stated his intentions, but he has to convince the general public that he is there for them.

'John, I am here for every man, woman and child. I will listen to every problem, proposal or idea that people want to raise. I am not acting for myself; I am standing for everyone who wants to be heard.'

The programme ends. Daniel lets out a big sigh. He thanks John for the interview and goes to join Jim.

'He's a strange one,' John says to his director, 'but he will be worth watching.'

Jim shakes Daniel by the hand, 'Well done, Daniel. You really kept your cool.'

They are pleased to get back to the house, especially as on leaving the studio they had to run the gauntlet of all the media waiting outside for them, they fired questions and cameras were flashing all round.

In the house their friends are waiting for them, with hot tea and congratulations.

'You must be absolutely exhausted, Daniel,' Daisy says as she hands him the steaming mug.

Daniel collapses in the chair. 'I suppose that is a taste of what is to come if I'm elected.'

'Not if, Daniel, but when,' Adam states, 'you were absolutely brilliant.'

The friends talk far into the night, but eventually they all drift off to bed. It is Election Day tomorrow and that will be the test of Daniel's commitment to the people.

At the farm, Johnny, Martha, Alf and I watch the documentary in silence. I know how Daniel is going to explain our sudden appearance and I am worried the affect of the revelation is going to have on the people I now live with and love.

They are all looking at me and I feel embarrassed.

'Well, that's a turn up for the books,' exclaims Alf laughing, 'you're a hippy. I would never have believed it.'

'Is that right then, Rose,' Martha asks, 'did you used to live in a commune thing?'

I answer nervously, 'Part of it I suppose, but we never thought of ourselves as hippies. We are just people who lived close to nature and away from the hustle and bustle of modern life. It was how we were raised and we never really thought about it. We enjoyed our lives, the freedom and the independence.'

'You must miss all your friends and family though,' Johnny says.

'We will always miss our loved ones, but we have each other and we made a joint decision,' I reply, 'but I found the transition to town life just too much, that's why I came back here. I hope that what you have heard today will not change your opinion of me.'

Martha gets up and hugs me, 'Silly girl, of course it doesn't make any difference; you are special to us and always will be.'

'I am so pleased, I don't know what I would have done if you had told me to leave.' I look at Johnny, he has been quiet and I am frightened that I have lost his friendship. Johnny looks up and gives her one of his beautiful smiles.

'Come on, girl, give me a cuddle. You really are something special.'

I smile with relief and go to Johnny and while we cuddle I can feel tears of happiness trickle down my cheeks.

'I think this calls for a celebration,' says Alf, 'what do you think Martha shall we open that special bottle of ours?'

'Any excuse, but yes, I'll go and get it. But you mind, Alf, only one glass for you.'

'Spoil sport.' Alf knows his wife is right; he does not want another funny turn.

Later that night when Martha and Alf have gone to bed, Johnny draws me close to him. I can feel my heart beating fast and I am frightened that Johnny can feel it too.

'I mean what I said earlier, Rose. You really are special, especially to me. I hope we have a long future together. Just tell me you feel the same.'

'Yes, Johnny,' I whisper, 'from the first moment I met you.'

We kiss with a longing that we both have hidden from the other. It is at that moment I know I have to tell Johnny the truth, but first I will have to discuss it with the others. I decide to go after the election.

Chapter Thirteen

Election Day has dawned and we are up early to catch the news on the television and in the newspapers. We wanted to see how the media has reacted to Daniel's revelations yesterday.

The comments are mixed, but that is normal because each publication has their allegiance to a particular party. On the whole though it isn't too bad at all.

Daniel and Jim have left early so that they will be at their local polling station when it opens.

'Here goes then,' says Daniel, nervously.

'Don't worry, Daniel, everything will be fine.'

It is a clear dry day, but not too hot so the polling station is very busy. It looks as if there is going to be a record turnout. Some people stop to talk to Daniel and some ask questions, but the day mainly drags out in front of them. The most important thing for the candidates is the results and Jim and Daniel are no different. Their impatience is increasing with every hour that pass.

They decide to visit the other four stations situated around the town, spending an hour at each one. They answer questions from the public and talk to the media. They snatch sandwiches and tea at every opportunity to keep them going.

At last ten o'clock arrives and the stations close. Now comes the tedious task of the count. Their friends have joined them at the local station and tensions run high. There are four candidates standing including Daniel and each polling station will be sending their results through to the town hall where the winning candidate will be announced.

'I think it's time we make our way to the Town Hall,' Jim suggests, 'I think they'll all be done in half an hour.'

'This is all so scary,' Daniel exclaims, 'if I lose our whole mission will be at risk, but if I do win there will be so much depending on us.'

'One step at a time, Daniel,' says Adam, 'we are all in this together, win or lose.'

When they arrive at the Town Hall they are surprised to see so many people. They practically have to wrestle their way into the building. Inside is no better, television crews have set up their cameras and the noise of a multitude of different presenters trying to weigh up the mood of the people and candidates is overwhelming.

Daniel keeps getting grabbed to say a few words live on camera. He is feeling very stressed, all he wants to do is to find somewhere quiet to gain his thoughts. However, even with all this pressure he still manages to smile and answer questions politely.

'Well done, Daniel,' Jim whispers in his ear, 'I've found us a retreat. Just follow me and keep smiling.'

Daniel did just that, he is so grateful to Jim; he always seems to be one step ahead of Daniel's thoughts.

The four candidates are called to the platform and the votes are read:

'Labour party, 14,320 votes,

Conservative party, 12,500 votes,

Liberal party, 11,775 votes,

Future party, 17,310 votes.

The Future party has a clear majority and will stand for this district in the next Parliamentary election.'

The speaker holds his hand out to a dumbfounded Daniel, 'Well done, Daniel, I wish you all the luck in the world.'

Daniel takes his hand and thanks him for his good wishes. Then Daniel turns to face the auditorium, the media and all the people are applauding. A smile creeps across his face as he realises that he has done it. He has actually done it. He shakes the hands of his opponents and then approaches the microphone.

'Thank you for your support, I will not let you down. My aim is to be the voice for everyone and each issue that is important to you is as equally important to me. I want to ensure that for everyone living now and for our future generations the future is good. Thank you again.'

Another round of applause starts as Daniel leaves the stage to join his companions.

'Let's go home,' Jim says as he puts an arm round Daniel's shoulders.

'But don't we have to speak to the press, or attend functions now?'

'No, Daniel, there is going to be plenty of that to come. For now I think home is the best place.'

Everyone agrees and they quietly leave by the side door.

Becky and Mary have laid on food. They have guessed, quite rightly, that no one has eaten properly all day. The children are fast asleep in their room, so the friends and Jim return to a peaceful house.

'This looks great. I didn't realise how hungry I am. Thanks, girls.'

'It is the least we could do. Well done, Daniel, I knew you would do it,' Mary says as she kissed him on the cheek.

'Rose phoned, she wishes she could have been here for you, but she says everyone in the village is really glad you won and so are she and everyone in the farmhouse,' Becky adds as she starts pouring out drinks.

Martha and Alf are getting their own party ready. Johnny has let them into a secret, he is going to ask Rose to be his wife, he has saved his money and bought a small sapphire ring.

Martha is having terrible trouble keeping the secret.

'What is the matter with you, Martha?' I ask with concern. 'You are all jittery tonight, are you feeling poorly?'

'Oh no, quite the opposite, I'm feeling on top of the world,' Martha answers, 'I'm so excited about your Daniel being elected, that's why we're having a bit of a party tonight. To celebrate.'

'Yes, it's great, isn't it? A party will be smashing. Shall I go and put on my best dress, Martha?'

'That's a good idea, I think I'll go and smarten myself up too.'

We both disappear to our rooms to get ready.

Johnny smiles and then asks Alf, 'You do think she likes me, Alf, don't you?'

'Are you kidding, son, she has been swooning over you ever since she first saw you.'

Johnny swells with pride.

'I have never seen two people so right for each other as you and Rose,' says Alf, 'well, not since my Martha and me.'

Johnny pours them both another drink while they wait for their women to return.

'They will take ages getting ready, so I will tell you one of my old exploits while their away.' Alf likes to tell stories from days gone by, he has embellished them so much that even he does not know whether they are true or not.

'I was out in the woods late one night looking for the fox that kept worrying my chickens. Well, I heard this noise, a kind of groaning, so I crept through the trees to have a look. I could see a clearing in front of me so I hid behind a tree. I was shocked; I had never seen a sight like it in my life. There were these people prancing around a small fire, they were dressed in weird cloaks and masks and making horrible noises. They seemed to be in a kind of trance.'

Johnny was astonished, 'Really, how frightening, are you sure you weren't dreaming?'

'I tell you, lad, it was as real as I'm sitting here. One of them looked up and straight at me. I turned and run as fast as I could and didn't stop until I got home and slammed the door shut. My heart kept banging for hours after that. The strange thing was, when I went back to the clearing the next day there was no sign that there had been a fire there. Now, what do you make of that?'

'How strange, Alf, I'll have to watch my step if I go through those woods at night.'

'You better had, my lad; I reckon it was one of them witch's covens!'

An hour later Martha and I return to the living room. The men look up and both are proud at the visions before them. Martha is wearing her favourite summer dress; it is cream and covered with little yellow flowers. I chose a dark-blue dress that enhanced my blue eyes. Martha giggles like a teenager when the men start to compliment them.

'Enough of that, Alf,' Martha chides Alf embarrassedly; 'let's start this party.'

'There is one more very important thing to do first,' Johnny says shyly. He comes over to me and takes my hand. My head is spinning. What is going on?

'Rose, I always enjoy being with you, I have never known anyone as special as you. I now know that I want to spend the rest of my life with you. Will you marry me?'

I am absolutely astounded, I know how I feel about Johnny but never thought for one minute he feels the same. I look at the man I love and nothing else mattered.

'Come on, girl, are you going to answer the man?'

'Alf, hush, let the girl speak.'

Johnny waits patiently for Rose to answer.

'Johnny, the answer is a definite yes,' I reply as I throw my arms around his neck. Tears are trickling down my cheeks.

'Don't cry, Rose,' Johnny says as he takes the ring from its box and slips it on to my finger, 'you have made me so happy; I will make sure that you never have reason to cry again.'

'These are tears of happiness, Johnny; you always make the sun shine for me.'

The next weekend Johnny and I go into town to announce our engagement to the others. I am worried that they will be angry with me, but it is important to have their blessing. Obviously about the engagement, but I also needs to tell Johnny where I really come from. I do not want to start our lives together keeping secrets from him.

'Well, this is an unexpected surprise,' exclaims Daisy and adds, 'and who is this gorgeous man?'

I proudly say, 'This is Johnny, my very important friend. We've come so that he can meet all my closest and dearest friends.'

'Who's that at the door, Daisy?' shouts Adam.

'Come in, Rose, we are all here and still reeling from Daniel's success at the polls.'

Everyone welcomes Rose; she is always sorely missed since she decided to return to the farm. Becky is out with the children, so this is an ideal opportunity for Rose to reveal the reason for her visit.

With refreshments distributed and people settling down I take a deep breath and start, 'I would like to introduce you to Johnny; he helps Alf on the farm and stays at the farmhouse with us.' I am not the type to make a long speech, so I just blurt out, 'Johnny has asked me to marry him and I've said yes.'

There is silence for a couple of seconds and then everyone is congratulating us.

'I have to admit,' reveals Adam, 'that I'm really surprised. I never thought that our shy Rose would be the first to commit to marriage, but I am so happy for you. The move back to the farm is the best thing that ever happened to you, Rose, you've blossomed in a way that we never thought you would.'

In a few hours everyone is relaxed, even Johnny, who has been terrified of meeting Rose's friends, but now he realises that they are a brilliant and intelligent bunch of people.

I have a quiet word with Adam in the corner. Johnny is a bit worried as he sees me looking agitated.

Adam and I return to the group.

'Johnny, I have to tell you something,' I say as I take his hand, 'it is something that you may find hard to understand, but it is something that you must know before we can continue with our plans.'

Everyone is silent, they know what is coming and they hope that Johnny will be able to accept the revelation.

'This all sounds very mysterious,' Johnny states jokingly, but inside he is getting concerned.

I start to relay our story and mission, Johnny sits quietly listening to the unbelievable words he is hearing. His head is buzzing, wondering whether this is some sick joke, but he knows deep down he is hearing the truth. When I finish everyone looks at Johnny to try to gauge his reaction.

'I don't know what to say. Is this all true?'

'It is, Johnny,' Mark answers. 'We know it is hard to digest, but we are still the same people on the outside, we just have a different past. Or should I say future. Rose is still the same person you fell in love with.'

'Do Alf and Martha know?'

'No. It will not be right to burden them with this truth. In fact, the only other people who know the truth are Mary, Mark's partner. Daniel's friend Becky, but not her children, of course and Jim, Daniel's agent.

'But, Mark, how have you managed to integrate in, what must seem to you, a very alien society?'

'It is not easy, there are so many things to learn, but we are blessed with high intelligence and the ability to learn extremely fast. We kept a low profile until we could safely mix with other people and the rest came easy. Our hardest task is fulfilling the mission given to us by our Elders.'

'Now that Daniel has been elected, will that make it easier for you?'

'We hope so, Johnny, but we are very limited in what we can do without raising suspicion. We will be trying to change things for the better for absolutely everyone, but it will be one small step at a time. Every time we are successful in our aims it will bring us closer to helping the future of our civilisation.'

Johnny thinks quietly to himself. It is a lot to take in. He looks around the room and he sees normal people like himself, it is very hard to think that have come from a life that he can't even begin to imagine. They are very sincere and their ultimate aim is for the good of this planet's future so he cannot fault their motives. He knows that his life has just changed in a dramatic way, even if he walks away now he will always know their secret. It will be better to be part of it with Rose by his side. He looks at me, my face is pale. He knows he loves me, so be it; if you can't beat them join them.

'Rose, I love you and I want to marry you. I will not pretend that I understand everything that has been said here. I can't even guarantee that there won't be times that I will find it difficult. But I am willing to take that chance – that is if everyone is willing to take a chance on me.'

The room seems to lift from a dark cloud and everyone is talking at once, welcoming Johnny in to their select club.

I have tears running down my face.

'Now are they tears of happiness, Rose, or sadness?' Johnny asks as he tries to kiss the tears away.

'Definitely happiness, Johnny.'

A little while later Becky returns with her children and they are introduced to Johnny. The children think it is great that they have another uncle and drag him outside to play football.

'You are so lucky, Rose. Johnny is gorgeous and so obviously besotted with you.'

'Thank you, Becky. Today was very hard but I'm glad it is over. Now we can plan our wedding. I'm so excited.'

The men take Johnny down the pub for some male bonding while the girls chat about wedding preparations.

Johnny and I get married in the little church near the farm. It is a beautiful April day and everyone from the village attends. Adam gives me away and Daisy is my bridesmaid with Tom and Charles following very proudly in their new suits.

The reception is held at the Dog and Gun. Alf and Martha held court; both of them proud of the happy couple. Martha has arranged the reception and made the wedding cake, Alf has seen to the beer and the wine for the toasts. They feel like Johnny and Rose's grandparents and are very willing to step into the role so that the lack of relatives is not felt.

Johnny has arranged a surprise honeymoon and whisks me away during the evening. He is taking me to Cornwall, he knows I will love the new experience of the wind in my hair and the spray on my face.

Everyone else are enjoying themselves so much being back amongst old friends that they decide to stay overnight, they find beds offered at the pub and scattered around the village.

Chapter Fourteen

There are people who are unable to accept differences in culture and feel threatened when they don't understand. These people use violence to voice their disapproval and try to eliminate nonexistent threat.

When Daniel came up for election his profile went over the web and so did that of us all. Then there is the obvious search for further information and any interesting misdemeanour related to any of them. Unfortunately the trail goes cold the night of the millennium, and that intrigues people. They dig harder and come up with nothing. Then rumours start − were we spies from alien countries or even from alien planets? Were we a secret organisation trying to infiltrate and destroy the British people? Most people are intrigued and look upon us as a refreshing challenge but a small core of people have banded together intent on getting rid of us.

These people have formed their own organisation O.U.S.T, Outsiders Unknown Should be Terminated. This group knew that we were going to be away at a wedding so they decide to leave us a message in our two homes.

One group go to the girls' flat and another group go to the boys' house. They break in and systematically destroy almost everything in both the homes by taking an axe to the furniture, pouring paint onto clothes and furnishings. They finish by spraying paint on the walls in every room and leaving a message in red paint across a mirror saying –

'GO BACK TO WHERE YOU CAME FROM. YOU ARE NOT WANTED HERE.' O.U.S.T

'Who could have done this? I don't understand,' Daisy says to herself through her tears, 'we have never hurt anyone, how can someone be so cruel?'

The phone rang. Daisy lifts the receiver, 'Hello.'

'Daisy, is that you?' It is Adam.

'Of course it is.'

'Is everything all right, you sound a bit strained?'

'No, it's not! We have had idiots in and they have completely trashed our home!'

'Oh no! Not you as well. Have they left a message?'

'Yes. I don't think they like us, and who is O.U.S.T?'

'I don't know but I've got a feeling we are going to find out. Don't touch anything, the police are coming round to take fingerprints and Daniel is on his way now.'

The next few hours are a nightmare. Both homes have police all over them trying to get fingerprints.

'Thank goodness Rose doesn't know what's happened.'

'I think it is best if we try to keep it from her. She was so happy going off with Johnny; it will be awful if this blights her memory of her wedding day.'

'Definitely,' agrees Mark.

It takes a week to get their homes back to some sort of normality; they even redecorate the worst affected rooms. Becky and her children are traumatised by the wickedness of the people that have inflicted such hate on her friends. She goes to stay with some army friends of hers in

Yorkshire because she does not want her children to be scarred by what has happened.

The police have not found any fingerprints as it seems the perpetrators wore plastic gloves. There are other traces of evidence that they are working on but they have said it will take a long time to sieve through their records.

Adam decides that it might be best if they get a bigger house and all live under one roof. It doesn't take them long, luckily, to find a suitable house on the edge of town, it used to be a small hotel and with all their wages combined they can easily afford the rent. The hotel used to be called 'The Phoenix', and they decide to keep the name with the hope civilisation will also rise from the ashes.

Moving day is a couple of weeks later and they all feel relieved to have a new start. When Rose and Johnny return from their honeymoon they send them their new address, and explain to Rose that it seems a better idea to live together.

Chapter Fifteen

'Have you heard about those poor people in Haiti, Daniel? They've been hit by an earthquake which was followed by floods, cholera and now a hurricane causing gigantic mud slides.'

'It puts our troubles into perspective,' Daniel states, 'and reminds us of the reason we are here. I think it's time we start being constructive, to prove that we are here to help and not to cause trouble.'

'Well said, Daniel! The problem is where do we start?'

'I would like to utilise the facilities and manpower we have in this area to help these people.' Daniel begins, thinking as he is speaking, until the whole plan starts to come into shape.

'The summer holidays are coming up. What I would like to do is approach all the big companies in the area to give a sizeable donation. We can select groups of unemployed and young offenders to send to Haiti, with trusted supervisors, of course, to help the people rebuild their homes and their lives. I feel that it will show everyone we send that they can do something worthwhile, they can learn a trade and hopefully gain some self-respect through helping others.'

There is silence.

'That's a big project, Daniel.'

'I know it is, Adam, but not anywhere near as big as the project we are here to implement. It will also prove to my voters that I am going to earn their trust in me.'

They make a list of perspective donors and Daisy starts to draft suitable emails to send out to potential funders.

Mark contacts the probation service for a list of people who can benefit from the experience and in turn will be beneficial to the project. Jim offers to do the same for the unemployed, many of whom frequent his café.

Adam is in charge of the legal aspect and will also use his contacts at the newspaper to get media coverage.

Over the next few days a group of ten young offenders and ten unemployed are sourced as possible candidates and four responsible adults volunteer to oversee the project in Haiti.

They now have to wait for funding.

Adam manages to get a large article in the local newspaper and donations of equipment, food, clothing and miscellaneous items are being delivered every day to The Phoenix.

The British people live up to their reputation and soon major companies in the area start to pour funds into the project. By the time the rescue group are ready to undertake their mission the national newspapers have picked up the story.

Daniel and Daisy are going to head the project and both are feeling nervous, neither has flown before and they find that more terrifying than what they will have to face in Haiti.

The night before they are due to leave the others who are staying behind help them check last-minute details.

Adam stands in the middle of the room and surveys the supplies. They are meagre but essential items that will be needed by Daniel and Daisy to survive.

'So how do you feel, Daniel?'

'Excited, Adam, but also terrified. I just hope that we can make some positive difference to those unfortunate people.'

'I'm sure you can. You will be taking materials for shelters, clean water, food and medical supplies.'

'We will be facing some heartbreaking scenes, children without families or homes, mothers who have lost their families, how can we give them hope?' Daisy exclaims.

'By being there and caring,' Adam replies and then continues, 'you will be a beacon of hope to all those who feel the world has turned their backs on them.'

The supplies for the victims in Haiti have gone ahead, some by ship and the rest by plane.

The following morning Daniel and Daisy are escorted to the local airport by their friends, everyone eager to portray positive thoughts. They are really surprised to see that so many people have turned up to see them off on their mission. The national media have all come out in force, cameras are flashing and microphones shoved under their noses.

Daniel and Daisy keep their composure and answer all questions politely and with a smile. They know how important it is to give positive vibes to the media, not only for the victims in Haiti but also for their own personal mission.

When they are finally seated on the aircraft they hold hands and then shut their eyes tight all through the take-off, not knowing what to expect. The noise is ear shattering as the plane speeds down the runway, then the nose of the plane lifts and they are in the air and everything feels calm.

Daniel opens his eyes first, he looks out of the window and gasps, 'Daisy, open your eyes, you have got to see this.'

Cautiously Daisy opens her eyes, 'Wow, we are above the clouds, and look down there you can just make out tiny ships on the sea.'

'It's great, isn't it? I just hope the landing is just as smooth!' Daniel says.

They have a long journey ahead of them, so they accept the meals being handed to them and then drift in and out of sleep.

Johnny and I return from our honeymoon glowing with health and happiness. We are absolutely amazed by all the things that have been happening while we have been away. I think it is a brilliant idea that everyone lives under the same roof, especially as our little tribe seems to be expanding. Becky and her children have returned from Yorkshire and love the hotel, there is so much more room.

I arrive at the Phoenix just after Becky's return from the shops.

'This is a smashing place, Becky. What made everyone decide to move?'

Becky remembers their vow of silence in respect of the awful break-ins. She feels bad about lying but knows it is for the best.

'It was a spontaneous decision, the place came on the market and it just seemed natural to go for it.' Changing the subject, Becky adds, 'So how was Cornwall? I've never been that far south but I'm told the beaches are lovely.'

'It was absolutely beautiful, I learned to swim in the sea and Johnny actually taught me how to surf. Although I seemed to be in the water more than on the board!'

'Have you heard about Daniel and Daisy flying to Haiti to help all those storm victims?'

I gasp, 'They flew? That was very brave of them. I don't think I can ever do that.'

'Why not?' asks Becky, 'I have flown loads of times. There's nothing to it.'

'I suppose it's something we are not used to, there's nowhere to go to in the little goldfish bowls where we used to lived. Which reminds me, Johnny took me to the Eden project. It is quite scary really, although it is an absolutely fantastic place, it reminds me of my old home. It is good that people are thinking of preserving species, but it also frightening that they feel they have to.'

Daisy and Daniel are relieved that the flight is over but are apprehensive of the strange country they have now arrived in. As they leave the plane the searing heat hits them. They look around and see that the task in front of them is massive. There is so much destruction and so many displaced people. The refugees from the string of disasters are not pushy or demanding. They just stand or sit in silence, looking with sad eyes at the aid workers. Hoping that somebody will produce a miracle to put everything back the way it was. Most of these unfortunate people are visibly starving, and some are obviously injured. Walking wounded that have been turned away from the overcrowded makeshift hospitals. Only the seriously ill or dying are taken in, and when one has died another will take their place immediately. There seems to be only one way out of these hospitals and that is through the back door which leads to the mortuary which is growing bigger by the hour.

The silence becomes unbearable, even the smallest of children have learned quickly that there is no point in crying, nothing can help them.

'Oh, Daniel,' Daisy exclaims, 'I knew it was bad, but this is heartbreaking.'

Daniel is also feeling the weight of despair, but he has to think quickly. He rallies their group together around their meagre luggage and the emergency supplies that have been donated. 'We can see that these people need help but we have to decide on the most direct and useful aid we can give them. I suggest that we source a suitable campsite, raise out tents and store the supplies. Then we can go out in groups to the aid workers that are already here and see whether we can find out where our help is most needed.'

Daniel is pleased to see that young offenders and the unemployed worked together well. It is amazing how all barriers melt when a greater need is evident. While their new home is being put together Daniel and Daisy meet up with the four adults who were to supervise the twenty volunteers.

There are two men and two women; all have been volunteers previously at different sites around the world where disasters have struck. Daniel is going to make good use of their experience. Alan and David have been on site after the Asian Tsunami had killed thousands of people and destroyed countless homes and businesses. Jean and Sam have attended the destruction after the floods in Chile.

Both couples agree that through their experiences they have realised that there are four main areas to address. Lack of food, lack of shelter, lack of clean water and lack of medical supplies. They also say that the majority of refugees would rather have structural help to show them how to return to a normal life than to let others do it all for them.

'They have lost their resources; they appreciate help in reclaiming the means to start again,' states Sam, 'you will find they are proud people and most of their misery is because they cannot provide the basic necessities for their families.'

'I agree,' says David, 'they need to be shown a plan of action and the basic means to implement it.'

'So what you are saying is if we enlist the help of some of the locals they might point us in the right direction to give maximum assistance with the supplies and manpower we have brought with us.'

'That's about it, Daniel. We will have to pick the right locals though, because even in times of desperation there will always be the odd group who are only out to make a profit for themselves.'

Daniel sighs, 'That's terrible.'

'Yes, it is, but it is a fact of life I'm afraid.'

'Well, I think it is time we went out with the others to see for ourselves,' Daisy suggests.

The adults each chose five volunteers and spread out amongst the carnage that lay before them. Daisy and Daniel visit the main rescue centres to see where they can help most.

Adam is pleased that the rescue party have arrived safely in Haiti, and is determined to keep their progress in the headlines. It is very important to maintain a good profile, if only to keep the OUST group away from their door. Unfortunately it is going to take more than good headlines to stop the hard-core of demonstrators from badgering them.

Their new address is soon public knowledge and hate mail starts to arrive. It is the first time that they have witnessed such animosity. Where they come from there are too few people left for petty squabbles and anarchy. There is a common aim to protect civilisation as it stands and to find ways to extend all life.

'I think we should ignore these people.'

'But what if they start to get violent again, Adam?' a worried Becky asks.

'I don't think they will. They know the police are watching them closely. I think it will be just a case of trying to wear us down.'

'It is very hard to ignore some of the things they are saying in their letters. I can't believe that people can be so cruel.'

'Unfortunately, Becky, that is how our world is evolving,' Jim remarks and then continues, 'there are people who are never satisfied with what they have, they always want more. Then there are those who do not understand people that are different from them, there are also people who are just downright violent and will join any cause that promises a fight at the end. It all comes down to unnecessary insecurity, a fear of the unknown and being beaten.'

'But surely, Jim,' Adam interrupts, 'the main aim will always be the preservation of the world we live in.'

'If only it was as easy as that, Adam,' Jim sighs and continues again, 'every country, every leader has their own interpretation. The main tools are power, money and knowledge. Money means power which then leads to more wealth. Wealth is gained by knowledge which then leads to power. The uneducated usually turn to violence to get power and money, but then so do some of the leaders of countries. Look into history − Hitler, Idi Amin, Saddam Hussain all ruled with violence and genocide. You can go further back into history to find even more notorious leaders. Even our own kings and queens thought nothing of decapitating relatives for their own furtherance.'

'What are you trying to tell us, Jim?'

'It's this, Mark. We know, through what you have told us of the future, that civilisation is going to suffer from global warming and of course the natural cycle of the Earth's life. We cannot do anything about the latter, but we can in a small part try to slow the effects of global warming. However, it will have to be a global agreement to make any difference and that is something that I cannot see happening. It will be very difficult to unite all the countries of the world to a common aim.'

Adam is quiet, he is thinking of the message that their Elders have managed to send them. The holes in the ozone layers that allows the full strength of the sun's rays to dry up the seas, lakes and rivers. The active sunspots that cause increasing number of violent earthquakes that shifted the Earth's axis and finally in the 27th century the meteorite that hit the earth with such force that most civilisation died.

'Adam, are you all right?'

Adam is knocked out of his thoughts, 'Yes I'm fine, Mark. I am thinking about the things Jim is saying. We came here to help the world, but the world has no idea that it needs saving. So we must seem like a lot of cranks, that as far as people are concerned, can be listened to or ignored, but either way it will not make any difference to their lives.'

'I didn't mean to belittle your project, Adam,' Jim declares.

'I know you didn't, Jim, and we are very grateful to be enlightened. We came to this time with a very naïve view of life. We knew that our mission was going to be difficult, but we thought that once people realised what we were trying to do everything would fall into place. In our time everyone is united with a common aim but, here and now, everyone has their own agenda. Each country, each tribe, each family, each person.'

Mark has been very quiet, listening to everything that is being said. He realises that they have come to this time with a very inexperienced impression. Adam is right; they thought that once they were listened to everyone would come forward to help. He understands that Jim is trying to show them that their mission is near to impossible.

'Okay, Jim, how do you think we should proceed?'

'Well, Mark, I feel that stabilisation is needed. I would love to be able to say that everyone will agree to the fair distribution of wealth and power, but I cannot see that happening. There is not enough trust in the world, plus there will always be some country or someone who wants more of everything. It will be a great step forward if there is a World Council, made up of a representative from every country, tribe and religion.'

'That sounds like a good idea, but how possible would that be?'

'Almost impossible, but only almost. It will take years of planning and also promises that it is not a trick for one single power to gain world domination. Now that Daniel has been elected locally he will need to be seen as trustworthy, which will mean a lot of hard work and positive actions. Then his next step will be to be elected into parliament, that's when it will get very difficult.'

'But do you think all this is feasible?' Adam questions.

'That is up to all of you. You came here to do a job. Are you going to do it or are you going to just infiltrate into our society and take what's on offer?'

'That's near the mark, Jim!'

'Not really, Adam, it's a fact of life. We all want an easy life and technology is handing it to us on a plate. We all know that people are dying violently and needlessly all over the world every minute of the day, we hear it on the news, we see the awful pictures of torn bodies, raped children, mutilated teenagers, starving babies and we say isn't that awful. Then we continue to eat our meals before we go out on a pleasant night on the town.'

'You don't hold your punches do you, Jim?'

'No, I don't, Mark, but then I am as guilty as everyone else. I left lecturing because I felt the words that I was teaching were just that, words. I wanted to show the students that they could make a difference through effort rather than spending years in university. Then I met all of you and find out about your world and your mission and I thought this is my chance to actually do something rather than spouting off and achieving nothing.'

Daniel and Daisy have been in Haiti for nine weeks, it has been a harrowing experience and now it is time to return to Britain. They have distributed the medical supplies, clothes and tools where they hope it will do the most good. People have been assisted in building new shelters and digging wells for clean water. It is obvious that the recovery for the inhabitants of this beautiful island will take months, maybe even years. The volunteers have worked hard together and hope that they have made some difference to the few, out of hundreds, that needed their help.

It is a very quiet and exhausted party that returns to Britain. They have all seen things they will never forget, but amongst the horrors they witnessed they each have a few special memories that will remain with them. An orphaned child who manages a weak smile, a man thanking them for helping to dig the graves to bury his family who had all perished. The joy of a woman who thought she had lost her family and her home being reunited with her six-year-old son. The list is endless and soul-destroying.

Each one of us has learned a valuable lesson. Jim has shown us that our original hopes to save the planet from the future we know is its destiny is as impossible as the antics of Superman in the comics. Everyone wants a happy ending but even though we have advanced knowledge, we know that no one can fight the force of nature. We have to stop thinking we have super powers and start thinking more realistically.

Daniel and Daisy have to admit that even though they have made a small difference to a few people in the ravaged Haiti, nature has beaten them. They return with a feeling that they have done the trip not only to help the refugees but also to help their profile.

Chapter Sixteen

The following evening we all meet and on this occasion we exclude our new friends. We feel we have to reassess our plans. We were sent by the Elders to try to help the planet but we know now that we will have to look at our objectives differently. The task is too big for us to make an overwhelming difference; we must decide what is feasible without allowing ourselves to be sucked into an apathetic attitude of 'we can see what is going to happen but what can we do?'

It is the first time for years that we have met without any outsiders present and it feels very strange. I have left Johnny at the farm and miss him terribly, but I can tell by Adam's tone that this meeting is a make or break situation for us and our future plans.

'I think we all have a good idea why I have called this meeting,' Adam looks around the room at us, then continues, 'our original plan was to save the world from its destructive destiny. It all seemed so easy when we arrived; we were young, enthusiastic and armed with superior knowledge. We were also extremely naïve. We are now wiser and more in tune with these current times. So we have to look for ways and means to implement our task within the boundaries open to us.'

Daniel is the first to speak, 'The way I see it is that even though nature is dictating future events, we are accelerating the process with our disregard to natural barriers.'

'Can you expand on that, Daniel?'

'Of course, Adam. The mudslides caused by heavy rain, kill hundreds of people in their shanty towns. If the trees and vegetation hadn't been taken away then they would have anchored the ground. It will also be helpful if the people affected were to be encouraged to build stronger homes in a better location.'

'That's a valid point, Daniel, but what about the people that are living on low-laying islands, what can be done to help them when a tsunami strikes?'

'I really don't know, we can't expect people to move away from the homes that their ancestors built, but it could come to that.'

'I think the best thing we can do is for each of us to list what we think are threatened areas and then give an idea of how it could be protected,' Adam suggests. 'You do all realise that this could be more than a one day meeting?'

'We sort of came to that conclusion, Adam, but I think it will be worth it, if it helps us to become focused.'

We all nod in agreement with Mark.

'Good. Then let's get to work?'

After a couple of hours of silence, we give our notes to Adam. While he collates them we busy ourselves with making sandwiches to keep us going through, what looks like being, a long brainstorming session.

When we all settle down again, Adam starts to read through his itemised conclusions.

'I don't know whether you will agree with my findings, but here goes:

1   Advice to be given in threatened areas

2   Stronger dwellings

3   Less clearance of wooded areas

4   Education on the ecological damage

5   Emergency plans put in place as required

6   World Government

'Not in that priority order, but what do you think?'

'Put down like that, Adam, it sounds simple but we all know it won't be. Why will people listen to us?'

'I can understand what you are saying, Mark, but what is the alternative? Could you imagine the reaction if we tell the world that we know what is going to happen because we have come from a time a thousand years in the future?'

Daisy sighs, 'I really don't know how we can proceed, except by tackling each problem step by step.'

'We could try advertising for volunteers to help in a fictitious project,' Daniel suggests, 'but it wouldn't be, it will be what we know is going to happen and see what people come up with.'

'You mean like a film of the future, but showing how people minimise the damage beforehand because they know what will happen if they don't.'

'Something like that, Rose.'

'That's a crazy idea, Daniel,' Adam says, 'but it could work. In these days everyone loves their films and television drama. Sometimes I hear people talk as if what they have seen actually happened. There seems to be a very thin line between fact and fiction.'

'Do you really think it would work?'

'It's worth a try, and if it does work then we can build on it. My main aim will be to set up a committee with a representative from every country, tribe and clan; this will form a World Government whose only interest will be to preserve all civilisations and environments on Earth.'

'So you're not aiming too high then, Adam?'

We all laugh and the mood lightens. We decide to expand on Daniels idea and see where it gets us.

Night has crept up on us so we thought we will give our brains a rest for the remainder of the evening. We can start a fresh in the morning.

The rest of the evening we enjoy catching up on everyone's news and experiences. It makes a change to be able to speak freely about the world we have left, our friends and the Elders. We did not realise how much we have each altered to fit into this strange life.

Little did we know that we are being watched and our conversations are being recorded. Trouble is brewing and it is coming from a direction we can never have dreamed of.

We go to bed full of good spirits and hopes for the future, whilst our adversaries smile at their target's innocence.

'Everything gone as planned?'

'Oh, yes. Much better than planned. You won't believe what we have heard tonight. These people are really something else.' He laughs at his private joke.

'I want everything you have; I want it here within the hour. We need to go through it before they wake in the morning.'

'Yes, sir, we are on our way.'

The concealed van slowly and quietly pulls away and disappears down the street into the night. The only living thing that sees the van leaving is a stray cat sitting on a fence.

The moon looks down on a peaceful night and all is quiet again, at least until tomorrow.

We are up early, encouraged by brilliant sunshine streaming in through the windows. It is really great being together again and we are fuelled by the excitement of moving our project forward.

After a noisy breakfast where all seem to be talking at once, Adam calls the meeting to order.

'I want to know how you all feel about Daniel's idea.'

There seems to be a unanimous agreement to give it a try.

'I think it can help to get the message across or at least get people to think.'

'I agree with Rose. I also think it will be fun to do, not only for us but also for the people who want to get involved.'

'Thank you, Mark. Does anyone else have anything to say?'

'Yes, Adam, I would like to add that we mustn't lose sight of our objectives. It will be fun to produce such a film but the message must not be lost in translation.'

'That's a fair point, Daisy, as Jim said; "we must watch that we do not lose our sense of purpose".' So it will be used as the next step up towards our eventual aim.'

The rest of the morning tasks are allocated between us all. We also decide to let our extended family know about our decision.

Chapter Seventeen

After a week of planning we manage to pull a business plan together with each of us working with our task to move the plan forward. We are quite aware that preparation is the key to success and we know that this stage is going to be lengthy. What we are not prepared for is the unexpected request that comes through the post later that week.

Adam opens up his letter first, he has noted the MOD logo and also that each of us has received the same type of envelope.

After reading the contents Adam feels his face drain of colour, he calls to us.

'What's the matter, Adam, you look terrible?' He does not reply, he just points to the other envelopes. We pick up our letters and read.

'I don't understand,' Daisy exclaims, 'what is all this about?'

All the letters are identical; they instruct each of us to attend a meeting at the Home Office the following day at 9am. Cars will collect us at 0830 precisely. We are to come alone, no partners or friends will be admitted to the building.

'They either think that we are able to help in a very important matter or our cover has been blown,' Adam states, 'I have a feeling though it is the latter.'

'What can we do?' I ask worriedly.

'There is nothing we can do. You can guarantee we are being watched.'

'At least we have a few hours to decide how we are going to respond to any questions,' claims Daniel.

'The trouble is,' says Mark, 'we don't know how much they know and, most importantly, how they are going to react to the information they have obviously obtained.'

We are all worried about what was going to happen but did not want to cause alarm to our extended family so we tell them that we have an important meeting to attend. We also tell them to carry on as normal until we are able to contact them.

It is not the best explanation but it is all we could safely reveal. The last thing we wanted is for our partners to be dragged into something distasteful. We agree that this meeting is going to be awkward at the best and extremely unpleasant at the worst. We have decided to divulge the whole truth and throw ourselves onto, what we hope will be, a rational and professional government.

The night is restless for each one of us; we know that in the past when a government are faced with the unknown, the members acted far from rationally.

The early morning sun sees all of us up and about, we have long given up any idea of sleep. We have all dressed in business suits, knowing that it makes us feel in control and confident. However, we are all wondering if that is how we will feel at the end of the day.

At eight-thirty precisely four black cars pull up, each car has blacked out windows. Two men in suits come out of each car; they look up and down the street and then walk up the path.

I have never felt so frightened. There are three sharp knocks at the front door. Adam opens it.

'All of you come out to the cars, two women in one car and a man each in the others.'

And that is all they said.

Daisy and I sit in the lead car; Adam, Mark and Daniel sit in their separate cars.

Johnny came up from the farm the previous evening, he could tell I was nervous and he wanted to be with me. Johnny, Becky, Mary and Jim watch from the window as the ominous cavalcade proceeds down the street.

Becky is crying, even though they have not been told anything to worry them; they all know that this summons is not normal.

'What is going to happen to them?'

'I don't know,' Jim admits, 'but at least we know where they are going and who they are with.'

'True,' Johnny says, 'but will they be moved?'

Becky starts to cry again and Mary comforts her. 'We know who will be interviewing them and they know we have rights. They have partners and close friends now; there is no way they can keep us from them. They have not done anything wrong. In fact, quite the opposite, they have helped more than their share.'

'Quite right, Mary, if we stick together we can monitor anything that goes on, and if we feel they are overstepping the mark, we will step in.'

Johnny smiles, 'You're quite the revolutionist, Jim, but I'm with you the whole way. I shouldn't be telling you this because Rose made me promise, but these are extreme circumstances. Rose is expecting our first baby.'

'That's absolutely great, Johnny,' Mary says as she kisses him on the cheek, 'congratulations.'

Becky comes forward and congratulates him also, Jim shakes his hand. 'Well done, Dad.'

The cars arrive at their destination just before 9pm. We have no idea where we are. There are wide stone steps leading up to double wooden doors framed by four stone columns. The doors open and a woman with a very severe disposition comes out to the car where Daisy and I are, she ushers us into the building. Then three men come out and took the boys separately from each of the three remaining cars.

'Where are you taking us?' Adam asks.

'No questions, please, just follow. Questions will be answered later.'

The girls are taken to two separate rooms. In each room there are two chairs and a table. Behind the table is a woman.

I enter my room.

The woman gets up and indicates to the spare chair, she shows no sign of friendliness, just strict authority.

'Please sit down, Rose.'

'Why are we here?'

'I have a few questions first. The sooner we get some answers, the sooner we can answer your questions.'

I have never felt so alone. I wish Johnny was by my side.

We are all asked the same questions. It seems we have been monitored by the Secret Service quite soon after we had arrived in the new millennium. The government have not seen us as a threat but are curious of our purpose. This is compounded by the lack of personal records to identify our origin. They have followed our movements closely and have only seen us doing favourable and caring actions. It has been noticed that a few people seem to resent us but nothing too serious has developed and now they see us comfortably integrating with new partners.

However, the 'powers to be' want answers, they want to know where we come from, how we arrived and what is our purpose?

We have talked about the probability of being cross-examined and we had all decided that if we ever found ourselves in that position, then the truth is the only option.

So in each of the five separate rooms the examiners are getting the same incredulous answers. After an hour, a break is initiated and refreshments are brought in to us, the interrogators leave the rooms to join their colleagues and compare notes.

'It's like a rerun of the 'Village of the Damned', except they don't all answer exactly the same.'

'I know what you mean, but I feel they all have one common aim, and that is to stop our planet ending up the way it does in their time.'

'This is all very hard to comprehend. Our task is to prove these people are not aliens bent on our destruction. Their story, however, is hard to substantiate one way or the other. We can only go on the way they have behaved since they arrived and we cannot fault the good work they have done. On the other hand, they have infiltrated our media and political system.'

'Do you not think they chose these avenues to enable them to be able to get their message across?'

'Possibly, but you have to look at it from every angle. I have to be a 'devil's advocate' here because I have to explain it to those at the top.'

'All right, let's go round the table here. Who believes their story and think they should be let go, and who thinks we should lock them up for tests and security.'

There is a lot of discussion and the main consensus is to let us go but on condition we have two operatives living with us to monitor our movements.

The next thing we know is that we are all herded into a big chamber, I am crying, not knowing what is going to happen to us, but the others manage to keep their emotions under control.

'We have got you all in here because we have come to a decision, we are going to let you go home, but on condition that two of our people move into your house.'

There is an audible sigh of relief. Adam stands forward.

'We would like to thank you for your trust and we will welcome two of your people in our house. We have nothing to hide and were sent here as your future generation to help you and our planet. We do not know what has happened to our people in the future, but we do know how our world came to be as it was when we left it. Our one and only aim is to slow down the inevitable.'

When we arrive back home we are exhausted. Our friends rally round us and are cautious not to bombard us with questions. We have had enough grilling. Johnny is pleased to see me but is worried about how pale I look.

'I think I will take Rose home, she looks absolutely shattered.'

'Good idea, Johnny, I think we can all do with a bit of 'down time' as well.'

Jim and Becky start to cook a meal. They think it best if they let us talk among ourselves about what we have just experienced. Later that evening their peace is shattered by a knock at the door. Adam answers it and they hear him ushering people into the living room.

The door opens and a man and woman enter the room followed by Adam.

'Let me introduce you to Mr and Mrs Smith, or Roger and Sylvia to us. They are going to be staying with us.'

They are all surprised to see their minders are elderly. However, it becomes obvious later in the evening that Roger and Sylvia have a wealth of experience behind them; they are also an extremely likeable couple and will fit into their household perfectly.

'Where's Rose?' Roger asks.

Daisy explains that I am the youngest and the frailest of them all. 'When we moved from the country to the town Rose became ill. We couldn't understand at first, but then realised she was having difficulty coping with the hustle and bustle of everyday life.' Daisy continues, 'She decided that she wanted to return to Alf and Martha's farm and since then Rose has thrived again. It obviously helped when Johnny came on the scene and now they are married and expecting their first child. They still live with Alf and Martha because they help on the farm. Alf and Martha never had any children and think of Johnny and Rose as their own.'

Roger and Sylvia exchange looks.

'We were led to understand that you all lived here. I'm afraid we will have to report this.'

'Sylvia, I know you will have to tell your superiors about Rose, but can I explain a bit further?'

'Go ahead, Daisy, I'm listening.'

'As we said earlier, Rose became ill and she wanted to go back to where we came from, when she realised that was impossible she started to kind of fade. We monitored her closely because we thought she was going to die. Then she made the decision to return to the farm, she always loved it there. We honestly believed that she was going there because she thought her days were numbered. You must realise that we had no idea how coming back in time would affect us, and as Rose was the youngest we thought the time travel had an adverse effect on her.'

'I'm still listening.'

Adam takes up the story. 'Alf and Martha love having Rose with them and soon Rose started to thrive. We all decided that we will continue our work here without Rose, she helps with fundraising and leaflets, but unless there is something very important that affects all of us we leave it at that. One other thing, Alf and Martha are both in their seventies, we did not think it appropriate to reveal our true identities to them. They accept us as their extended family and we are very fond of them.'

'We will tell our superiors your concerns about Rose. Does her husband know where you all came from?'

'Yes, Johnny knows.'

'I think that's enough for tonight,' Sylvia states. 'Where's our room, I'm shattered.'

Daisy shows Roger and Sylvia where they will be staying and then left them to settle in.

Mark is saying goodnight to Mary, who unfortunately has to work on the night shift. Becky is checking on her children. The rest of them are talking quietly in the living room.

'Well, what do you think?'

'I don't know, Daniel. It all seems too straightforward. I think we are going to have to keep our wits about us. We know we are not going to do anything wrong, but are they thinking if they give us 'enough rope we will hang ourselves', as the saying goes.'

'Adam, I can understand why you feel cautious and I know that strange things go on that we commoners are not in the know about. However, we are not in a position to question their motives and I do not think they should be aggravated. I think that for the moment we should ride it out and see what their next move is going to be.'

'Wise words, Jim. Tomorrow is another day, let's see what it brings.'

The next few days are weird for everyone, the atmosphere is tense. Roger has gone to report their findings in respect of Rose to his superiors; Sylvia tries to help with the chores.

They feel that they are under a microscope and every move and word is being documented and dissected, which, in fact, is exactly what is happening. Then they realise that they have been lucky to have had so much freedom for so long. It is obvious that the further they move towards the aim the more they are going to become noticed. So they decide to use it to their advantage and see what help they can get from the hierarchy.

Roger returns from his meeting with the good news that I can stay at the farm, but someone will be moving to the village to keep an eye on me.

'We would rather you didn't tell Rose.'

'We have no problem with keeping that secret,' Adam replies, 'Rose poses no threat to anyone and she will get very upset if she thinks that someone is watching her. It could even make her ill again, especially as she is pregnant. So you can depend on our discretion.'

'Thank you, that is much appreciated,' Roger says, and then continues, 'I have been asked if you can come to a meeting, Adam. They have requested you because you are the oldest and seem to have the respect of all your friends.'

'If that's what they want, that will be fine by us. Have you any idea what the meeting will entail?'

'They want to know as much information you hold in respect of the circumstances that contributed to the world we know now changing to the world you lived in.'

'They're not asking much then! It will take time to get all the information collated, but I'm sure if we all pitch in we can produce a feasible document that can explain the pattern of events.'

'I'm sure it will prove very interesting. I'm finding it very hard to digest what you have told us so far, but I am an optimist and I am enjoying your company so, for me, I'll go with the flow. However, you must be prepared for criticism and possibly complete denial to believe what you tell us.'

'I hear what you are saying, Roger, we understand that it will be difficult to envisage the full extent of destruction that will become the planet. We had the same problem coming from our time into yours, but I have to admit that once we got over the initial shock, our move was by far the best. We, however, cannot show you our time; we can only describe how the few of those that remained survived.'

Roger bows his head and replied quietly, 'It must have been awful for you.'

'It was all we knew. We had no idea what had been lost over the centuries. I suppose, in a way, we are the lucky ones, our Elders chose us to come back to your time and we have seen a much better way of life. However, our ticket is one-way. We said goodbye to the people and the life we knew knowing there was no return.'

'You were so young, were you not frightened.'

'I suppose we were a little apprehensive, but mainly we were proud to have been chosen for such an important mission. We had been well briefed but nothing could have prepared us for everything we were to experience.'

Roger nods. Their conversation is interrupted by the arrival of Becky and her children. Enough for one day he thought.

It is late afternoon and the house is in pleasure mode, a brief respite before the evening meal is prepared. As the others start to come home the noise increases, everyone starts chatting about their day and the funny little things that happened. Roger and Sylvia enjoy the downtime with everyone else and soon the atmosphere lightens, by the time dinner is served everything has gone back to normal and the new habitants of the house feel they are no longer the enemy, but part of the family.

Adam is given a week to prepare the information for the meeting. He wishes he has something more tangible to produce but, unfortunately, all he has is his experience and the notes he has made from the unexpected communication sent to them from the future years. Everyone chips in with their memories and facts that they have gleaned from things happening globally in the present day and what they learned in their own time.

The night before the meeting, after the children have gone to bed, they all sit down to go over the notes. Roger and Sylvia are included as they will know the best format to present the document. The session is long and arduous but finally they come up with a report that they are all happy with.

'Well, I don't know about anyone else but I think we deserve a drink,' Daisy decides as she heads for the kitchen.

The suggestion is unanimously agreed and Daisy returns with a bottle of white wine and a bottle of red.

Sylvia accepts her glass of red and says, 'Just to help me sleep, of course.' She raises her glass and winks at the others.

'Of course, Sylvia.'

The all raise their glasses, and repeat.

'To a good night's sleep.'

They talk for another half an hour and then start to disperse to their separate rooms. Each one of them wondering how the meeting will go tomorrow and what will progress from there.

In their bedroom Sylvia and Roger are still discussing the day's events.

'What do you think, Sylvie?'

'I really don't know. They are a smashing group of people. They have witnessed so much. I do not think they are a threat, but they may have to be guided. The project their Elders have given them is massive. Let's hope that some good will comes out of their mission.'

Chapter Eighteen

The ominous black car appears at 8am to transport Adam to what is going to prove the most important meeting of the project. Adam tries to look confident as he leaves the house, but in reality he feels that this is a make or break situation. He hopes that the papers in his hand are adequate for the meeting ahead.

A little time later the car pulls up outside the same building that we had been taken to previously. He is politely ushered into a waiting room, his report is taken from him for photocopying and he is told that he will be collected when they are ready for him.

Adam looks out of the tall window; it is a beautiful day, brilliant blue skies with a few fluffy white clouds lazily gliding across the horizon. The trees are in full leaf and are gently swaying in the breeze. Someone is sitting on a lawn mower and the faint smell of newly cut grass wafts through a slightly open window. Adam admires the colourful flower beds around the house, and on distant hills he can see sheep and cows grazing. How different this all is to the world he was used to seeing. He hopes that their mission can delay the inevitable for as many years as possible.

Adam is knocked from his thoughts by a polite receptionist requesting he follows her. He is shown into a large room; there are paintings of what must have been important people around the walls and an impressive fireplace to his right. The natural light comes from towering windows opposite the doors and in front of the windows are people seated at a long table. There is just one chair on his side.

A man sitting opposite Adam stands and introduces himself.

'Hello, Adam, I am the Chairman of this committee, my name is Steven.'

Adam steps forward to shake Steven's hand.

'The people you see at this table come from different organisations, they all have an interest in what you are about to tell us. I will not go through their names as they are all wearing badges but I will tell you who they are representing. But first let me give you back your report, we have all got a copy and have briefly gone through it. After the introductions we would like you to explain in your own words the contents.'

Adam is feeling very intimidated, there is a mix of men and women in front of him, some in uniform, some in suits and others dressed very casually.

'Well, here goes, you will have seen that we have the three main forces represented Air force, Army and Navy. Representatives from the World Health Organisation, the World Meteorological Organisation and the United Nation for the Co-ordination of Humanitarian Affairs or UNOCHA for short. We also have some much respected scientists and MPs.'

'Good morning,' Adam says, 'it is a pleasure to meet you.'

'Please sit down, Adam, and we will commence. Would you like to talk us through your document? I should tell you that we will be recording this meeting for members who are unable to attend.'

During the first hour Adam explains what the conditions were like in our time and why we were chosen for the project. He tells his audience that the Elders could see our stark world deteriorating faster than anticipated and they felt that they should at least try to warn their ancestors of the consequences of misusing the planet's natural resources. The Elders knew that the planet would have its own natural lifespan but things were happening too fast. Adam explains that the scientists had developed a time capsule that would allow people to travel back through the centuries, but they were unable to make it a return journey. That is why we were chosen. As young adults it was thought we could cope with the transition better. As our intelligence is high compared to the intelligence of people in this day and age, integration and the formation of a project would be relatively straightforward.

His audience are listening intently as Adam gets into his stride. He describes how we lived, how there were other pods, similar to the one we lived in, scattered over the Earth's surface. How we communicated to each other and the few natural things we were able to preserve. Adam also describes what it was like outside the pods: the barren red earth, steaming geezers, brown skies, the horrific atmospheric storms and the poisonous gases seeping into the atmosphere.

As Adam talks the room is deathly quiet. To most people listening it seems as if they are listening to passages from a horror story, to others it is as they would have predicted but even more extreme.

Steven is the first to speak. 'Adam, what you describe is beyond our comprehension. It reminds me of the documented birth of our planet, but you are describing its death. I think we shall take a break here, have some refreshments and start again, say, in half an hour.'

Everyone nods in agreement and the quiet is replaced by scrapping chairs and excited chatting as everyone leaves the room.

Adam looks around and feels a bit lost, and then he notices a young woman approaching.

'My name is Maddy, short for Madeline; let me show you where they have disappeared to. There is a canteen just down the hall where we can get a drink or you could sit on the terrace.'

'The terrace sounds good, will you join me?'

'I'd like that, Adam, it's just through there,' Maddy pointed to two open patio doors, 'what would you like to drink and I will bring it out?'

'Just still water will be fine, thanks.'

Adam walks out to the terrace, glad to get some fresh air at last.

A few minutes later Maddy returns with their refreshments. Adam notices she has a nice smile.

'There you go, Adam, you must need this.'

'Yes, thank you,' he replies as he takes the proffered drink, 'I have to admit I'm finding this very stressful. What is your role in this meeting, Maddy, if you don't mind me asking?'

'Not at all. I am, I suppose, an independent observer. I did a degree in global environmental changes and followed that by doing a personal study of the cause and effect of ecological damage caused by our misuse of natural resources. I have been lucky enough to have been funded to travel all over the world to aid my study. I have also seen some horrible consequences of our greed and heavy-handedness to obtain what we think is important.'

'So you must be well aware of what I am trying to explain at this meeting.'

'I do know what you are saying and it will be my responsibility to translate your words in a way that will be acceptable to the 'powers to be'.'

'And do you think you can?'

'I have to be honest, Adam, everyone has their own agenda and, probably deep down, they know the truth in your revelations. However, they will try to bend and twist it so that they can still benefit from financial rewards, power or whatever they find is personally beneficial to them.'

Adam sighs, 'I suppose this group of people are just the tip of the iceberg, if we are lucky enough to get global interest, there will be hundreds of people trying to grab their bit of the cake.'

Maddy laughs, 'You certainly have a deep understanding of this generation of your ancestors.'

At that moment Steven, the chairman, approaches them, 'Glad to see you two getting on, you have a lot in common, even though it's a few centuries apart,' he winks and smiles, 'are you ready to continue, Adam?'

'Raring to go, Steven,' Adam replied even though it was a lie.

They return to a noisy meeting room, but as soon as they enter a hush falls over the room. Adam sits in his chair opposite everyone and Maddy takes her place at the end of the table.

'You have described why you were sent, now can you explain why your particular destination was chosen and how you were prepared for the type of life you would be facing?'

Adam takes a deep breath, 'Of course, Steven.' He realises that the report he and the others have spent hours over is just a reference, they wanted to hear everything first hand. It is going to be a long day.

During the next few hours Adam explains how the cottage had been located through looking at historical records, then he continues by describing the difficulty we had coping with the elements, cooking raw ingredients and ingratiating ourselves in the local community. He also says how helpful and kind people were to us and because of their kindness it made it easier to accept our new environment. All the time Adam is speaking he notices people scribbling madly on notepads, which makes him realise that soon he is going to be bombarded with questions.

Steven is conscious that the amount of information being given is generating tension on both sides of the table so he decides to interrupt at a convenient pause in conversation. 'I think it might benefit everyone if we break for dinner now. Shall we say to reconvene in two hours, that will give us all time to not only digest our dinners but also what Adam has so kindly relayed to us so far.'

Maddy approaches the rather exhausted looking Adam. 'Do you want to join me for dinner? I know some where quiet we can go.'

'Sounds good to me, lead the way.'

Adam follows his new friend through the tall glass doors into the garden; they go over the lawn to a wooded area which miraculously opens up to a small clearing. There is a table and two chairs to one side and a small pond spouting a stream of water two feet into the air.

'This looks nice, but how are we going to get anything to eat?'

'No problem, Adam, what do you fancy, the full menu or a nice light salad followed by a disgustingly sweet dessert?'

Adam laughs, 'It's obvious what you will prefer, is the salad to compensate for the disgustingly sweet dessert? I'll have the same, with some still water.'

Maddy uses her mobile to order the food. While they wait they talk some more, but not about the meeting. Just idle chatter.

'So, Adam, have you got anyone special?'

'No, only my housemates and their partners and friends, I seem to be too busy looking after everyone else.'

'It is a shame, everyone should have a friend they can talk to, nothing to do with responsibilities, just for fun.'

'Sounds good, have you anyone special in your life?'

Maddy smiles, 'No, I have to admit that I'm just like you, I don't seem to find the time for relationships.'

Adam hears a rustling in the trees and then sees two waiters bringing their salads and drinks.

After they have gone Maddy said, 'I hope you like prawns, they are my favourite.'

'I've never had them before, but I'm sure they will be great.'

Back at the house the disciples are waiting anxiously for Adam's return.

'How do you think it's going, Daisy?'

'I wouldn't even like to hazard a guess, Mark. I'm glad it wasn't me that had to go, it must be very stressful.'

They are interrupted by a loud banging at the front door.

Roger and Sylvia come rushing out of the room.

'Be careful opening the door,' Sylvia whispers.

'Can you see who it is from the window?'

Daisy cautiously looked out, 'It's Jim, Roger, he looks really agitated.'

Sylvia opens the door, 'Whatever is the matter, Jim, you're shaking, come in.'

'It's Daniel he's been knocked down by a car, he just stepped out of the café and a car mounted the pavement and came straight at him. He looks really hurt; an ambulance has taken him to the hospital. The car just disappeared down the road, it all happened so fast.'

'Did the police arrive, Jim?'

'I think they went straight to the hospital, Roger, after asking a few witnesses what they had seen.'

'Right, Sylvia, you make the necessary phone calls and I will go to the hospital.'

Daisy and Mark accompany Roger to the hospital and Jim follows in his car. Roger explains that they will transfer Daniel to a military hospital where he will get better treatment and no awkward questions will be asked. The police will also be informed that the situation is being dealt with by the government. The last thing they want is for our identity to become public.

News of the accident has come to Steven's attention, but he decides to keep it to himself for now, he wants Adam to complete his story and he is aware that if Adam knows about Daniel he will leave the meeting immediately to be by his friend's side.

Everyone is returning to the boardroom after their two-hour break, Adam is feeling far more relaxed, he has enjoyed the meal and has enjoyed Maddy's company even more.

'Are you ready to continue, Adam?'

'Let's just get going, Steven.'

Adam informs the committee of all the activities we have been involved in. He also admits getting the appropriate identification documents for everyone from someone of dubious reputation.

'Ah,' interrupts Steven, 'that's how that group O.U.S.T' got to know about you.'

'Yes, I suppose so. In hindsight that was a bit irresponsible, but we did not know what else to do.'

After another hour Adam finishes and the meeting opens for questions. This is the bit he is dreading.

The questioning is not that bad after all, the facts are all documented in the papers in front of them, and so he is only asked questions on a personal basis. He is asked things such as: what did he think of the world he had come into, did he think the future can be changed. Does he regret not being able to go back to the year 2999 and has he any other regrets?

Adam answers as well as he can but finished by saying, 'I don't know whether the place and the people we left still exist, it was our destiny to come here. We were privileged to be given that chance. I hope we can make a difference but only time will tell in the end.'

Steven stands and thanks Adam for his time, the committee applaud and Adam hopes that is a good sign and not just politeness.

People start to leave the room. Maddy approaches Adam, he smiles.

'Will I see you again, Maddy?'

'I hope so, Adam.'

'Can I interrupt,' Steven says, 'I have something to tell you, Adam.'

'Of course, Steven,' Adam then turns to Maddy, 'hope to see you again soon, Maddy.'

She smiles and nods then disappears through the door.

'What is it, Steven?'

Steven tells him about Daniel and Adam feels the blood drain from his face.

'Where is he, can you take me to him?'

'There is a helicopter waiting outside for us now.'

They go out the main doors and the thud, thud of the rota blades is deafening, the displaced air is violently blowing the trees and plants. Adam has never been in a helicopter before, it looks so small. He did not think twice, he runs after Steven with his head bowed down away from the spinning blades and jumps in the open door. As soon as he is belted in his seat the helicopter rises vertically, spins round and speeds off into the blue sky.

Daniel is in the A & E, he is still unconscious and the doctors are trying to find the extent of the damage. He obviously has a broken arm and a broken leg, and there is a bad injury to his head, but they are worried about any internal bleeding.

'Nurse, can you phone X-ray, we need to take this young man up there immediately.'

The nurse comes into the emergency room. 'Oh my goodness it's Daniel. Whatever happened?'

'Do you know the patient, Mary?'

'Yes, he is a friend, what happened?'

'Hit and run it seems. The police may want to talk to you, so another nurse will accompany him to X-ray.'

Mary watches Daniel disappear through the swing doors and turns to face the police. She is in shock and is in no mood to be bombarded with questions.

Just as she is about to explain how she knows Daniel, the outside doors bang open and Adam, Daisy and Mark rush in. They are followed by the man she knows as Roger and two military men.

Roger shows the policemen his I.D and explains that the military are going to take over the investigation. The police are not very happy but know they have to step down.

Mary tells Roger that Daniel has gone to X-ray, but he is still unconscious and looks badly hurt. She then goes to join her friends. It's obvious that Daisy has been crying and Adam and Mark are both in shock.

'I'll go and get you a hot drink,' Mary offers, 'go and sit in the office over there and I'll be back in a minute.'

Roger is talking to the Registrar on duty.

'We know this lad and we will take him to the Military hospital.'

'Have I any option?'

'No, I'm afraid not.'

'Well, you will have to wait until we can stabilize him sufficiently for travelling,' the Registrar says rather haltingly.

'Of course, we don't want to cause poor Daniel any more damage. We have an air ambulance on standby outside; just let us know when you feel it is safe.'

Roger goes to join the others in the office while the two military men stand watching by the exit doors. The medical staff feel uncomfortable having them there, they are not showing any weapons but it is obvious that they are armed.

Within the next hour Daniel is transferred to the air ambulance and taken to the Military hospital. His friends are advised to go home and wait for news. They are not very happy being dismissed but do as they are told. Roger is going with Daniel and he promises them he will keep them updated.

Daniel is in hospital for three months recovering from his injuries and his friends are finally, after waiting two weeks, allowed to visit him. It seems that tests were done to see how or if his bodily make-up is different from humanity today. Adam is not pleased that Daniel has been used as a guinea pig while being unconscious, but it is done before anyone knew.

Roger is very open with information and that is appreciated.

'Daniel can come home at the end of the week, Adam. Are you going to tell him or the others about the tests?'

'No, not yet. There are too many other things to consider at the moment.'

'I think that is very wise.'

'Daisy and I are going to visit Daniel today. I have not long to go before my baby is born, only another two weeks to wait. I want to see Daniel before I go into hospital myself.'

Roger laughs, 'You won't have much time to yourself once the little one arrives. Are you still all right about going to the Military hospital to have your baby?'

'Not really, especially as Martha wanted to deliver the baby at the farm, it is tradition. But I realise that it will be best for me and the baby to be at the hospital and Johnny agrees.'

'That's good, but you do understand that they will probably take tests again.'

'It's not what we want, but as long as they don't do anything that will harm me or my child we have to go along with it.'

'While I remember, Adam, I have a letter for you.' Roger took an envelope out of his pocket and handed it to Adam.

'Who's this from?'

Roger just grins and leaves.

Adam tears the envelope open and smiles when he sees who the letter is from.

'Dear Adam,

It seems a long time since I last saw you. I thought we got on rather well and I hoped to see you again, but so far our paths have not crossed. If you feel the same maybe you could meet me on Wednesday at that little café in town, say about 4pm. Until then, take care and I hope to see you soon.

Maddy'

He has been thinking about Maddy quite a lot lately and so is delighted to get this invitation. It is Wednesday tomorrow so he must make some excuse to disappear so he can meet her. Adam is a very private person and did not feel he wanted to tell anyone about Maddy yet.

Adam escapes about midafternoon the next day, he makes a futile excuse but the others realise that he wants time to himself. He arrives at the café just before four; Maddy is not there so he orders a coffee and opens the newspaper to do the crossword.

A few minutes later the door opens and Maddy stands there beaming at Adam, she hadn't expected him to turn up. She is very pleased he has.

Adam looks up and sees her, she looks even better than he remembers, her dark hair falls over her strong shoulders, she is tall and athletic. It is obvious she takes good care of herself; he feels embarrassed by the quickening of his heart and hopes she does not notice. Adam smiles and goes to her.

'It's really lovely to see you again, you are looking well.'

'Thank you, Adam, it's nice to see you again.' She looks down at the crossword, 'I hope I'm not disturbing your concentration.'

'Of course not,' Adam says as he folds up the paper, 'what would you like to drink?'

'A coffee will be fine, thank you.'

Adam orders two more drinks.

'So, what have you been up to, Adam, and how is Daniel?'

'I'm glad to say Daniel is recovering well and is due home any day now. We are busy getting a welcome home party organised.'

'And how is Rose, her baby must be due quite soon now?'

'Definitely a mother in waiting and her husband Johnny can hardly suppress his excitement. They make a good couple.'

'Have any of the others found partners?'

'Mark met Mary, a nurse. They have been together for ages. She is very nice, but I've no idea how serious it is. You must understand that one-to-one relationships are alien to us. We don't know of the protocol to follow.'

'It must be awkward for you all, but Johnny and Rose have got it right. You know what they say, 'love conquers all'.'

'Is that what they say? If only life was that simple.'

'It can be, Adam, if you give it a chance. Anyone else?'

'There's Becky, she lives with us and her two boys and young daughter. Poor Becky, on the morning of those awful floods she got a letter saying her husband had been killed in action in Afghanistan. Then that evening her home had been washed away by the floods.'

'That's terrible, so what happened?'

'That night we were all out trying to help the victims and Daniel was in the café with Jim dishing out hot drinks. Daniel noticed this poor girl sobbing in the corner cuddling her three children. He took drinks to them and stayed with them for the rest of the evening. They had lost literally everything, what could we do? They have lived with us ever since and it is our pleasure. The children keep us grounded and remind us the reason we have to continue with our task.'

'Do you think Daniel and Becky will ever get married?'

'I feel that Becky is still grieving for everything she has lost and Daniel is giving her the necessary space, but there is closeness between them and the children, so who knows?'

'What about you, Adam, have you anyone special in your life yet?'

'I have our ever-growing family, so I really haven't had time to think about.'

'Would you like to have a special friend?'

'You are not slow in coming forward,' says Adam laughing.

'I am a very direct person, Adam; I like you and want to get to know you better. Life is too short to beat about the bush.'

'That's very refreshing, Maddy. I don't think I could handle anyone complicated. And, yes, I think I could do with a friend. It will be nice to be able to escape into normality every now and then.'

'I'm glad that's sorted. Is there anything you want to know about me?'

'Absolutely loads, but we have all the time in the world to swap life histories,' Adam replies, but continues cautiously, 'there is just one question and I would like an honest answer.'

'Don't be scared, Adam, I am always honest, and if I am unable to answer I will tell you why.'

'You haven't been put up to this by the military or the government to see whether we are telling the truth or pose a danger to anyone?'

'Adam, my interest in you is strictly personal; I think you are a wonderful person and I want to spend a lot of time with you.'

'I'm not that great, Maddy, but the thought of spending more time with you will make my day.'

'Smashing. As it's a lovely day out there why don't we go for a walk in the park, feed the ducks and hold hands?'

'Maddy, you are completely crazy, but I like your ideas.'

They spent a pleasant couple of hours walking, talking and laughing. They promise to meet up again soon and they swap phone numbers.

Adam feels as if he is walking on air as he returns home, he enters the house with a comforting warm feeling inside and a smile on his face.

Daniel's arrival home is celebrated with a party; everyone is pleased that they are all together again. However, the merriment proves to be a little too much for me.

'Johnny, I think I had better sit down for a bit.'

I'm not surprised, Rose, you have been dancing around like a teenager.' Johnny leads her to a vacant chair. 'Now you just rest for a while, you will soon get your breath back.'

I take a deep breath and try to concentrate on what is going on around me, but I am having pains in my side and they seem to be getting stronger. Sylvia notices my discomfort and sits down next to me.

'Are you all right, Rose, you look a little pale.'

I smile, 'I'll be fine, I've just got a bit of cramp that's all.'

'And how regular are these cramps?'

'They come and go.'

'I think your baby is trying to tell you something, Rose.'

'It's too early, Sylvia, it's probably nothing.'

'I think we had better make sure. I will ask Roger to call an ambulance.'

I am shocked and very frightened.

'Now don't you worry, nothing is more natural than child birth. I'll get Johnny.'

Johnny is by my side immediately, concerned about me but also beaming with pride at the thought of being a dad before the night is through.

The ambulance arrives very quickly; it came so fast that we think it was waiting outside just in case. Everyone gives words of encouragement to me as I am helped into the ambulance. I feel so nervous.

As the others file back into the house, they are joking.

'Well, we get one back and lose someone else,' Daisy says laughing.

'Yes, the hospital will be giving us season tickets soon,' Daniel replies.

Roger and Sylvia exchange furtive looks, they know that the Military hospital wants to test all of them, but they didn't know how to break the news.

'I'm sure Daniel is feeling tired, so now is as good time as any to tidy up and get some rest,' Adam suggests, 'it will be a long night for everyone, especially for Rose and Johnny.'

They all agree and soon the house is silent.

Johnny holds my hand, he is worried, I have been in labour for five hours and each pain seems stronger than the last. I am absolutely exhausted my face contorts with the pain and my hair has become tangled with sweat. A nurse comes in.

'Can't you do anything to help her?' he pleads.

'Everything is going great, you can't hurry a baby, it will come in its own time.'

Johnny has seen animals born and it never seemed as tortuous as this, he feels so helpless.

The nurse examines me. 'I think we are almost there.'

Thank goodness Johnny thought. He didn't believe he could bear to watch Rose suffer anymore.

An hour later Johnny sits with his baby son in his arms while I look proudly at them both. I recover extremely quickly, considering what I have endured the last few hours. I smile in contentment. I have never felt so good. My husband. My son. We are now a proper family.

'I think mother and son should rest now, and you look as if you could do with some sleep as well.'

'I think you're right,' Johnny agrees, he bends down and kisses me tenderly and then kisses our new baby son. His journey back to the house is done in a dream with Johnny sporting a wide grin.

Although it is still very early when he opens the front door most of the others are bustling around making hot drinks and breakfast.

'Johnny, is everything all right, how's Rose? You look exhausted. Sit down I'll make you a hot drink.'

Daisy rushes into the kitchen and Johnny is too tired to argue, he collapses into the nearest chair. Soon he is surrounded by people asking questions.

'Give the poor man a chance,' Adam says.

Daisy gives Johnny his drink and he proudly tells them all about his new son, and how clever his beautiful wife has been to produce such a gorgeous baby. Johnny soon takes to his bed to catch up with some sleep, but not before he phones Alf and Martha to tell them the good news. Martha cries with joy and says she can't wait to see them all.

Roger and Sylvia have decided that in the light of Daniel coming home and the added good news of the new baby that now is as good a time as any to tell them that they are all to be tested. They know that the news will not be welcome as it will seem an infringement of our privacy. If only they can understand that it will be mainly for their own benefit.

The next day as they are sitting having breakfast Roger clears his throat and starts, 'I'm glad we are all here and in such good humour because I have something I need to tell you.'

'That sounds ominous, Roger; I hope you are not going to put a dampener on our good mood.'

'I hope not, but I've been asked to tell you that while Daniel was being treated in hospital, a few tests were done.'

'Well, that's normal isn't it?'

'Not these tests, Mark.'

'What do you mean, Roger? Come on spit it out?'

'Before they could treat Daniel they had to find out if his body make-up had evolved, considering how far in the future you lived and in the conditions you were surviving. We had to make sure that any treatment we gave would not harm Daniel and also whether the doses would be affective.'

'So Daniel was used as a guinea pig.'

'That sounds rather cruel, the medical service were only doing what they thought was best. The same will be done to Rose and her son. You must understand it is only for the right reasons.'

There is silence. Sylvia is the next to speak.

'If they hadn't taken samples and followed through with tests our doctors might have done lasting damage. Your bodies have evolved and the doses we would have normally given would have paralysed Daniel.'

'Is that true or are you making excuses?'

'Daisy, Roger and I have always been completely honest with all of you; we have even told you things we shouldn't have, why should we lie now?'

They could not argue with that, in fact Roger and Sylvia have become part of their extended family.

'We believe you, but I have a feeling that is not the end of the matter.'

'You're right, Adam. They want to do the same tests on all of you. Just in case any of you need treatment in the future, they want to be prepared. I will also admit that they want to understand why you have evolved to such a great extent, especially your IQ.'

'Great. Now we are going to be guinea pigs as well!'

'Don't get heated, Mark,' Adam advises, then turns to Roger. 'Will this be a one-off or a continuous stream of tests going on for years?'

'I don't know, Adam. I hope it will be just one round of tests for you all, but I will try to find out.'

'Fair enough, Roger. Until then let's concentrate on having Daniel home and look forward to seeing Rose and her baby.'

Roger sighs, he really likes these people and he hates having to tell them things that he knows will upset them. Sylvia leans over and squeezes his hand.

They all take turns to visit me in hospital and are amazed how well I look, the girls coo over our baby and the men congratulate Johnny on having such a strong and handsome son.

I chide the men, 'Anyone would think he has done it single-handed,' I exclaim.

I am due home at the end of the week. Daisy helps Johnny to choose some new baby clothes and a pram for our son. We have been caught out with his early arrival and all our provisions for him are still at home on the farm.

At last baby and I are discharged from hospital, the plan is for us to stay for a week in the house and then travel home to the farm. However, Martha cannot wait that long to see the baby, so she and Alf are going to make one of their rare visits to the 'big town', as Martha calls it.

Roger and Sylvia are warned again that Alf and Martha have no idea of our origins and that's the way we want it to stay. So they decide that Roger and Sylvia will be introduced as friends whose house is being repaired after a bad water leak.

We return to the house to see a great banner displayed from the top windows, saying 'CONGRATULATIONS'.

I had to laugh, 'I would have been mad to expect a quiet welcome.'

'Come on then, my baby son,' Johnny says as he carefully takes the sleeping baby from my arms, 'let's meet the rest of the family.'

'They're here, they're here!' Becky calls; she has been so excited to welcome another baby into the house. It is a positive against all the negatives that have happened in her young life. She has thanked God many times that she had met Daniel on that awful day and has been welcomed into this strange family. Things have not been easy, but she knows it could have been a lot harder. Her sons settled down eventually and are thriving at school and little Jenny is loving nursery. Becky has no idea what the future holds for them, but at the moment life is good.

Daisy hears Becky and rushes to open the door.

'Come in, Rose, we are so pleased to have you home.'

The girls have made up the crib with lovely blue linen and sitting in the corner of the bed is a cuddly blue toy rabbit.

I carefully put my new son into the crib.

'I'm so pleased to be out of that hospital,' I said, 'don't get me wrong, everyone was extremely kind, but I was beginning to think that my son and I were pin cushions. There were so many tests.'

'Forget about that now, we are all together again,' Johnny says as he gives me a cuddle.

'Have you thought of a name for the little one yet?'

'Yes, we have, Becky,' answers Johnny as he looks at me, 'you tell them, Rose.'

I am sitting by the crib, softly stroking my son's blond hair, 'We are going to call him James. It's a good strong name and just seems to suit him.'

They all nod in agreement and raise their mugs of tea, 'To James and a long healthy life.'

The next day Martha and Alf come to stay. Martha is overcome with emotion when she sees baby James.

'Do you want to hold him, Martha?' I ask her. 'He is due a feed, do you want to give him his milk?'

'Are you not feeding him, Rose?'

'No, unfortunately my body has not produced sufficient quality milk to sustain him.'

'That's a shame, but I will love to give him his bottle.'

The others go about their day-to-day chores and Adam, Johnny and Mark take Alf to the pub to 'wet the baby's head'.

'What a bonnie baby, Johnny, you must be really proud.'

'Yes, I am, Alf; I hope Martha wasn't too upset about Rose having the baby in the hospital.'

'No, I convinced her it was for the best. But why a military hospital, is something going on that I should know about, you haven't joined the army, Johnny?'

'Of course not. It's all rather complicated, but everything is sorted now, so there is no need to worry.'

'Fair enough,' replies Alf, but deep down he knows something is going on, but did he really need to know? Everyone seems happy enough and that will do for now.

Chapter Nineteen

It is now well into the second millennium, the world is still being ravaged by floods, earthquakes, tsunamis, droughts, riots and wars. We have a task to fulfil, the Elders had put their trust in us but the remedy we thought would come easy is as fragile as a flame in a hurricane.

The government have tested all of us and have only found an extreme increase of IQ and a slight change in the body make-up. We are also being continually grilled about our previous lives and we are expected to produce a miracle cure to the world's troubles.

Since Daniel's accident he has tried to fulfil his role as representative for the people's voice but the government is making it very hard for him to speak to his voters liberally. Representatives insist on coming with him to meetings and that is not giving him a very good profile.

Johnny and I and our son James are living contentedly on the farm, just taking one day at a time. Martha and Alf both died the year before. Alf had died peacefully in his sleep and Martha joined him a few weeks later, some saying it was from a broken heart. She just could not go on without him. The farm had been bequeathed to us.

Johnny is slowly building up the property and I have opened a little shop in one of the barns to sell our products direct to the public. Things are going well and even James in his tender years is learning how to look after the animals.

Mark and Mary decide to marry at a register office, it is, as they both wished, a very quiet affair, just a small reception at a local hotel. However, everyone is very surprised when Adam turns up at the wedding with a girl. He has been seeing Maddy for some time and really enjoys her company. He thought it was about time we met her. She was welcomed into our group. We are all pleased that Adam has found a friend.

'You are a sly one, Adam,' remarked Daisy, 'I would never have thought you had time for the ladies.'

'I made sure he had time for me,' Maddy replies as she held Adam's arm tightly.

'Well, I think it's great, but I must admit I feel a bit left out in the love stakes.'

'Your time will come, Daisy, and I bet it will be worth waiting for,' Adam says grinning.

Back at the farm there is a much unexpected development.

'Come on, James, eat your dinner,' I plead, 'your dad will be home soon and will want some peace and quiet.'

The door to the cottage opens and Johnny comes in looking extremely agitated.

'What is the matter, Johnny?'

'You know that deserted cottage way off in the top meadow, you know the one you used to live in with the others?'

'What others?' James asks with a mouthful of dinner.

'Hush, Johnny,' I said, and then turn to James, 'I think you've had enough now, go and have your bath and get ready for bed.'

'Do I have to?'

'Yes, your dad's had a long day; I will be in to tuck you up in a while.'

James reluctantly disappears out of the room.

'What were you saying, Johnny?'

'I think some more people are in that abandoned cottage.'

I am not concerned, they could be travellers, but it did seem odd after all these years. I get Johnny's dinner on to the table, all the time wondering if it is possible that the Elders had found a way of sending more people through the timeline.

'I'll take James to the village tomorrow to stay at one of his friend's houses for a while and then we can go and investigate.'

'Do you think we should be prepared for trouble, Rose?'

'No, I doubt it; they could just be some kids who have decided to opt out for a while. As long as they are not doing any damage I can't see any harm in them staying there.'

'You're probably right. This dinner's good, Martha certainly taught you well.'

I fake a curtsy and say, 'Well, thank you, kind sir.'

We both laugh and forget about the intruders.

The next morning I take James to visit one of his friends and by the time I arrive back at the farm Johnny is ready to go to investigate the cottage.

It is a fine spring day and the views are as beautiful as ever, the cottage appears in the distance and they can see washing blowing on a line near the back door.

'It looks like you are right, Johnny, there's definitely someone living there.'

'What shall we do, shall we be furtive or just go straight up and knock on the door?'

'Johnny, you are daft we are not in the commandos,' I answer smiling, 'let's just knock on the door.'

We cautiously approach the cottage and I knock on the door, it swings open. It seems deserted but the table is laid and a half eaten meal is on the plates. One bedroom door is open and Johnny looks in.

'No one in there, Rose.'

'Hush,' I whisper, 'can you hear that?'

We stand quietly and then we hear soft crying, it seems to be coming from the other bedroom.

I slowly turn the handle and open the door. The sight that greets me is unexpected and heartbreaking. There are three children cowering in the corner behind the bed, they look absolutely terrified. There are two girls of about seven and one of them is cradling a little boy about two years old. I slowly approach them.

'Don't be afraid, we are not going to hurt you.'

One of the girls tries to make a run for it, the girl holding the toddler starts to cry louder. Johnny catches the fleeing girl.

'Now what are you running from, young lady, we are not here to harm you?'

It takes a while to calm the children down, but eventually I manage to get them to sit at the table to finish their dinner.

I know where they have come from. I find it hard to believe, but I recognise their mannerisms and they must have seen something in me. They seem to know that I am the same as them.

As I fuss around the children I ask, 'Are there more of you living here? You can't possibly be living here on your own?'

'Yes, there are three more of us, but they are trying to find some food.'

'So what are your names?'

The girl that had tried to run said, 'I'm Violet, and she is Julia and he is Isaac.'

'What lovely names. I'm Rose and this is Johnny.'

'Are you the Rose they told us about?'

'Now that depends, who told you what, doesn't it?'

Johnny is standing in the corner watching incredulously at the scene unfolding in front of him. He finds it hard to believe that these children and more have been sent from a future a thousand years away. Their parents must have been extremely desperate to send their children on a journey that might have never ended. Was it better than what they would have faced in their time?

I am startled by a loud banging outside, and then a voice shouts.

'Who's in there? Come out with your hands up, we're armed.'

I look at Violet, 'Is that the others?'

'Yes.'

'Go and tell them we are coming out.'

Violet goes out to speak to the new arrivals, Johnny looks through the window.

'They have sticks, but I think we will be safe. There is one girl and two lads and they all seem to be about the same age. Eleven, I would think.'

Johnny and I go out to join Violet.

'Hello,' I said cautiously, 'we have only come to see whether you need anything.'

'Who are you?' asks one of the boys.

'My name is Rose and this is my husband Johnny. We own the farm down in the valley. We know this is Violet, Julia and Isaac, but what are your names?'

The tallest boy says, 'I'm Steven, he is Antony and she is Laura.'

'It is a pleasure to meet you all,' I reply.

'How did you know we were here?'

'Why don't we go inside and talk, we mean you no harm.'

The boys go first and Violet and the other girl follow Johnny and I.

'I hope you haven't hurt Isaac or the girls,' the tallest boy says.

'Of course not,' says Johnny, 'why would we do that?'

'Just asking.'

'Have you been out hunting?' I ask.

'We didn't have any luck today.'

'Why don't you all come down to the farm and I will make you a proper meal.'

'How can we trust you, it might be a trick.'

'Don't be daft,' Johnny says exasperated, 'we are just offering you a meal.'

'All right then.'

So we make our way back to the farm, followed at a distance by a strange procession of children.

'You must be patient with them, Johnny. They are very young and have been through some terrible things.'

'I know you are right, Rose, but it is a little frightening for me, knowing where they have come from.'

'What do you mean?'

'It's obvious. They have come from the same place as you and the others. Except even further in to the future. They are younger than you all were when you arrived here. Who knows what has changed since you left. They seem a bit feral.'

'That's only because they are younger. They just need a bit of love and kindness.'

Later, when things had settled down I contacted the other disciples; I am not sure how to approach this new development.

'I can't believe what you are telling me, Rose,' Adam replies, 'the Elders must have been desperate to send these children through the time tunnel.'

'I know, and they are so young, they have turned practically feral, but they are good kids and they were told to find us.'

'That was a tall order, but I suppose it is hard to imagine the millions of people in this world,' Adam says, 'they must come here, we have plenty of room. We can decide our next step once they have settled in to their new environment. Do you think you can convince them to move here, Rose?'

'I think so. They seem to know a lot about us. It will just take them some time to get used to us and the 21st century. Will you tell Roger and Sylvia?'

'I will have to, they are bound to sense that the six new arrivals are the same as us. I am sure they will follow our lead and if we want to keep it quiet for a while they will understand.'

During that evening I explain to the children that there is not enough room for them all on the farm. We will take them to meet the rest of our group who live in a big house in town.

'We might not like it there,' whines Julia.

'I'm sure you will,' I reply patiently, 'you will get the chance to meet lots of people and see and do things you would never dreamed existed.'

'If it's that good why don't you live there?'

'We have this farm to look after, Antony, I'm sure you must understand that being the eldest.'

'I suppose.'

'Is it a long way and will we see you again?'

'It's not that far, Laura, and yes, of course you will see us again. Johnny and I are always visiting the town.'

'What shall we take with us?'

'Only things that are important to you.'

'The Elders sent something to us after we arrived here. They had shown it to us the day we left and said if we found you we were to give it to you. Shall I go and get it?'

I try to hide my excitement and surprise at hearing what Steven has just said.

I say calmly, 'Yes, I think that may be a good idea, Steven.'

There is great excitement in town, Adam is grateful that they have taken over the abandoned hotel as their new home, it seems that the extra rooms will soon be filled. We have all agreed to give the hotel a new name to make it feel more welcoming. The name is going to be 'Providence'.

Daisy with Becky's help get the rooms ready and aired. They put Steven and Antony together, Violet and Julia are in the next room and Laura, because she is the eldest girl, will have Isaac sharing her room.

Johnny and I will be arriving later that day with the children.

'Do you want us to make ourselves scarce?'

'That might not be a bad idea, Roger. These children have been through a lot; they are so young and tend to be distrustful. It will be better if they get used to us gradually.'

'I can understand that. We will go out and get the shopping and arrange to have the sign for the new name made; when we come back you can introduce us as extra helpers.'

'Would that be all right, Sylvia?'

'No problem, Daisy, we don't want them to be frightened of us.'

Roger and Sylvia are true to their word and leave for town an hour before we arrive.

Becky has made some cakes and sandwiches. The house has the welcoming smell of home cooking by the time Johnny and I arrive with the children.

Steven and Antony are very rebellious when they come in, the girls are timid, Laura won't let go of baby Isaac. We give them space and are pleased when they accept food and drink.

'Well, you have certainly had some journey,' Adam tentatively observes.

'We managed,' replies Steven

'Rose told us to bring this,' says Antony as he held out a box to Adam.

The box is wood and covered in carvings. It is obviously important as it is richly decorated.

'Do any of you know what is inside?'

'No,' says Laura, 'we were told to keep going to our arrival site to see whether it had arrived and if it was there we were not to open it, but to give it to you if we found you.'

Adam takes the box and looks at the others. He can see they are as baffled as he feels.

'I think we will open this later. We would all like you to tell us what is happening back home.'

'I don't know. There is someone here who is not one of us.'

'Would you like them to leave, Steven?'

'Yes.'

Adam looks at Becky, 'Would you mind, Becky?'

'Of course not. I will take my children to the park. They can do with some fresh air.'

They hear the front door close.

'Is that better?'

'Yes.'

'So what can you tell us?'

Laura is the first to speak. 'Things were getting worse. We had heard that some of the pods had caught fire. The temperature of our world was rising faster, more in some places than others.'

I am sitting quietly in the corner of the room and Johnny is next to me holding my hand. There is no way that he can comprehend what he is hearing.

'People were dying of the heat and no more babies were being born,' continues Laura, 'we were the youngest so they agreed to send us to you. It is our duty to let you know what was happening.'

Violet starts crying. Daisy goes to her.

'You are safe now, Violet,' she says as she puts her arms around her.

Violet shrugs her off. 'We might be but what about the ones left behind? They are probably all dead.'

There is silence in the room. There is nothing that can be said. We realise that they have all been thrown a lifeline at the expense of hundreds of other lives.

Gradually people start to return to the house, Roger and Sylvia are first and they show everyone the new plaque that they had made to hang over the front door. The new arrivals cautiously accept them, especially as they realise that they are part of the family. They have never experienced being round people that old before and are intrigued by their grey hair and love their sense of humour. In their world people died quite young; there was hardly anyone older than forty and if some did last longer they were put in the equivalent of nursery, but for old people. They seemed to lose their ability for reason and therefore had to be separated from normal people until they eventually died.

It is decided to hang the new sign immediately and Roger insists he will be the one to do it. There is great excitement as we all crowd around; Adam hangs on to the ladder to keep it steady, and as the sign is at last hung on to the hooks there is a loud cheer. It is at this point Becky and her children turn into the drive, followed closely by Maddy and Jim. Mary and Mark arrive a few minutes later. 'Hey, can we join the party?' Mark shouts.

We all go inside. It is with great relief to Adam when he notices the children have let down their guard. They have seemed to pick up on the fact that they are with friends, even the 'strange ones', as they call them, are accepted.

Mary and Maddy have been shopping for Laura, Julia, Isaac and the young Violet. Mark and Jim have bought clothes and electrical gadgets for Steven and Antony. So while Sylvia and Daisy busy themselves in the kitchen preparing the evening meal, everyone else is surrounded by bags full of goodies.

'Are these ours?' asks Laura, holding a pair of jeans and a red T-shirt up against herself.

'If you want them,' replies Daisy.

The children dive into the bags laughing and exploring everything. They have never seen so many clothes and toys. Steven and Antony are amazed with the IPods, Kindle books, CDs and DVDs.

By the time our meal is ready everything has been divided between them and tidied away into their respective bedrooms.

The meal is accompanied by a great deal of chatter. This is the largest gathering there has ever been around the table. All friends eating and drinking together.

'This is better than Christmas,' I exclaim, 'I wish James was here as well,' I continue wistfully.

'We will make sure he is next time, Rose,' Johnny replies squeezing my hand.

'What's Christmas?' questions Julia

'Don't be daft, Julia; we did it in our history lessons.'

'I didn't, Laura, I'm not as old as you. I only got as far as The Great Explosion.'

We exchange glances at this reference.

'I'm sure each one of us has things to learn and things to tell. There is plenty of time to catch up with each other,' says Adam, 'now if we have all finished eating I think it's time the children bath and went to bed. It's been a long day.'

Steven and Antony protest, but they have to admit they are tired and like the others they are eager to get to their rooms to go through all the new things they were given.

Becky and I help Violet, Julia and Isaac to settle, and soon even the boys are quiet. Becky checks on her children and once she is satisfied they are asleep she joins the rest of us in the living room.

'Come and sit with me, Becky,' Daniel says.

'Are you sure it's all right. I thought you would have a lot to talk about, and you have that box to open.'

Adam speaks first, 'We have decided that there will be no more secrets, Becky. We are all in this together, there are many things to consider and we are going to need help in deciding the best route to proceed.'

Becky smiles, 'I'm so pleased that you want my help, I have felt a bit like an outsider and I will be honoured to help in any way I can.'

Daniel gives Becky a hug. 'Well, you are one of us, and while we are on that subject I was going to ask you to marry me and I'm hoping you are going to say yes.'

The room goes silent. Then Becky throws her arms round Daniel and shouts, 'YES. I thought you would never ask.'

We are all pleased and congratulate them, and just for a little while the important business is forgotten as wine is poured and toasts are made.

After about half an hour Adam clears his throat to get everyone's attention.

'Right, friends and family, we have things to discover. Tomorrow is another day, but now we have to find out what our world is doing in the next millennium.'

Adam collects the strange wooden box from the shelf. 'Are we all ready?'

He carefully feels for a catch to release the lid, but cannot find one. 'I don't know how to open it?'

Sylvia comes forward. 'This is all very weird, but I think I know how to open it, Adam.'

We look at Sylvia in amazement.

'I really don't know how your Elders came by this box, but I have seen similar ones before. They were made in China centuries ago to store important papers. The easy way to describe the box is that it is a puzzle box. You have to move each panel in the right order to get the catch to click open.'

'Do you think you can do it, Sylvia?'

'I will give it a good try, but each box has its own secret combination.'

Adam hands Sylvia the box. She studies it carefully, turning it around and upside down until she is satisfied that she has taken in all the symbols and drawings. Then she looks again, but closer this time.

We watch intently as Sylvia slowly slides a small section on the side of the box, then she turns the box and did the same on the next side, and then again on the following side. We all expect her to do it again on the remaining side but she turns the box upside down and studies the underside. Sylvia pushes a section of the pattern and it goes in, she then turns her attention to the top of the box. There are more carvings on the top than anywhere else and as she studies the patterns we hold our breath. Then suddenly she presses down on the right hand corner and the box springs open.

'Wow!' Daniel cries, 'how did you know what to do, Sylvia, it all looks very complicated.'

We all agree and look at Sylvia as some kind of a miracle worker.

'I suppose it is, but I have studied these boxes they have always intrigued me. You have to understand a bit of the old Chinese language and also know the rotation of all the different periods in their history. Then you have to work out what they are trying to tell you.'

'So what were they trying to tell us?' Mark asks.

'It's a bit sad really, are you sure you want to know?'

'If it is part of the message our Elders sent then we must decipher everything, Sylvia.'

'This is the message, "Confucius says there is a time for all beginnings and there is a time for all endings." It is rather poignant and rather sad. But let's hope it means whatever ends something beginning will follow.'

'Well said,' remarks Adam as he takes the open box from Sylvia.

The first thing Adam sees is a piece of paper which he slowly unfolds, the writing is done in handwritten script, he glances at it and realises that it is his duty to read it out aloud to everyone. Adam also knows that it will be the hardest thing he has ever done.

The others are watching him closely and can see the emotion overwhelming him.

'Would it be easier if I read it, Adam?' Roger asks. 'I can see that you are going to find it very difficult.'

Adam looks at Roger; he pauses and then replies as he tries to control his tears. 'I think that may be a good idea, Roger.' He hands the document to his friend and then Adam goes to Maddy and holds her hand tight.

Roger looks around the room at the eager faces of his newfound friends and he feels pride at the trust they bestow on him. He knew from the first moment he and Sylvia had met these strange people that they are definitely special, he also knows that his life will never be the same again and nor will theirs.

The room is full of expectation, fear and a kind of longing to hear what has been said in the letter. Our feelings are full of mixed emotions and the tension is electric. He has quickly skimmed through the letter and is aware that some of the contents are going to be painful for his friends, it will not be easy for him either so he will translate the comments quickly and clearly.

Roger starts to read the message from the future to us.

Our Dear Children

If you are reading this then we know you are all together and for that we thank God. We think it's time to relay everything we can to help you in your quest. We realise now we no longer have the luxury of time, therefore this note will be brief, but together with the other contents of this box we hope that it will give you the insight you need to continue.

We have concocted a 'time capsule', except instead of being opened by future generations this will be open by our ancestors, I hope the irony will not be lost on you and that you all find the contents useful.

We scoured our private museums to locate the easiest method to transport everything we wanted to send to you and we came across 'Memory sticks'. After some research we managed to relay onto these 'sticks' all the information we have at hand and some personal messages as well. What a delightful and apt name these contraptions have, now we will always be in your memories, but such a shame you are unable to do the procedure in reverse.

There are four Memory sticks in this box each numbered in the order we would like you to view them, please do as we ask. Make sure you fully understand the contents of each one before moving on to the next.

We have also enclosed some items that you may find interesting, humorous and even useful.

It would seem that we have not got much longer to wait before we join those that have gone before us.

Please accept our fondest love and know that we will always be with you during all your endeavours, your sad times and your moments of jubilation.

Yours forever and beyond

The Elders

25th December 3012

The silence in the room is only broken by the soft sobbing. Even Sylvia is dabbing her eyes. Roger is glad the letter is finished; he did not think that he could have gone on for much longer without betraying how it was affecting him. He places the letter back in the box and hands it to Adam.

'Thank you, Roger, we appreciate you doing that for us,' Adam tells him and then trying to change the mood he continues, 'let's see what else they have sent us.'

He puts the letter on the table and then takes out the four Memory sticks; each numbered as stated, and puts them next to the letter.

'How clever of the Elders to think of the memory sticks,' Daisy says, 'so come on, Adam, what else have you found?'

Adam takes out a gold locket; I look at it in shock.

'That's mine; I thought I had lost that ages ago. It is very special to me, I was told that it belonged to my mother and that it had been passed down to the first daughter in the family for centuries.'

'Well, you had better take it, Rose, and this time look after it properly,' Adam says jokingly.

I take the locket into my hands; I open it and see that the picture of a woman is still in it. I never knew who the woman was, and at the time it had never been important to me, just special. I now secretly vow that I will try to find out who she was.

The next thing that Adam pulls out is a small shiny stone, it is the colour of the bluest sky and when he holds it up to the light he sees it contains the shadow of a flower. It is quite beautiful.

'Now who does this belong to?' Adam asks as he looks around the room.

A muffled voice answers, 'Me.'

We turn round and see Steven looking embarrassed at the back of the room. 'I couldn't sleep. I wanted to know what is in the box.'

'Are the others still asleep?'

'I think so,' he replies rubbing his eyes.

'Come and get your trophy, Steven, it really is very beautiful.'

Steven reluctantly makes his way to Adam and takes the stone.

'You shouldn't be shy about liking nature, Steven, if it wasn't for things like this we would have never been here in the first place. Nature is our life's blood.'

Steven shyly smiles and goes back to his seat feeling very proud.

Daisy stands up before Adam can say anything else and declares it is time for a refreshment break. Her suggestion is met by instant agreement. Some of us retire to the kitchen but most of the men start to discuss what has been revealed so far. Roger looks at the memory sticks, 'It's amazing that these are in such good condition after all those years. How clever your Elders are to preserve such important items.'

'I suppose it is no different from the preservation of items from the ancient Greeks and Egyptians that are in the museums now.'

'I never thought of it like that, Daniel. It is hard to imagine that things made today will have the capacity to last hundreds of years. I bought Sylvia a new washing machine last year and was told it only had a five-year life!'

An hour later they return to the box of treasures, each one wondering if they had something special hidden in its depth.

Adam holds up a piece of paper, it is neatly folded and held together with a piece of gold thread.

'Does this belong to anyone?'

'Open it up, Adam.'

Adam carefully unties the thread and unfolds the paper. We gasp in astonishment. It is a picture, immaculately penned and then coloured with the lightest watercolour wash, and it portrays the home we had left. The detail is perfect, from the people, to the glass cover that protected us from the ravages of the outside world.

'Have we an artist among us, or is this beautiful piece of art from someone unknown?'

Daniel speaks up. 'It's mine, Adam. I gave it to one of the Elders before we left, how kind of them to send it back to me. You will notice hidden among the sketch of plants in the bottom right-hand corner is my name.'

'So it is. I am sure everyone will agree that this is absolutely fantastic and we will have it framed and hung so that we will always have a bit of home with us. How do you feel about that, Daniel, will you let us do that?'

'Of course,' Daniel replies as he comes forward to get his picture.

The last object in the box is a surprise to all of them; it is contained in a red velvet pouch. Adam slowly takes it out, it is a disc about 6cms in diameter, it is edged with a gold rim and the back is gold with the sun and its rays etched into it. The front is a mirror. It looks like a woman's elaborate handbag mirror, however, we know it isn't.

'Well, I never thought I would ever see one of those again!' exclaims Daisy.

'What is it? It looks like a very expensive mirror to me.'

'You are half right, Sylvia; we know it as a Magic Mirror.'

'That sounds intriguing, why magic?'

'We used it as you would use an encyclopaedia or the internet. We asked it questions and the answers would come up in the mirror.'

'Do you think it will still work after coming through the time zones, Adam?'

'I suppose we can give it a try. Just something simple though.'

'How about what is 10×10?'

'Go on then, Sylvia, you ask?'

'How do I do it?'

'Just look in the mirror and ask the question.'

Sylvia takes the mirror and looks into it; she feels rather stupid talking to it but says, 'What is 10×10?'

There is silence in the room and then a light shines from the mirror. Sylvia is so shocked she nearly drops it, but when she looks into the reflection she sees the number 100.

'I can't believe it still works,' Adam says in amazement. 'You have future technology in your hands, Sylvia.'

'Is this for real, Adam?'

'Yes, Roger. This device was originally designed to help with simple calculations but it was found to literally absorb information and so it was used to store data. I'm not sure how it works as it was invented by our top scientists, but I know that it stores information in the same way as our brain does. Once seen never forgotten, and it retrieves information quicker than our brain ever can.'

'It is absolutely marvellous. I'm sure our scientists would love to get their hands on it, but for the moment I don't think they need to know of its existence, I just have the feeling that would be wrong.'

'You are probably right, Roger, and I appreciate your confidence in this. Its existence must not go beyond this room, for now anyway.'

Everyone is in total agreement.

'There must be hundreds of questions we would all like to ask, but I think we must be very careful. The Magic Mirror deals with facts and there are some things we might not want to know. We must remember that it has facts stored from the far future; we must be really careful and be fully prepared for the answers it gives. This is not fantasy, anything it tells us actually happened including the consequences.'

Adam let this information sink in before continuing.

'However, I don't think it will do any harm to test it with a few simple questions. Does anyone have something they would like to know?'

Jim comes forward, 'I've got a question, Adam.'

Adam hands Jim the mirror.

Jim looks into the mirror and asks, 'Are we going to have snow this winter?'

The mirror flashes again and when Jim looks into the refection he sees the words '*YES LOTS*'.

He laughs and hands it back to Adam.

'I'll have to get a snow shovel then, and maybe a sled.'

'How does it keep charged, Adam?'

'In the same way we use solar energy, but it goes a step further and takes energy from everything that lives.'

'Even us?'

'I suppose it does, but because it can collect energy from so many sources its effect is negligible on any one thing.'

'Can I ask something, Adam?'

'Of course you can, Mary,' Adam says as he passes the mirror to her, 'but remember to be careful.'

'I will,' she replies as she looks into the mirror, 'I would like to know if we will ever find a cure for cancer?'

The mirror glows for a few seconds and when Mary looks into the reflection she sees the words '*YES SOON*'.

She smiles and gives the mirror back to Adam.

Before any more questions can be asked we becomes aware of what only can be explained as an overbearing silence. The birds have stopped singing. Then there is a deafening roar followed by a trembling thunder. We sit still waiting; no one knows what we are waiting for, then it comes. The whole house shakes. Things crash off shelves in the kitchen, we can hear pictures falling off walls, the very chairs we are sitting on move and then all is quiet again. The whole episode takes only a few minutes but to us it feels like hours. The children come running in from their bedrooms; some are crying others look confused. Noises start again in the street; we can hear people shouting to each other. Above that, we can hear the birds singing their evening songs again. The children are taken to the kitchen for hot drinks and to reassure them that they are safe.

'What was all that about?'

'I think we have just experienced an earthquake.'

196

'That's ridiculous,' exclaims Roger, 'we don't have quakes like that in England.'

'It seems we do now, Roger,' states Adam, 'I think we had better check for damage in the house and then see what's happening outside.'

We are lucky there are only minor breakages in the house, but when we go outside it is a complete different story.

A large crack has appeared in the road and a car has nosed down into it, the occupants have managed to scramble out with only a few cuts and grazes. Down the street a tree has been lifted by its roots and has fallen onto the front of a house, demolishing part of the upstairs. A water main has burst and a column of water is shooting ten foot into the air soaking everything in its vicinity.

There are people huddled together trying to comfort the weeping, others are standing alone looking around in complete shock.

We split up and try to help our neighbours in any way that we can.

The damage is not as extreme as we first thought, but the people we help are not used to such natural disasters and fear is their worst enemy, especially as there are a few aftershocks to remind them what has happened. It is late into the night before we wearily make our way back home. The emergency services are stretched to capacity but eventually they arrive. They move the people from the damaged house into temporary lodgings while they shore up the front of the building then start to saw the tree into pieces. Gas mains are checked and electricity supplies, everything seems to be in order. The water board set about mending the fractured pipe.

Peace arrives in the street in the early hours. We collapse into bed, we are too exhausted to even think about what has happened.

The next day dawns sunny and bright, the street looks like a patched up wounded army. The news is relaying the events of the previous night, over and over again. Some people are saying that the earthquake was caused by underground exploration, others are blaming the collapse of old mine shafts, but it soon becomes evident that the area covered by the quake is too extensive to blame any particular party. There is scientific proof that it was caused by plates shifting under Britain, but what made them move is still being investigated. It is going to be a long drawn-out process.

A week goes by before we gather together again and the talk is still about the earthquake.

'Do you think we can ask your mirror why the quake has happened,' asks Sylvia, 'there are so many theories.'

'We can ask but we must always be prepared for the answer. Remember the mirror deals with facts.'

'I understand that, Adam, and if everyone else is in agreement I would like to take that chance.'

We all agree.

Adam takes the mirror in his cupped hand and asks, 'What caused the recent earthquake in Britain?'

There is the familiar flash of light and then the words 'SUNSPOTS' appear.

'I can't see why sunspots would affect movement under Britain.'

'They wouldn't directly, but if they caused extreme movement of the Earth's plates in Europe the result would be a rippling affect over thousands of miles.'

'I can understand what you are saying, Adam, but that would have to be a very strong pull by the sunspots and I know there is a hole in the ozone layer but surely it is not big enough to allow so much power through.'

'What can I say, Roger, there can possibly be two reasons, or a combination of both. The hole in the ozone layer is getting bigger and/or the sunspots are increasing in velocity.'

'Both of those explanations are scary.'

'I know, Daisy, but I think it is time to see what the scientists are saying. I don't want them to know about the mirror, Roger, is there some other way we can relay this information over to your superiors?'

'I can understand your reluctance to let them know of the existence of the mirror, if they had it they will use it to its full extent and try to clone it's properties. So for the moment it stays here. I can tell them that you remember certain facts from your history lessons, but you realise they will have you in to glean every last bit of future knowledge in your head. Are you ready for that?'

'I can do that, but I wouldn't want any others to be grilled. I can say that as I'm the eldest so my knowledge of history goes back further than theirs.'

We object to Adam taking all the stress yet again, but he insists and we eventually give in.

'So when will you contact your superiors, Roger?'

'When is best for you, Adam?'

'Give me 24 hours and I will be ready.'

'I haven't a problem with that. Do you think the mirror can give us any more information? I know for a fact that when they hear from me they will have a car outside in five minutes and I also know they will question you until you want to scream.'

'That sounds pleasant, Roger. I suppose we can try, however you will have seen that the answers are very brief, factual, but brief. We need to be able to ask the appropriate questions.'

'Why don't we all write down what we think are relevant questions,' suggests Sylvia, 'then we can work out the best way to get as much information as possible. By the way, Adam, how is your knowledge of history for this period?'

Adam laughs, 'About as good as your history of medieval times, Sylvia.'

'That good!' Sylvia replies smiling.

We all sit down to write our questions and half an hour later there is a pile of papers on the table. Adam collects them up and looks through them.

'Some of these are the same; some are too complicated to get a simple answer.'

We decide to put similar questions in one pile and then sort through the rest in degrees of relevancy. When this is done we find we have four questions that are factual and could produce useful information.

It is agreed that Adam did the asking this time, so he picks up the mirror and looks at his reflection and asks, 'Can we prevent the Suns overactivity from harming our planet?'

The answer is '*NO.*'

There is alarm on Roger and Sylvia's faces, but we already know the damage that is going to occur.

Adam asks the next question, 'Can we slow down the Global Warming?'

A flash and then the answer '*YES.*'

Adam pauses and looks around at his fellow companions, and then he continues, 'How can we slow it down?'

Another flash and then '*STOP AIR POLLUTION.*'

There was a second blinding flash '*GROW TREES.*'

'That's telling us,' remarks Roger.

'Is there another question, Adam?'

'Just one more, Daisy.'

Adam continues, 'If we do what you suggest, how much longer will that give our planet?'

'*FIVE HUNDRED YEARS.*'

'That's not bad, but can you ask just one more thing, Adam?'

Adam gives Roger the mirror. 'You ask it, Roger.'

Roger takes the mirror in his hand, 'How many countries would have to deplete their contributions towards Global Warming?'

The mirror shines brightly in Roger's hand. '*EVERYONE!*'

A small voice at the back of the room says, 'I find this all very scary.'

Daniel puts his arms around Becky, 'Don't be scared, Becky, we have a good chance to delay the inevitable, I won't let anything happen to you or your children. Don't forget we were sent to help, and help we will.'

Becky looks up at Daniel and smiles, she has every confidence in him and his companions but it did not stop her from being scared.

'I think I'm prepared for the interrogation, Roger, but just give me tomorrow to put some matters in order then you can phone them first thing on the following day.'

'Sounds fair to me,' replies Roger, 'so are we all ready for a slap-up meal. I think it is time Sylvia and I repaid your generosity so we have booked a meal in that big hotel across town.'

'Sounds great, do you mean all of us though?'

'Definitely, even young James is coming over from the village.'

I look up, 'Really, how did you manage that?'

'I think 'them up above' should start to show their appreciation so I ordered a car to get James. You can talk to him if you want.' Roger dials a number on his mobile and says a few quiet words, and then he gives the phone to me.

'Hello, Mum, it's me. We are all going to a big dinner, I'm nearly there.'

'Oh, James, I have missed you, see you soon.'

James arrives and tells them there is a posh coach outside.

We all bundle into the coach with a lot of laughing and squealing. The children have never seen anything as luxurious, there are televisions fixed to the back of every seat, curtains up at the windows, even a toilet and wash-room at the rear.

Roger has chosen the best hotel in town for this meal, we have the dining room to ourselves and over the next two hours we are offered many different courses of every type of food imaginable.

'You are really making them pay, Roger, this must cost loads.'

'You are all worth it, Daniel, it's about time we showed how much we appreciate your Elders sending you to help us. I am going to make sure that you get a good hearing and that your advice and suggestions are acted on. Now let's raise our glasses for a toast.'

We raise our glasses some containing wine, some fruit juice and some squash.

'Here's to the future of our Planet and long may it last.'

'Here, here!'

Chapter Twenty

Adam makes the most of his day; he gathers a few clothes together and some personal belongings. He has a feeling that he could be away for more than a few days. He speaks to the others and it is agreed that Johnny, James and I will go home and the rest of them will continue as normal. Adam promises he will be in contact as much as possible but he takes Mark aside and gives him the mirror for safe-keeping.

'I want you to look after this, Mark, put it somewhere safe and I trust you to only let it be used in a severe emergency.'

'You can trust me, Adam. What if Roger and Sylvia want to know where it is?'

'Just tell them that you don't know and that I told you I had put it somewhere safe to protect it and us. I hate to deceive them but I think if word got out about it then their superiors will put pressure on them and their loyalty will be stretched.'

'I understand.'

Adam spends the afternoon with Maddy, she is like a breath of fresh air and it helps that she knows the kind of things he is up against. She understands our task from the future and she knows what the government here is capable of.

'Don't worry too much, Adam; just tell them as it is. I'm sure they will listen, or the majority will anyway, but there will always be at least one sceptic. However, you will be relaying facts and if they want to close their eyes to that, for whatever reason, that is their problem and you just insist on speaking to someone higher.'

'I wish you were coming with me, Maddy, I always feel more positive if you are near.'

'I promise you, Adam, I won't be far away. Now let's just enjoy our walk, it is a beautiful day and I am with the most handsome man in Britain, what more could I ask for?'

'Only in Britain!'

'Don't push your luck, Adam, I don't often give compliments!' she shouts as she starts to run down a hill.

Adam chases after her, with the two of them laughing and running until they collapse on to the soft grass.

They lie next to each other looking up at the blue sky and watching the white clouds glide across. They can smell the sweetness of freshly mown lawns and they can hear the birds chattering in the trees above them.

'Have you ever recognised shapes in the clouds?'

'What do you mean, Maddy?'

'Look at that one over there; it looks like an elephant with big ears and a trunk.'

'So it does, I've never really noticed before. That one over there looks like a castle from a fairy tale.'

'Now you're getting the hang of it. Look there's one that is an angel.'

'That's our guardian angel, Maddy.'

'You old romantic, Adam, but let's hope it is.'

The following day Roger phones his Headquarters to tell them Adam wants to come in to see them as he has some information regarding the earthquake. Also about other similar events that are happening in increased frequency.

Within ten minutes of Roger's phone call a car arrives outside and two men come to the door.

Adam just has time to say his goodbyes before he is whisked off at speed.

The house seems empty and his friends try to go about the normal routine, but each and every one of them cannot alleviate the feeling of doom.

Adam is feeling apprehensive as he is driven to his destination. The men in the car are silent and this adds to his discomfort.

They stop outside the familiar imposing building and a tall suited man comes down the steps and opens the car door.

'Welcome, Adam, I'm Chris, we have been waiting for you, we are very eager to hear your news.'

Adam follows Chris into the building. There is a staircase in the centre of the expansive hall, above it is a large chandelier, its glass crystals are glinting in the sun shining through the magnificent window at the top of the stairs. Adam is guided to one of the many double doors that lead off from the hallway.

Inside the room there are half a dozen men sitting around a shiny mahogany table. Adam remembers thinking that there is obviously no expense spared for the elite of this country.

As they enter the men stand up and introduce themselves to Adam, it is apparent from their titles that they are all military and a couple are from the MI6.

Adam realises that they still think the battle in front of them can be won by force.

After refreshments have been offered the meeting begins.

'How would you like to do this, Adam? Shall we ask the questions and you give us the answers. Where you can of course. Or do you want to talk first and then we ask questions?'

'I think it will be better, Chris, if I tell you what our scientists deduced from our history and then I will try to give you answers to your questions.'

'The floor is yours, Adam.'

Adam sees notebooks opening and a recorder being activated. He clears his throat and starts.

'There is an increasing amount of activity in the sun, sunspots are being projected far more than ever recorded. This activity will continue to increase over the centuries and there is nothing we can do to stop it, it is a natural progression of the life of the sun.'

'Will that alone affect our planet?'

'Yes. It can buffet us a bit but not enough to knock us off our axis. The main problem is the hole in the ozone layer; this allows the sun's activity to get through our natural defences. The increase in earthquakes is caused by the sun's adverse activity shifting the plates, which means that any area over our world's surface can be prone to disruption. I needn't tell you that earthquakes can be followed by tsunamis and there will also be greater risks of volcanoes erupting. Even the ones we think are dormant.'

'That's a pretty scary picture you are giving us, Adam.'

'Chris, this is not fantasy; I deal with facts as I know them. You want to know the truth and I am telling you. What you decide to believe is entirely up to you.'

'Fair enough, Adam, please continue.'

'The situation I have just described gets worse. The hole in the Ozone layer increases as we continue to use fossil fuels and other harmful gases. The bigger the hole becomes the more the Sun's activity will be able to enter our atmosphere and damage our planet.'

'Your scientists, Adam, did they come to any conclusions as to how we can save our planet?'

'Over the long term, and I am talking about thousands of years, this planet will eventually succumb to its natural progression. However, if we look after what we have now we could prolong the inevitable by about 500 years.'

There is silence in the room. Adam knows the future of the planet because he has been there and lived it, but to the men listening to him it must seem like complete fairy tales. Their faces portray disbelief but their bodies look distinctly uncomfortable with the possible truth in the facts they are hearing.

'What can we do to prolong our time?'

'The solution is in our hands but with technology and science progressing at the rate it is and the increase of the human population it will be a bitter pill to swallow. The only way that any progress can be made is for every single person, in every country to pull together for the one aim.'

'That will be impossible, there are so many conflicts going on around the world and so many different political and religious priorities. I cannot see a 100% agreement of working together.'

'I say again that I can only give you the facts. It will not work unless every single person strives for the same aim. Some countries will be affected by the necessary changes more than others, and there will be disagreements, but it has to be agreed by everyone otherwise the whole thing will be a waste of time.'

'So, Adam, if by some miracle we can pull everyone together what do we have to do to save the Earth, or at the least prolong life as we know it?'

Adam sighs, 'I don't have miracles. The way forward is logic, we know the Sun is becoming more active and we know there is an ever-growing gap in our protective Ozone layer. The cause is being accelerated by harmful gas emissions and deforestation. We also know the remedy but we can't do too little too late. The urgency of our actions must be accepted by absolutely everyone of Earth's society.'

Adam is getting weary, how can he get them to understand that this is not a game. This is life and death of a planet and everyone on it.

Chris stands up, he can tell how frustrated Adam is getting and he can see that they are only going around in circles. Decisions have to be made but by a larger group than those in this room, but he has to have more than words, if only they had proof of the things Adam is telling them.

'Thank you, Adam. We appreciate the information you have given us. Our problem is trying to convince our government, let alone every governing body in the world, that the information we have is fact and not fiction. If only we had concrete proof of the destruction that awaits us if we don't remedy our ways.'

'Isn't it proof enough seeing the increase of natural disasters over the planet? They must have noticed that we are all experiencing crazy weather patterns.'

'They will have what they call 'logical reasons' for every occurrence and it will be swept under the carpet with every other unexplained phenomenon.'

Adam sighs again and sits down heavily in his chair.

'You look exhausted, Adam. We will get a car round to take you home. You have given us a lot to work on, but if anything else comes to mind will you contact us?'

'Of course and thank you, Chris, we promised our Elders that we will try our hardest to steer the planet away from destruction, but we can't do it on our own. Your help will be invaluable.'

Adam is very grateful to be returning to his friends. He is not sure how helpful that meeting has been. The first priority when he gets home is for them to see what is on the memory sticks the Elders have sent them. Maybe they will give him more information to relay over to the government.

That evening, when everyone has assembled, Adam tells us what has been said at the meeting. He is obviously frustrated that more proof is needed before any action is taken.

'Adam, you must remember that we mere mortals cannot begin to imagine what you have seen and what you know. We are living in a fairly stable environment that is being rocked by some unusual events. Our way of dealing with it is to alter a few things here and there to compensate for our over-indulgence and hope that is enough.'

'But don't you see, Maddy, it won't be enough.'

'I can see that because I know you all and I can see how desperate you are to try to stop the inevitable carnage. However, to convince the whole world enough to make them turn their backs on ancient beliefs, religion, power struggles and whatever else they fight about and bring them together as one you will have to produce tangible evidence to back up your words.'

'I realise that now and that is why I have called you all together. You didn't mind coming back here, Rose?'

'Of course not, Adam.'

'We are going to see what is on these Memory sticks. We will then have to decide whether there is anything feasible enough to persuade them of the truth. We will also have to decide how and when we let them know that we have visions from the future.'

We all settle down for a very long evening.

We have managed to set up a large screen so we can all see the contents clearly. Adam inserts the first Memory stick. Nothing happens for a while and we thought it had been damaged, but then the screen flashes white and a few dots speed across it followed by a type of rushing noise. Then we are transfixed, we are looking at Marco, the senior Elder.

'Hello, my brave disciples, if only I could see you. We have used this first M.S to let you see our world as it is now. We will take you on a tour around our home and introduce you to some old friends.'

The tour takes in the laboratories, kitchens, dining rooms, living quarters and dormitories. We notice that there are not many people in any of the rooms. The next part shows the gardens, animals, insects and birds. This leads on to the religious rooms and finally the meeting room. The meeting room is full of people we know, much older than we remembered, but then of course many years have passed.

Adam pauses there and turns to his friends.

'It's a bit disturbing for us, but to our extended family it must be very confusing. Has anyone got any questions?'

'It seems to be like a commune, Adam, is there more than one for each country?'

'Roger, in our time there are no countries, just pockets of civilisation dotted around the planet and surrounded by a raging barren landscape. We are all equal in our quest to survive.'

'Are you able to communicate with others?'

'Sometimes, Sylvia, but mostly the disturbances of nature ruin transmissions. We do try to keep up-to-date with occurrences all over the planet; it is very much hit-

and-miss. Shall we continue, I have a feeling the next bit could be very entertaining.'

Adam is right, in the meeting room are some friends we have left behind and the banter is lighthearted and jovial. Only we can tell the emptiness that lies behind the teasing and jokes, everyone else laughs and remarks what a lovely friendly group they were.

Daisy decides it is time for a break. She notices that the children have been very quiet and is worried that they are getting upset seeing their home and their friends.

'I need some help in the kitchen, Violet, Julia, Laura why don't you all come and see what we can rustle up to eat and drink?'

The girls move, somewhat reluctantly, but once they are in the kitchen they brighten up a bit. Daisy gives them all a job, Violet toasts the bread, Julia prepares the cups for coffee or tea and Laura pours out fruit juice.

Daisy smiles, 'You are great helpers, I'll have to get you in the kitchen a bit more often.' Then she notices that Violet has traces of tears on her cheeks.

'What's the matter, Violet, please don't cry. I know everything is strange for you, but you are among friends and we will always be here for you.'

'You don't understand,' Laura shouts, 'most of the people you saw in the Meeting Room are gone. We know that because it happened before we left.'

Daisy gathers the girls round her, 'That's awful, I'm so sorry we had no idea. You must decide if you want to continue watching or is there anything else you would rather do?'

'Can we talk to Steven and Antony?'

'Of course you can, go and take them to one of your rooms.'

The girls scurry out and got the boys. They all disappear into one of the bedrooms.

When Daisy comes from the kitchen with the drinks and toast Adam gives her a questioning look.

'So what's up, Daisy, are they all right?'

'We should have pre-warned them, you see these recordings were done before they left. I have an idea that things were very bad when they were sent away. I don't think they need to see any more as the poor things have experienced the worst for real. The girls are very upset.'

'I never thought, but you are quite right, what are they doing now?'

'Trying to decide what they want to do while we watch the rest of the recordings.'

'I know,' pipes up Sylvia, 'Roger and I can take them bowling and then a pizza. We can see the rest of the recordings another time.'

'Sounds like a good idea to me,' agrees Roger.

The elderly couple leave the house with five excited children and the rest us sit down to watch the second MS.

This recording starts with one of the Elders explaining that they had managed to design protective suits that allow them to venture outside for a maximum of two hours. The volunteers have to wear oxygen tanks as the air outside is acrid and poisonous.

The scene commences with the men preparing to enter a neutral chamber, the inner doors closes, the men test their oxygen supply and mount their mobile transporter, and then the outer door slowly opens.

They face swirling brown and orange dust that clings to their suits and threatens to mask their visors. The ground stretches out in front of them; a series of undulating mounds of orange earth and rocks, the sky is a dirty red.

There are no clouds, no life, just a never-ending desolate landscape.

Although we have seen all this before it was from the safety of our pod.

We never realised the extent of the destruction. How could we when we were in a safe environment, to us it was like looking at a report of a natural disaster on the news. It happened somewhere else, it would not affect us.

We all watch silently as the men turn the camera to the pod. It is an amazing construction built mainly of glass and steel. It was built in the hope it would last for centuries or until the planet is able to safely support civilization again. There are signs of some surface damage but miraculously nothing serious. The air inside is crystal clear and as the men move round they see the botanical gardens containing trees, flowers and fruits. There are birds and insects flying high to the roof as if they are frantic to get outside, that would mean immediate death, but how can they know that. Further on are small fields with a few sheep, a couple of cows and some horses, then in the farmyard section there are ducks, chickens and pigs. A pond nearby has swans and geese swimming around, completely oblivious to the destruction a few feet away on the other side of the glass.

As the men reach the far side of the pod the scene inside changes, this is where research is carried out, first comes the laboratories, then the archives followed by the Elders private domain. The important decisions will be formatted here. Only the Elders have the full knowledge of the cycle of destruction.

The kitchens and dining rooms are next, the dormitories and the Meeting room are situated in the middle of the pod, so cannot be seen from outside.

The men have circumnavigated the pod and still have some oxygen left in their tanks so they decide to approach the first mound and climb up to the top.

The view from there has never been seen before, they hear one of them exclaiming, 'Oh no!' and when they see the scene he is looking at they realise his dismay.

Stretching out in front of them is a scene from hell. To the right is the pit of a volcano spewing out red hot lava and rocks, to the left is a broiling lake of putrid chemicals coming from the depths of the Earth. The most frightening scene is that the lake has overflowed and a toxic boiling river is heading towards their pod.

We hold our breath; we now know why the remaining children had been sent to us. The pod would never be able to withstand the danger that is now heading towards it.

'I'm so glad the children did not see this.'

'How long do you think they have, Adam?'

'It's hard to say, it depends on how much more of the chemicals are still to come up and whether the river continues on its straight course.'

The recording went on for another twenty minutes. We watch the men rush back to the pod and into the inner chamber. The outer doors slide shut and the men take off their protective clothing. It is hard to tell whether the men's eyes are wet through the exertion or whether they are crying.

The screen goes blank.

'I feel sick,' I said as I rush to the bathroom.

'You had better make sure she is all right, Daisy.'

'We've left it too late to help them!'

'It's never too late, Mark. We haven't seen the other two recordings yet.'

'I think we shall call it a night. I'm sure everyone will agree that we've seen enough for one day.'

We did agree with Adam. We did not feel as if we could watch any more destruction today.

Our timing is perfect because Roger and Sylvia are just returning with the children.

'That was great,' says Antony as he bursts into the room, 'I'm pretty good at bowling.'

'How was your pizzas, Julia?'

'Smashing, I've never tasted anything like it before.'

The children are so happy chatting that they did not notice the mood in the room, but Roger and Sylvia do.

'Come on you lot time for bed,' Sylvia orders as she ushers them to their rooms.

Roger sits down with the others. 'So how did it go?'

'Horrible,' I said as I returned from the bathroom with Daisy.

Roger raises his eyebrows, 'That bad?'

Daniel is the first to speak, 'It was unbelievable, Roger. It does not matter how much you prepare yourself, when the inevitable actually happens the pain is excruciating.'

'I'm so sorry. It must have been awful for you to see. Have you seen all the recordings?'

'No, we have just watched the second one.'

'Well, in that case there must be hope otherwise they would not have been able to record the third and fourth ones.'

'You have a point there, Roger, but I warn you to be prepared when you watch this one, it's pretty harrowing.'

'We have finished for tonight. I think it's time to lighten the mood.'

'Good idea, Adam, there is nothing we can do now, so who's for a drink and a game of scrabble?'

'Drink yes, Mark, but scrabble, I don't think so!'

There is a ripple of laughter.

The next day turns out to be a beautifully warm sunny day and Becky says she will take the younger disciples and her children on a train ride to the coast.

'Are you sure, Becky, they will be a bit of handful?'

'I'm sure, Daniel; I don't think I can watch any more of those recordings. I know the reality of what they show, but the truth is proving a bit more than I can cope with at the moment. Anyway what can be more distracting or more fun than being with the relevant innocence of a gang of children at the seaside with ice creams, donkeys and sandcastles?'

'Put like that I'm tempted to come with you, Becky.'

It doesn't take long to get them all ready for their day out, they are so excited they wouldn't stop chattering. Becky soon has them under control and then they are gone.

'I think we should finish watching the recordings, do we all agree?'

'I think it will be best, Mark,' replies Adam and he goes to set up the screen again. Roger and Sylvia have watched the recording they had missed. They had found it extremely distressing and hard to comprehend. It was as if they were watching a film; however they were actually watching the planet they lived on in its dying moments.

Adam starts running the third recording. It starts with one of the Elders smiling.

'You are probably wondering why I'm smiling. It has been some time since we made the last recording because we have been monitoring what we have called the river of death, for obvious reasons. Some of our people volunteered to go outside at regular intervals to try to work out how fast it was flowing. Yesterday a miracle happened the river has changed its course, it must have come up against some kind

of obstacle and now it looks like it will bypass our home by a safe margin. So once again we can breathe easy.

However, our scientists are busy trying to research why we are unable to reproduce any more, this problem is also affecting all living creatures under our dome. Our crops are not doing too well either. We think it might be something to do with our air quality and the increasing heat.

It is for this reason we have decided to send you our youngest children. Baby Isaac was the last child born and there is no sign that any other children will follow. Look after him and of course Violet, Julia, Laura, Steven and Antony. They are brave children and so young to have such a journey but I'm sure you will find them delightful company.

This recording will show the start of their journey to you. It will also document the basic changes we have had to make to balance the conditions that seem to be affecting us now.'

The scene changes to the deportation chamber, they see the young children assemble at the departure point. There are only half a dozen people behind the protective screens, some of the children are silently crying. The lever is pulled and just before the children vanish they can see Julia holding out her hand for help. Then they are gone.

Becky and the children get off the train, Steven helps her with the pushchair, little Isaac is still asleep. Tom and Charlie are holding Jenny's hands and the other children stay close to her. This is all very new to them, they have never seen a train before and now they have actually travelled on one.

'There are so many people,' whispers Violet, 'where do they all come from?'

'Don't worry, Violet; they are all doing the same as us. They've come to enjoy a day at the seaside.'

'What's so special about the seaside?' asks Antony.

'What a daft question!' retorts Tom, 'it's smashing here, you wait and see.'

They come out of the station and go down the main road towards the front. There are many shops selling buckets and spades, souvenirs, rubber rings and other tempting treats.

Becky buys a couple of buckets and spades, and rubber rings in case they want to go into the sea and she has bought a digital camera to record their day out. Then she buys some food and drink so that they can have a picnic. Because the sun is so warm she errs on the side of caution and also gets some sun screen.

When they finally arrive at the beach the children's faces are a picture.

'Wow! Look at that. I have never seen so much sand and look at all those children. They are all so happy.'

'Of course they are, Steven. Everyone enjoys a day out at the seaside. Young and old.'

'We'll never find a place to sit, there are hundreds of people.'

'Don't worry, Julia, there is always room for a few more. Come on, Steven, help me with the pushchair it's impossible to wheel it over the sand. Mum has enough on her hands carrying all the shopping.'

'Thanks, Tom,' Becky says as she slips her sandals off so that she can feel the warm sand seeping through her toes.

It isn't long before they find a nice space to sit in. Julia wants to sit closer to the sea but Becky has to explain that they are better on the dry sand in case the tide is due to come in.

'What do you mean?'

'Twice a day the tide comes in closer to land and twice a day it goes out again. It's pulled by the moon.'

'Why does it do that?'

'Do you know, Julia, I'm not sure. We will have to ask the others when we get home.'

'Shall we make some sandcastles?'

'What's sandcastles?'

While Becky explains to the girls how to make a sandcastle she sends the boys off to find shells and stones for decorations.

The day goes better than Becky can have hoped, the boys go paddling in the sea while the girls help her to make a massive castle decorated with the stones and shells the boys have collected.

'What made these pretty shells, Becky?' asks Laura.

'They are the homes of sea creatures; they use the shells as protection, just like tortoises do.'

'But where have the creatures gone, the shells are empty?'

'Sometimes when they outgrow their shells it falls off and they grow a bigger one, or they might have been eaten by another creature or bird, or simply died of old age.'

'That's sad.'

'It is sad but that is the way of the world, everything is born, grows, then gets old and then withers away. If that did not happen then the world would be so overcrowded it could not support everything.'

'Is that what is happening to our world?'

'Nearly, Julia. We have become so clever at inventing new gadgets, medicines and biological aids that we have forgotten to take into consideration the natural balance of our world. The population is increasing and people are living much longer so we need more food. Forests are being cut down to make way for additional areas to grow food. There are more factories spewing out harmful gases and the same goes for the millions of cars on the roads all over the planet.'

'Do they not realise what they are doing?'

'They are beginning to realise that the planet's atmosphere is changing, but many countries are refusing to believe that it is their activities as well as others that are compounding the problem.'

'How can they be made to take notice?'

'That is a very good question, Laura. That is why the Elders sent the others back in time. They hoped that the people living now will listen and act on the information they are given, but it seems that they are going to take a great deal of convincing.'

'I can't understand why, Becky, it is common sense.'

'It is for all of you because you have experienced the results of ignoring the obvious, but for the people living in this day and age with all the benefits and beauty around them it is very hard to accept that it will ever disappear.'

'So it is hopeless.'

'Nothing is ever hopeless, Laura. Now come on let's go and join the boys and have a paddle in the sea.'

They went to join the others splashing around in the sea.

Back at the house the mood is low. They have finished watching the third recording. It shows them a dwindling population and the only flora and fauna that are surviving are those which are used to tropical conditions. Many of the animals are dying and the birds are fighting against the heat. They are even trying to break through the glass as if they think it might be cooler outside. The increased heat is being caused by the volcanic activity and also the River of

Death. The Elders hoped that as the river wound its way past their refuge the heat might start to subside. Unfortunately it is taking too long and there are many deaths in the community. Mainly the very old and sick.

The Elders still maintained a positive outlook and insisted that they are doing tests to combat the negative activity outside. They have managed to contact another refuge and are exchanging information and remedies with them. It seems that this other place has also experienced a similar catastrophe and they have managed to neutralise the affects so the Elders are acting on their information.

Becky and the children are packing up their things after a long and very enjoyable day. She is hoping that the children have seen that they can still enjoy themselves and that there is still a lot to look forward to.

When they leave the beach they buy some rock and postcards of the sea so everyone at home will know where they have been.

'What is this rock for, Becky?' Violet asks.

'It's a kind of old tradition Violet. Every seaside town makes their own rock and they have the name of the town all the way through it.'

'What do you do with it?'

'You eat it. It's very hard and sweet and comes in lots of different colours and flavours, not really good for the teeth, but nice anyway.'

They arrive at the rail station and sit and wait for their train. Becky knows they have about half an hour before their train is due so she sends the boys off to get some comics to read. The journey home will take about two hours and she doesn't want them to get bored.

A few minutes later the boys come back escorted by the Rail Police.

'Are you in charge of these lads, madam?'

'Yes, officer, what's wrong?'

'They don't seem to understand that they have to pay for things?' he says sarcastically. 'They just choose what they want and then walk out of the shop.'

'I'm so sorry. I gave them money, but they have not got used to the concept of using it.' She gives her sons a scornful look.

'I'm sorry, Mum, we hadn't realised what they were doing. Tom and I were looking at the music DVDs.'

Becky looks at the police men she feels completely flustered – how can she explain to them that the boys have no idea how to use money. Then she has an idea.

'These lads were found living on their own, their parents had abandoned them but they were rescued by the social services and they now live with our family. They did not know they were doing anything wrong. I will pay for anything they have taken.'

'Under the circumstances we will overlook it this time, but we strongly suggest that they are taught that nothing in this world is free.'

'Thank you, officer, we will make sure that they are fully prepared the next time they go shopping.'

The officers walk away and the long awaited train arrives. Once they are all settled Becky takes a deep breath. She has never been so embarrassed.

'I'm sorry, Becky; we did not mean to get you into trouble.'

'Don't worry about it, Antony. There is so much that we take for granted, it must seem so alien to you. We will make sure that you are fully aware of all the weird things we do in this day and age. It will be advisable for you to remember what that policeman said and that is 'that nothing is free in this world.' That doesn't just mean cost but also consequences.'

The children settle down to read the comics and the younger ones fall asleep.

In the house we are settling down to watch the last recording. We are feeling apprehensive; we did not think it is going to be very pleasant.

'Are we all ready?'

'Let's get this done, Adam.'

The recording starts once again with one of the Elders talking. He explains that things have taken a turn for the worst. The river has changed course again and is now heading straight for their home, they can also see that the volcano is getting increasingly active and their outer shell is being bombarded by ash and red hot rocks.

There are only a hundred people left alive and they have accepted their fate, so it is agreed to do as much filming as possible before sending the box through the time zone later that day.

The pictures that follow show the River of Death approaching, it is bubbling with heat and an orange gas is hovering over it. We can also see missiles being spurted out from the volcano and see them smash into the glass domes. It is terrifying to watch and we are all deathly quiet.

The scene changes to the day-to-day routines still being carried out within the pod. There are some exceptions; all the living things they have spent so much time nurturing and protecting are now slowly being put to sleep. It is the only way they can stop them suffering a horrific death. The people in charge of this awful task are visibly crying.

Many of the artefacts collected and saved for hundreds of years are being packed into lead boxes and put into deep pits, just in case. People are doing their tasks without talking, each occupied by their own thoughts. They have been given choices of how to die, not something any of us would want to contemplate.

As the recording is drawing to a close an Elder comes on to the screen once more.

'We have shown you enough, there is little more to say except we love you all. We never expected miracles, just do your best, have a good life and remember your old friends.

May God be with you.

Goodbye.'

The screen goes black. There is a heavy silence in the room.

Sylvia is the first to speak. 'That was absolutely terrifying. It makes me wonder why we waste our time in fighting each other; there will never be a winner.'

'How right you are, Sylvia. I hope you will all agree that these recordings must be seen. Its proof of what you've been saying, Adam. They will have to believe you once they have witnessed what is on these MS.'

'Do you really believe that, Roger. I bet their first reaction will be that we have concocted those images somehow. Even if they do believe us do you really think the rest of the world will come together as one to save the planet?'

'It is all we have; we must give it a try.'

At that moment Becky and the children come in the front door. They can be heard laughing and fooling around.

We are relieved by the distraction.

'I am absolutely exhausted,' exclaims Becky as she collapses into the nearest chair, 'I must have been mad to suggest it.'

'Didn't you enjoy it then, Becky?' Daisy says as she offers her a cup of tea.

'Actually I did, but shoot me if I suggest it again!'

Daisy laughs as she ushers the children through to the bathrooms to get ready for bed. She promises them some supper and a warm drink if they hurry up.

'What was it like, Daniel?' Becky asks, referring to the recordings.

'Not very nice, Becky, in fact I think it affected us all very badly.'

'I'm so sorry. I don't know what else to say.'

'I think your timing is perfect. We have just finished watching the last one as you all came home, you diverted our attention. When the children are settled you must tell us all the things you did.'

'Actually I can do better than that, Daniel; I bought a digital camera and took loads of photos. We can download them on to the computer and look at them later.'

'Brilliant idea, Becky.'

The children, thankfully, are exhausted by all the fresh air and excitement of their day out, so they go to bed earlier than usual. We are drained by the events that have unfolded from the recordings, so after we have eaten and settled down for the evening we are more than ready for some light relief.

Becky starts by saying she had been caught unawares by everything that has to be explained to the new arrivals.

'It is so weird, we take so much for granted but as the day drew on I got used to the questions and tried to prepare in advance. There was one embarrassing moment when Steven and Antony were escorted back to me by the rail police. They had been in the shop to buy comics for the journey home. I had given them money but they did not understand the concept of exchange. Poor dears they were so ashamed but we soon sorted the problem.'

'You did marvellously, Becky,' Daniel says giving her a hug, 'but we will have to make sure they understand how we conduct ourselves in this century.'

'We will make that a priority, Daniel; we can't have them arrested again.' Adam continues, 'I have downloaded your pictures, Becky, are we all ready?'

We spent the next couple of hours looking at the photos Becky has taken, it is lovely seeing the children splashing around in the sea and building sandcastles. They really enjoyed the Punch and Judy show and the ride on the donkeys. The fish and chips followed by ice-creams also went down well.

'How on earth did you manage to control them, Becky, they all seemed delirious with excitement?'

'It wasn't that bad really, Daisy, if things started to get out of control there was always something new with which I could divert their attention.'

When the picture show has finished we slowly dispersed to our beds until the only ones left were Adam and Roger.

'Have you thought any more about the recordings, Adam?'

'It seems we are going to have to let them know about our new arrivals if they are going to even start to think the recordings are genuine. I really didn't want the children to go through all the examinations and tests.'

'I know, but I think it is going to be inevitable. I feel it will be worth the upheaval to them if the recordings are accepted as bona fide.'

'I know you are right, Roger, but I think it will be prudent to wait until after the weekend. It will give the children a chance to settle down a bit more and give us the chance to explain a few more necessities to them.'

'That seems fair enough, Adam, but don't leave it any longer than that, because I swear my bosses think I've joined the other side!' Roger replies with a wink.

Adam laughs, he really likes Roger, he seems like a father figure to him and makes Adam feel he isn't alone in making important decisions.

Chapter Twenty-One

The next day is Saturday so Johnny, James and I return to our farm and Mark takes Steven and Antony shopping. Julia, Violet and Laura go girly shopping with Daisy. This is their baptism to current day life.

Becky and Daniel take her children to the park and then to Jim's café for dinner. It is a favourite haunt for them as that is where they had first met.

Jim is pleased to see them and makes a fuss of the children. He looks older than usual today.

'Are you all right, Jim, you look a bit done in?'

'I have to admit, Daniel, watching those recordings gave me nightmares, it makes me think what is the point of things.'

'Never had you down as a defeatist, Jim. There is always a reason for everything, the inevitable is always just round the corner, you have had the misfortune to actually see it. That doesn't mean that we can't do something to delay it.'

'You are all so brave and so positive. You are right – I must stop these negative thoughts. I'm behind you every step of the way.'

'That's more like the Jim I know and love, now where's our dinner?'

Jim smiles and goes off to fetch their meals.

'Do you think he is all right, he does look a bit rough?'

'Yes, he'll be fine, he just needs something to cheer him up, and normality should do it. I think we should plan our wedding. How about asking him to give you away?'

Becky's eyes sparkle, 'You don't think it's too soon for us to get married?'

'It can never be too soon for me, so what do you think?'

'It's a great idea and I will love having Jim give me away.' Daniel leans over to give Becky a kiss.

Jim is delighted when they ask him to give Becky away; they talk about the wedding while they eat. Tom, Charlie and Jenny are all for a big party, especially when they realise that they will each have a special role to play. They have grown to admire Daniel, even though he seems a bit strange sometimes, but most importantly he has made their mum happy again.

When they leave the café they are pleased to see Jim look more like his old self, with a big smile on his face and a spring in his step.

There is chaos that evening in the house; everyone wants to talk about what they have done that day. The girls give a fashion show with all their new clothes that they have been buying. The boys want to show off their new mobile phones, DVDs and CDs. However, it is all topped by Daniel and Becky's news that they plan to get married in three months' time.

'That's brilliant, Daniel, we can all do with a celebration, there's too much doom and gloom around lately.'

'What's a wedding?' a little voice asks.

They all turn round to see Julia looking very confused.

Becky laughs, 'Oh, Julia, there is so much for you all to learn, but a wedding is most definitely the most exciting.

Tomorrow I will tell you everything it involves, you will love it.'

True to her word, the next morning Becky gathers the girls together to show them weddings on the internet. They look at dresses and churches then Becky takes great pains to tell them the significance of the service. They love to see the celebrity weddings and Becky has to explain that ordinary people didn't go quite that mad.

'Will you have bridesmaids, Becky?'

'Probably. I would like to have my daughter Jenny as one, but then I will have to have someone to watch her because she will probably run off.'

'I can watch her,' says Julia shyly.

'What a good idea and what about Violet and Laura. It will be smashing if you all agreed to be my bridesmaids. How lovely you will all look.'

The girls' eyes gleam.

'Would we wear special dresses, like the ones on the internet?'

'I'm sure something can be arranged.'

The girls run off to tell everyone, they are so excited. Becky hopes she has not overstepped the mark.

Later that day everyone sits down to discuss more serious matters. Adam is going to release the recordings tomorrow and his visit will include disclosing the arrival of their newest members. He knows that they will then be called in for examination and he wants to prepare them.

'Why do we have to go to this hospital, Adam?'

'It is because we have come from the future and our bodies have evolved. They have to take tests and samples in case one of us needs medical treatment. There is a possibility that the doses they give in this time could be either harmful to us or not strong enough to cure us.'

'But you have been, so why have they got to test us?'

'You six arrived quite a few years after us, Antony, so they have to test for any changes.'

'Will they be doing it to little Isaac?'

'Yes, Laura, but he won't be harmed. Rose's son James had the same tests as soon as he was born and he has not suffered any effects from them.'

'How long will we have to stay there?'

'Only a couple of days. I have to go tomorrow as well and I can stay with you if you want.'

'We are going tomorrow?' exclaims Violet, 'what about the wedding, we will miss that?'

'Of course you won't,' says Becky putting her arms around a distraught Violet, 'it takes ages to plan a wedding and I promise I won't start until you all come back.'

'Promise?'

'Of course.'

The next day the weather is gloomy which reflects everyone's mood. Three black cars arrive at ten o'clock precisely and five unhappy children, the baby and an apprehensive Adam are whisked away.

Adam is pleased to see that Maddy is in the car carrying baby Isaac and has the two younger girls with her. At least they are familiar with her which may make the tests less daunting for them. Adam, on the other hand, is dreading the reaction when the recordings are shown, and he is not looking forward to seeing them again himself. He cannot believe that these people are going to actually see their planet dying.

Thankfully for everyone the two days pass quickly and soon they are greeting everyone home again.

The young children look exhausted and their faces are pale. We know exactly what they have been through so a special meal has been organised for their return and a light-hearted DVD has been chosen for them to watch.

'How did it go, Adam?'

'As bad as I expected. However, Chris was there, I'm glad to say, he seems easy to talk to and is willing to accept the answers I give as probable. But we will talk about it when the children are in bed, Daisy.'

The children enjoy their meal and settle down to watch the film. They have not said much since they came in and that worries Becky.

'Everything all right, Laura?'

'I suppose. We don't have to go there again do we?'

'Not if I have anything to say about it. Try to forget it now. Tomorrow you can help with the wedding plans.'

Laura gives a weak smile. Becky hopes they will all recover after a good night's sleep.

Adam waits until we have settled down for the evening before he starts to tell us what has gone on over the last two days. He knows that Roger and Sylvia have been contacted in respect of the validity of the recordings.

'I'm sorry if the two of you were reprimanded for keeping the new arrivals secret, Roger.'

'Don't worry about it, Adam. We were told to use our own initiative and that is what we did, so they will have to get over themselves. I'm just glad that we talked them out of withdrawing us and putting new people in our place.'

'Did they really want to do that? That would have been awful.'

'We did say that it would have been a grave error as you all trusted us, and of course we promised to behave in the future,' Roger says with his customary wink.

'Come on then, Adam, what was their reaction when they saw the recordings?'

'They watched each one without a word, but I could tell by their faces that they didn't want to believe what was unravelling in front of them. We had a break between each one but not a question was asked. By the middle of the first afternoon we had seen them all. They dismissed me for an hour while they talked about the evidence put in front of them.'

Adam sips his drink before he continues. 'They actually said, "you don't expect us to believe what we have just seen?" I told them that was their prerogative but the recordings are genuine.'

'They then start bombarding me with questions. When they finally stopped I was absolutely shattered. I had noticed that the whole meeting was being recorded, so when we finished for the day I expect they went through everything again.'

'It all sounds terrible, Adam. Weren't you tempted to lose your cool?'

'Many times, Daniel, but what would have been the point?'

'Do you want to stop there for a break,' suggests Daisy, 'who wants a snack and a drink?'

An hour later everyone is curious to hear more of the grilling Adam went through.

When they were all settled down again Adam continues.

'The following day they wanted to know how we had got our information and how we communicated with the other pods. I could only give them my limited knowledge because when we left we were too young to be involved in the complex running of our home. They also wanted to know how long our world had been in the destructive state we had left. I told them that people had been living in our isolated pod for over a hundred years. I knew the number of pods scattered over the planet's surface had been reduced drastically within that time, due to the Sun's immense activity causing massive storms wiping out fifty percent of survivors.'

Adam pauses before going on. 'They were asking me questions that were best answered from our history lessons. I'm glad I can remember those lessons. What I couldn't answer is the precise moment the destruction all started. They seemed to think it was a specific point in history; they did not seem to understand that the destruction was done over years through mistreatment of natural resources. The accumulation of overworking these natural resources. That the increasing use of deathly fuels and chemicals combined to destroy our natural protection from the Sun's over activity.'

'If they are asking these questions they must believe what they have seen,' states Mark.

'So it will seem. I just got the feeling they would have felt more comfortable proving it was all lies than the alternative, which will mean they have to face the inevitability of their actions and try to find a way to combat the continual destruction.'

'That sounds about right, Adam. They will be terrified of trying to explain it to their bosses, let alone the rest of the world.'

'What do you think then, Roger, what will they do next?'

'It's hard to say. At the moment they will be running around like headless chickens. So I suggest that we just carry on as normal until we hear from them again.'

The next day is a much brighter day in every sense of the word. The sun is shining, the birds are serenading the world and Becky is enlisting everyone to help her plan her wedding.

It is just the diversion that is needed. The children are a bit hesitant to start with but soon they join in with the others choosing clothes, food and venues. Daniel and Becky have decided to get married in the village near Rose and Johnny; they will be married in the old church there and have the reception in the local pub, The Dog and Gun.

The other big event which is being continually shown on the news is the Olympic Games. England has been chosen as the host country and London the main host city. It is shameful to admit that the excitement of relaying the preparations for the Games sometimes overshadows harrowing disasters throughout the world. People just did not want to know about disasters they just want to hear about the positive things of life

The day of the wedding dawns bright and sunny; Becky has chosen an ivory dress and all her bridesmaids are dressed in pale blue. Young Mary, Julia and Laura join her daughter Jenny as bridesmaids and I am maid of honour. Everything goes smoothly and the reception afterwards at the Dog and Gun is a resounding success. It is lovely seeing all the children laughing and playing together, no one can have guessed the literal age difference between some of them.

The villagers have done us proud as usual; all the houses have been decorated outside and everywhere is covered in flowers. Mark and Mary announce at the reception that they are soon to become parents and everyone is delighted by their good news.

It is definitely a day to remember.

Chapter Twenty-Two

The return to the house is an anticlimax, especially as news is coming in about a cyclone hitting the Indian coast. This news not only knocks stories about the forthcoming Olympics but also all the wars, killings and droughts off the front pages for a few days. Unfortunately the latter are still continuing.

Roger receives a call from Chris asking for Adam to return for another debriefing. It seems they have gone through all the data that they have received and they want to talk to Adam again before they move the information higher up the ranks.

'I really don't how much more I can tell them, Roger.'

'I know, Adam, but the good thing is that they are obviously taking things seriously now. They must believe the recordings are genuine because they will not dream of moving it higher if they have any doubts. They just want to get their facts straight. You think they are tough interrogators; they have to face worse than that when they start revealing the facts.'

'I suppose you are right. Do you have any suggestions, Roger?'

'What about the magic mirror, Adam?'

Adam hesitates. 'With respect, Roger, I still don't think that is a good idea. It will not help them and it can end up being used as either a party trick or, even worse, for the wrong reasons. I will prefer its existence to be kept within these walls, for now at least.'

'Sylvia and I will abide by your decision on that. So I can only suggest you answer their questions as fully as you can. No one can expect more than that.'

Once again Adam is whisked off in one of the black cars. He wishes this wasn't happening and hopes that Chris will be chairing the meeting.

On his arrival Adam is shown into the same meeting room, there are only four people there including Chris, two men in uniform that Adam does not recognise and a woman who looks vaguely familiar.

Chris immediately gets up to welcome Adam. 'Nice to see you again, Adam, please sit down.

Adam does as he is directed.

'Let me introduce you, this gentlemen is Harry and is a member of our armed forces,' Harry nods to Adam, 'and this other gentleman is Vic who is with the air force.' Adam acknowledges Vic; he wonders why the military are being involved. Were they still thinking the battle in front of them can be won by force?

Chris continues, 'And this lovely lady is Helen, she is one of our top scientists and has been specialising in natural disasters for the last twenty years. She has been monitoring cause and effects of the chaos that seems to be escalating all over our planet.'

That's more like it, thinks Adam.

Chris hands Adam the memory sticks. 'We thought you might like to have these back, they must mean a lot to all of you. We have, of course, taken copies.'

Adam accepts the gesture, but knows that they must have been scrutinised for evidence of fraud.

'Have you anything you would like to say, Adam, before we get down to business?'

'Only that I am curious to know of your truthful reactions as to what is on these recordings.'

'That's fair enough, shall we go round the table, Harry, you can be first, what did you think?'

'My first reaction was this has to be an elaborate hoax. However, the more I watched, the more it seemed to be too complicated to be made up. It is hard to comprehend that we were actually watching our planet as it will be in a thousand years. That's a long time ahead. How do we know that the destruction is caused by what we are doing now? Something could happen in the next five hundred years that causes the Earth to terminate.'

'Fair comment,' replies Adam, 'but you see I have come from that future world and in our history lessons we were taught what led up to the decline of Earth. That is why we were sent back here, to try to stop the rot from setting in, so to speak.'

'But you were just young teenagers when you arrived, what made them think that you would be capable of such a huge task?'

'We wondered that as well, why was such a huge responsibility handed to us? Then we realised that our mental capacity was far in advance compared to today's standard. Also, I think they knew their decline was inevitable and they wanted the brightest and youngest students to have a chance of experiencing a normal life, with a slim chance we could possibly do something here and now to prolong their lives.'

'Thanks, Adam, what about you, Vic, have you something to say?'

'Yes. How long were people living in pods?'

'From our history books I gather it must have been a few hundred years.'

'Why did they send the last six children to you?'

'Basically to save them from watching their world being destroyed. They were the youngest; the rest of the people knew their fate and had accepted it. The animals were slowly being put to sleep and I believe that everyone had the means to end the agony when they thought they could bear no more.' Adam lowers his head.

'Are you all right, Adam, this must be very painful for you?'

'Let's just continue.'

'If you are sure.'

Adam nods in reply.

'Right, Helen, it's your turn.'

'Hello, Adam, I will try to keep my questions factual. Do you know how in advance the pods were built and were they built because of an impending holocaust?'

'Well, Helen, it took sometime before all the countries came together to try to preserve the planet. There was so much suspicion. Countries or sometimes just the leaders thought that it was a ploy for a world takeover, financially and politically. Then they had an unmistakable wake-up call. The Sun's activity increased at an alarming rate and harmful rays and missiles shot through our already damaged Ozone layer. The victims were central Europe, millions of people died and the land was left a barren, burning mass. That's when they started to build their refuges, some countries were more advanced than others, and at this point our world came together as one, the more advanced helped their neighbours. If only they had come together sooner.'

It is obvious that Adam is emotionally affected by this recollection.

'I think we shall break there, see you back here in an hour.'

The others left, but Chris comes up to Adam. 'Will you be all right to continue?'

'Yes, in a while, I just want to be on my own for a bit. Will it be okay if I go to the gardens?'

'Of course, I will send someone out with some refreshment for you.'

Adam walks slowly through the trees, he is calmed by the sounds of nature around him and he hears the splash of water as it flows over the rocks into the nearby lake. He cannot understand why people are so willing to lose all this beauty. The only things that concern them are power, wealth and pleasure. He sits down by the lake and if by magic a young girl appears before him with a tray of food and drink. She did not say anything but just places the tray on the ground next to him, then disappears before he has time to thank her.

He must have fallen asleep after eating because the next thing he knows he is being gently awakened.

'Do you feel better, Adam?'

Chris is hovering by him. 'Yes, thank you, Chris, is it time to go back?'

'Fraid so, are you ready?'

'As I'll ever be.' Adam gets up and bends to pick up the tray.

'You can leave that, someone will come for it.'

Adam follows Chris back to the building. When they enter the room the others are waiting for them.

'I think Helen has a few more questions for you, Adam.'

Adam smiles at Helen, 'Fire away, Helen.'

'You say that finally countries come together to help each other. Does that mean there were quite a few pods scattered over the planet?'

'Yes, there must have been well over a thousand scattered around the main countries, each holding about twenty thousand people with archives and flora and fauna of that region. There is another development I have not mentioned before and that is the spacecrafts.'

They all look up at once.

'Spacecrafts?'

'Yes, that's right. When it finally dawns on the bigger countries that there is a strong possibility that the place they call home will decline fast, they decide to build large spacecrafts to send the chosen few to inhabit another planet.'

'Which countries were these?'

'You must remember this was in my history books and happened hundreds of years before I was born. I think I'm correct in saying four crafts left Earth, one each from America, Russia and China.'

'What about the fourth?'

'That contained representatives from the poorer countries and was organised by the British and French.'

'Where were they all heading?'

'I'm not really sure; the information is a bit sketchy as it was classed as top secret. Nothing was ever heard from any of them after they went off the radar. So they could have started another Earth somewhere, or they could have all gone to different planets, or they could have all died. We never found out.'

'Have you anything else to add, Adam?'

'Just one thing really, will it be feasible to draw all the countries together or will it be as it was in my history books?'

'That's a tough one, Adam. It all comes down to money, scepticism and power.'

'So no change there. I don't understand how all the different countries can come together for the Olympic Games where billions of pounds are spent, but they can't come together to save their planet.'

'That unfortunately is the way of the world, Adam.'

'But don't they realise that all the power and wealth in the world will be useless when they are standing on a burning planet!'

Adam continues, 'It would seem that the attitude is "live for today and let our descendants go to hell." Because that is exactly what is going to happen. I know that because I was there and if it hadn't been for the Elders I would be walking around with a pill of death in my pocket just as all my friends in the future are doing.'

'Point taken, Adam. We have to answer to our superiors now. We will appreciate you staying for a night if you don't mind. We feel it is important that you are on hand to strengthen our case.'

'I'm sorry, Chris, I didn't mean to take it out on all of you. It must be very hard for you all to take this in and believe it. To tell you the truth when we first arrived in your time we thought we had died and gone to heaven. Everything is so beautiful. All I am describing to you of our life is a literal hell on Earth.'

Helen comes to him, 'Thank you, Adam. We do appreciate how hard it must be for you.'

The others left the room leaving just Adam and Chris.

'Can I phone home, Chris?'

'I don't think that would be a good idea. We don't want to worry them and you will be going home tomorrow.'

'This is all top secret then?'

'For now, and we don't fully trust the phones, we never know who is listening.'

The next day the meeting convened but instead of the military personnel there were two men in suits with Helen and Chris.

'Good morning, Adam, I hope you slept well.'

'Yes thank you, Chris.'

'Good. Now let me introduce you to Malcolm and Peter. They represent our Government and have just a few more questions to ask you.'

Adam acknowledges the two new faces and smiles at Helen. He really didn't know what more they can ask him, but obviously something is niggling them. Peter is fidgety; he looks as if he would rather be somewhere else and Malcolm just stares at Adam as if he is an alien.

Chris can obviously feel the tension in the room so decides to get the meeting started.

'Have you got a question, Peter?'

'Adam you are rather vague about the spacecrafts that left Earth. Surely there is something more you can tell us?'

Adam sighs and thinks here comes trouble.

'We only learned about the spacecrafts from our history lessons; if there was more information available it was never made common knowledge.'

'You must have gleaned some idea of the direction they were heading?'

'There was a great deal of speculation. We know that a planet with similar properties to Earth and that orbited a Sun like star was discovered 600 light years away. The problem was of course the distance. The people travelling would have long died before they got anywhere near it. So it would be their future descendants that would actually explore and possibly inhabit the planet. The only bonus to such an enduring journey would be that humans would have a chance to start again. The downside would be that such descendants would only have experience of surviving in a spacecraft. They would have records etc., as to life on Earth but would that be sufficient.'

'Malcolm, have you anything to ask?'

'Well, Chris, it's all very sketchy and it's as if we are questioning someone about a science-fiction book, but yes on that basis I have some things I would like to know.'

'Adam, if these spacecrafts left Earth for pastures new did they overcome the problem of distance and if so how?'

'Once again I have to stress that any information I have gleaned was done by speculation of tutor and students. You must understand that it is the same as trying to get to the truth of religion. It all happened hundreds of years ago for my generation and although our historical documentation is way in advance than in the Biblical days, it has been distorted by the writing and rewriting of facts.'

'So we will take that in to consideration, Adam, please continue.'

'It was thought that a way had been found to jump in and out of time zones without harming the structure of the spaceship or its crew and passengers. In this way they could travel through space in years rather than hundreds of years, so it would be possible for them to reach an orbiting habitable planet within their life time. Official records on this were never clarified so I cannot give you any more information.'

'Why were these spacecrafts sent on a one-way mission?'

'After central Europe had been destroyed by the Sun's activity the world's governments at last took the threat to their planet seriously, much too late to save the majority of people but soon enough to save thousands. The first option was the building of the pods which you already know about. That, however, was deemed necessary for the ordinary people but the wealthy, higher class and cleverer people did not relish the idea of being herded in with the common folk. So they decided to use their money, position and brains to do something for the elite, so to speak. That is where the spacecrafts came in; they were financed and researched by the highest grade of people. These people would rather take their chances in space than dying on a burning planet in a glass shelter with common people.'

'That is rather a harsh statement, Adam.'

'I'm just saying it as it was taught to me. I have no experience of any class or wealth divides, in my world everyone is equal. I do know that there were a number of learned people who opted to stay on Earth and helped with the problems that were then occurring daily. It was because of them that we were able to advance as far as we had. As for the rich, well there was no place for money by this time, the enemy was nature and you cannot bribe nature, you just have to work with it.'

'Helen, have you any questions?'

'Sorry, Adam, I know you are exhausted but I do have some questions that I hope you will be able to answer.'

Adam looks at her, 'I'll try my best, Helen.'

'Firstly, how did they choose appropriate sites for the pods, were they chosen because they were near natural resources?'

'That was the idea at the beginning; however, it was evident that any natural resources would be disappearing as the Earth was becoming increasingly damaged by the ravages of the Sun. The plans changed quickly to ensure that each pod would be self-sufficient, air quality, water and food production were the first on the list and then everything else stemmed from there. If you can try to imagine that each pod was a satellite surviving in what was literally "hell on Earth". There was a communication system between each of the satellite dwellings but by the time I left it was hit and miss because the conditions outside were getting increasingly worse. We had no idea how many pods were still surviving.'

'That must have been awful for you all.'

'It was the way we lived, to us it was normal and until we arrived here in your time we thought we had a pretty good life in our world.'

'Just one more thing, Adam. The people that lived in the pods, how were they chosen?'

'They were not chosen, Helen, they did the choosing. Many people were being killed daily because of sudden volcanic eruptions, tsunamis, earthquakes and hurricanes etc., so the number of people remaining would have all been able to live comfortably in the pods that had been built. However, there were many people from across the nations that for religious reasons, personal beliefs of all different kinds and through sheer stubbornness to acknowledge what was actually happening refused to enter the pods.'

Helen sighs and wonders what she would have done.

'Is that everyone finished?'

Peter and Malcolm shrug and Helen nods.

'I think that's it then, Adam. I would like you to just wait an hour or two before going home, just in case there are any more things that have to be raised. Would you like to have some dinner down by the lake, I think there is someone waiting for you there?'

Adam looks up in surprise, 'Who's that then, Chris?'

'Just go and have a look, Adam. Your meal and a bottle of good wine is waiting for you.'

Adam smiles and rushes out to the lake. When he gets nearer he sees a table and two chairs and sitting in one of the chairs is Maddy.

She gets up as Adam approaches, 'I've been waiting ages for you.'

Adam hugs her, 'You're a sight for sore eyes, Maddy. How did you get in?'

'I've still got my ways, Adam,' she replies smiling.

They have just finished the pleasant lunch when they were disturbed by Chris approaching.

'Well, Maddy, how nice to see you again. How are you?'

'Keeping busy as usual, Chris. Have you finished with Adam now?'

'I think so. He has given us a lot to work on, but I think the ball is in our court now. So if you are ready to go home Adam I will send a car round for you.'

Adam collects his stuff from his temporary room and heads for the waiting car. Maddy is standing at the door.

'Are you coming back with me, Maddy?'

'Unfortunately not, I have a few more things to do here, but I will come to see you this evening if that's okay?'

Adam kisses her cheek, 'Of course it is, see you later then.'

Chapter Twenty-Three

When Adam arrives home it seems deserted, Daniel and Becky are on honeymoon with her three children and Daisy has taken all the new disciples to the zoo. Jim is working in the café, and Mary and Mark are at a pre-natal clinic.

Adam collapses into the nearest chair.

'That bad?'

Adam looks up to see Sylvia hovering over him.

He smiles, 'I've had better days, I could kill for a decent cup of tea.'

'Your word is my command,' Sylvia says as she heads for the kitchen. Then Roger appears.

'You look exhausted, with a bit of luck they will give you a bit of peace now.'

'I hope so, Roger, there really isn't much more I can tell them. I kept getting the feeling that they were waiting for me to produce a magical solution to the inevitable problem. They do not seem to want to acknowledge that they will have to do some serious talking, and more to the point, some serious action if any progress is going to be made.'

Sylvia agrees, 'You are quite right, Adam. However, there has never been any one country or any one single person throughout history that has managed to unite the whole world. The Romans tried through domination, Germans tried twice through domination and genocide. Even Britain had it's go with the commonwealth, and there are many other countries that have tried through war and genocide to conquer their neighbours. But to get everyone in the world pulling in the same direction will be an absolute miracle.'

'So what next?'

'Well, Adam, I think the Olympic Games could hold the key.

Almost every country in the world will be participating in the games here in Britain. There will never be a better chance to get all the heads of states voluntarily in one place.'

'That's brilliant, Roger. Do you think that it will be possible to arrange a World Summit in Britain before the Games?'

'Who knows, we can only find out by trying. There's still a few months before the Olympics start, maybe if they can get all the information together. They will have to have a logical argument to present. Then arrange a meeting a couple of weeks before the games actually start. I'll have a word with the bosses.'

Roger disappears to his room and Adam goes to unpack his clothes, he is relieved that he is home again.

Daisy and the children return from the zoo, they are all very excited about all the animals they had seen. They have changed dramatically in the last few weeks, their cheeks are glowing with health and they are no longer withdrawn and suspicious. It is a great improvement.

Mary and Mark come home. 'Hey, look at this picture,' says a proud expectant dad, 'we've hit the jackpot, we are going to have twins.'

'Who is going to have twins, I'm the one that will have to do all the hard work!' Mary replies, but she is smiling.

Mark gives her a hug, 'Who's my clever girl?'

Everyone crowds around to see the photo taken of the scan.

'That's brilliant, Mary; do you know when they are due?'

'Not yet, Daisy, but it will be early September.'

'I think a celebration dinner is called for,' says Daisy, 'who's going to help?'

Maddy arrives just in time for dinner. Adam is really pleased to have her by his side again.

Later that evening Roger gives his account of his talk with his bosses.

'They are in full agreement of the idea but they seem unsure how to proceed with the presentation. I told them that I was willing to go in and help if they needed more inspiration. They did suggest that you go back, Adam, but I know how you will feel about that idea.'

'Thank you, Roger. I am not ready to face another inquisition, but we can go through some ideas together here.'

'We'll leave it for tonight, Adam, but if we can pull some things together in the next few days. They want me to go at the beginning of next week.'

'No problem, Roger.'

The rest of the evening they spend watching old films and drinking wine. Adam and Maddy go into the garden for some quiet time together.

Roger and Adam use the next few days to try to come up with a convincing dialogue. They want to pre-empt any doubts to the contents of their presentation and use as much material as possible taken from the MS recordings. When they both feel happy of the contents they file it away until Roger is due to leave.

Johnny, James and I come to stay that weekend to catch up with all the news. I am delighted to hear about the expectant arrival of twins, that kind of occasion never happened in our future world. If two embryos were formed in conception the weakest was always terminated. There was not sufficient reserves to care for a poorly child. It would not have been fair anyway because life was hard and demanding.

James goes off to play with the other children in the garden; there are enough of them for a small football team, the noise is horrendous.

'Thank goodness we don't have close neighbours. It is lovely to see them all playing together though,' remarks Adam.

'Now they are out of the way we can ask you how you got on, Adam.'

'It was gruelling, Rose, but I'm hoping it will not be repeated.' Adam continues to explain about the idea of having some kind of World Summit before the Olympic Games.

Roger leaves the house the following week for his meeting with his superiors. He takes the notes that he and Adam have put together to help with the foundation of the proposed Summit. Roger has asked Adam for one favour before he went. He wants to know what the Magic Mirror predicts the result of the Summit would be. Adam is reluctant at first, and then he agrees to put the question forward. He holds the mirror in his hand and asked whether the Summit will be successful. The answer is vague, it just says '*possibly*'. Roger looks disappointed, he thought that a more positive answer would have appeared. Adam explains that there are too many variables to the question, too many voices to be heard, too many ideas and too many sceptics. So Roger has to accept that at least the answer wasn't completely negative.

Roger was gone for nearly two weeks and Maddy had to go back to work but she promised Adam that she would return as soon as she could. There are ten weeks before the Olympic Games are to commence and eight weeks before the proposed Summit.

However, the house is getting ready for another big occasion, this year marks the Diamond Jubilee of the reigning Queen and there is going to be many events all over the country to celebrate at the beginning of June.

Daisy has put forward the idea of opening up their gardens to all of their neighbours and having the biggest party ever. She reckons we can erect a big screen for people to see the celebrations that will be happening all over Britain and we can hire a marquee in case the weather turns nasty. We can also hire tables and chairs and the children can help with the food and the decorations. We can get commemorative mugs and coins to give all the children to celebrate the day.

'I think it's a great idea, Daisy,' Mark agrees, 'but it is going to take a lot of organising, not to mention money.'

'There is enough of us to arrange everything and it will be a great diversion from the Summit,' replies Daisy and then adds, 'it might also be our last chance for normality, because once the Summit meets I feel our lives are going to change.'

'You might be right there, Daisy.'

By the time Roger returns the house is filled with homemade decorations as well as flags, tablecloths and commemorative gifts.

'My goodness, what's going on here?'

Sylvia greets Roger and then explains, 'We are getting ready for the biggest party you have ever seen. This is for our Diamond Jubilee party.'

Roger notices how flushed Sylvia looked, she is obviously enjoying herself.

'Can anyone join in?'

'It is the rules of the house, all hands to the pump, Roger.'

That evening Roger tells how the meeting went.

'It was all very tense. I felt the same as you did, Adam, it seemed as if they were waiting for me to come up with a miraculous solution.'

'Have they started contacting Country Leaders yet?'

'I'm sorry to say they haven't. They have no idea how to phrase the invitation.'

'Why don't they just say it is an official greeting to the Games? That way they can get people to attend without raising suspicions.'

'That's not a bad idea, Adam. The good news is they have come to an agreement on how to present the problem. They are going to show edited highlights from the Memory Sticks and back it up with information that you have all given.'

'Sounds good so far, but I have a feeling there is more.'

'Sorry, Adam, but you are right. They must back up everything they will be revealing, which means they will have to release information about all of you.'

There is a groan from the back of the room. Roger turns round to face Mark.

'I'm sorry, Mark, but it was inevitable sooner or later. If they can't back up what they show and the information they give it will be seen as a big hoax.'

'I know that, but it means we will be treated as freaks.'

'They will not allow that to happen, you will all be under high security protection. There is more, I'm afraid, they want the media to attend the meeting.'

'Why? Won't that put us under even more pressure'?

'Actually, it is a clever ploy the government use. If there is something going on that will upset the people they release the information at the same time as something positive. And what can be more positive than the Olympic Games?'

'Will it work? Will it take the pressure off us?'

'It usually does, although a small number of people always pick up the ploy but their voices are usually lost amongst the positive revelations. Only time will tell.'

Adam speaks up, 'Will they want us at the Summit?'

'I think you can take that as a certainty. They may have questions fired at them that only you can answer.'

'Will they want all of us, even the children?'

'I think so. I know this is going to be horrible for you all but this is the chance you have been waiting for; you will be able to explain to most of the planet the consequences of our actions on the environment. You can give this planet another five hundred years of life.'

'Well, at least we know what is coming,' sighs Adam, 'will you let them know our idea about wording the invitations, Roger?'

'I'll do that right now,' Roger says as he leaves the room.

There is not much more any of us can say, but we all have our own thoughts and reservations about the Summit. The one thing we did agree on, and that is Roger is right, this is the opportunity we have been waiting for. It is just that we have not realised how intrusive it will be.

By the time Roger has joined us again the mood has lightened a little.

'What did they say, Roger?'

'They thought it is a good idea and they are going to start preparing the invitations. They actually said it was so simple they were surprised they hadn't thought of it. Then excused themselves by saying that it is possibly because they are so busy. They couldn't see the wood for the trees!'

Adam smiles. 'Come on then who wants a drink? I've bought a new DVD for us to watch, it's called *Back to the Future*!'

Mark throws a cushion at Adam's back as he disappears into the kitchen laughing.

The next day we gather the children together to explain about the Summit and that they will all probably have to attend. Steven and Antony can see the positive meaning of this but the girls are not very happy. They are obviously frightened of the consequences.

'Do we really have to go, Adam?' Violet asks.

'I'm afraid so, Violet, but we will all be together and we have the benefit of experience behind us. Considering what we know and what we have gone through we will be foolish to let them intimidate us. We may be young but we know what we are saying is true, if they are stupid enough to ignore the obvious warnings there is nothing more we can do.'

'But what if people try to kidnap us to get the upper hand in the knowledge stakes?' a worried Julia asks. 'We know from our history books how countries and dictators have tried to get the upper hand to reach domination.'

'We have been assured that we will be protected at the highest level, but I will be foolish to say that our lives here won't be forced to change.'

'You are saying that we are going to be put into hiding?'

'I hope it won't be as bad as that, Laura, and I hope that eventually things will calm down enough for us to return to a near normal life. We must think about Rose, Johnny and James, they will have to leave the farm, it will be too exposed.

'I think Rose and Johnny are already training up a farm manager, so at least the farm can keep going while they're away.'

'That's good, Daniel. What we must all remember is that we were sent here for a reason and we now have the perfect opportunity to see it through. I know it won't be pleasant but if it gives the Earth and its inhabitants another five hundred years − surely it is our duty to do our utmost to help.'

There is no arguing with Adam's logic.

We have all benefited from the affluence of the 21st century now it is our turn to repay in full the opportunities we have gained from being sent back from the future

We have now resigned ourselves to the consequences and, hopefully, the benefits of the Summit, but that is weeks away yet. We all agree to concentrate on the forthcoming Jubilee party at the beginning of June.

Roger is able to procure funds from his superiors. He thinks that their generosity is based on keeping us on side and the good publicity that will be generated for all concern.

'We don't care what their reasons are,' laughs Daisy, 'we have never had an opportunity to experience such a celebration, and as far as we are concerned we are going to make sure it will go down in the history books as the biggest event of the century.'

The grounds of our home are big enough to hold at least two hundred people comfortably but more at a squash, so we decide to not only invite neighbours but everyone that has made an impact on our lives since they arrived in the 21st century.

Our men are put in charge of procuring a marquee, large screen, commemorative mugs and coins, as well as tables, benches and chairs.

Us women take on the catering, disposable plates, beakers and cutlery. We design the invitations and list people we want to invite. The younger members are in charge of the decorations, some to be made and some to be bought.

'This is absolutely great, I have never enjoyed myself so much,' admits Sylvia. 'Do you think we can be ready in time?'

'Where's your faith, Sylvia?' retorts Daisy, as the two of them scan recipe books to sort out the menu. 'Wouldn't it be fun if we could mix the type of food across the years? Starting from sixty years ago up to the present year. The style of food and cooking has altered dramatically over the years.'

'That's a good idea, Daisy, we have to remember that when our Queen came to the throne there was still some rationing so the variety we have now was practically non-existent.'

'Let's be methodical then, we will start at 1952, then list every year and put a typical dish down for each one. So, Sylvia, I'm relying on you and your memory, what did you eat in 1952?'

'Cheek of it, how old do you think I am?'

They both end up giggling.

'This doesn't sound very productive. What are you two doing?'

'Hello, Jim, we have hit a stumbling block, but I'm sure you can help.'

They explain to Jim what they want to do with the menu and they gratefully accept his expertise in catering.

Tom, Charlie, Steven, Antony, Violet and Laura are given some money to see what kind of decorations they can buy. They all find it very exhilarating to be given such responsibilities. Everyone is extremely pleased to see how Jenny's children have become such firm friends with the new children. When they return they are laden with red, blue and white balloons, streamers, flags, serviettes and many small memorabilia of the occasion.

'Wow, you've been busy, are you sure you have enough?'

The children collapse on chairs; they are all flushed with excitement and the effort they have put in to buy so much.

'We still have some money left, Daisy, so we can get some more.'

'No, I am only joking, Steven. We will work out how far all this will go first.'

At that moment Adam walks in, 'We've got the screen and the marquee sorted,' he then notices the exhausted children and their piles of shopping, 'you've been having fun. It all looks great. Do you know what; I think it is definitely going to be the best day ever?'

Within days of the invitations being sent the replies start pouring in, it seems that everyone wants to attend our Jubilee party. The neighbours offer their help with the food and a local music group say they will play for nothing.

We are overwhelmed with people's generosity and with just a week to go before the celebrations are to start everything is falling into place perfectly.

'I can't seem to control James, he really is excited.'

'Don't worry, Rose, this is a once in a lifetime experience, let him enjoy himself.'

'I suppose you're right, Daisy, James isn't used to having so much attention and having so many children fussing around him. It's really nice to see all the children working and playing together, it's still hard to believe that they are born centuries apart.'

'Yes, it is weird, but children are all the same underneath, it's just their different life experiences that separate them.'

I look down at the baby I am holding, young Isaac is fast asleep. I am grateful that he will never remember the carnage he left when he was propelled back through time.

'Roger, do you know where Sylvia is? She disappeared ages ago; I hope all this commotion is not proving too much for her,'

'I shouldn't think so, Daisy, she has never been happier since she has met you all and she is really looking forward to this party. I'll go and check our room.'

Roger quietly opens the door to the bedroom and he finds Sylvia crying on the bed. He goes over and holds her in his arms.

'What's ever the matter, Sylvie?' he asks as he smooths her hair from her eyes, 'please don't cry.'

'I was watching the news, there's been another big earthquake in Thailand and people are terrified that a tsunami will follow. The last time that happened hundreds of thousands of people died. It is so awful, the world is going mad and all people can worry about is money and power, while the poor and innocent are dying.'

Roger sighs, 'You must try to be positive, you and I can't make a difference on our own. We are lucky to be with some marvellous people whose only aim is to try and alter the destruction. They have the knowledge we just have to help them to get people to listen.'

'I know you are right, Roger, but sometimes it feels like walking against a sea of self-imposed ignorance.'

Roger cannot argue with that. Everyone is out to get as much as they can and to hell with the consequences.

'Look, Sylvie, our job is to help these people with their given task and that will be our part in helping everyone in the world and the future generations. We can do no more, I wish we could. Let's not worry too much now, let's just see what happens at the Summit. Until then, we have a big party to arrange and Daisy asked me to look for you. It would seem your expertise is needed.'

Sylvia smiles; she knows her husband is speaking the truth, as usual.

'Give me a few minutes to tidy myself; I must look a mess.'

'You never look a mess, my dear.'

'Away with you and your blarney,' says Sylvia, 'tell Daisy I'll be there in a minute.'

Roger leaves the room and Sylvia wistfully pulls a comb through her hair. If only life was that simple, she thought.

I have put Isaac down in his cot and I go in search of James, I have not seen him for a while and think it is time I reined him in for a bit. It is getting near his teatime and soon after that he will be going to bed. I know there will be no chance of settling him unless I can calm him down.

No one seems to know where James is and I am getting worried, I ask the children and the adults but he has not been seen for over an hour. Then I realise that Antony has disappeared as well. I am not quite sure whether I am pleased that James could be with an older boy or not.

Antony is still getting used to this strange world and James is a bit young to try to act the superior.

When the others realise the problem a search party is formed and a plan of action is implemented. After a thorough scouring of the house and gardens, the women start to knock on every door in the street, their neighbours are really helpful and some even join in the search.

Johnny and I are with a number of others searching the park, it is getting dark and I am really panicking.

'Shall we phone the police, Johnny?'

'I think Roger's lot will be more helpful, they have many more facilities at their fingertips. I'll go and find him but you go back to the house in case James and Antony turn up,' suggests Johnny. 'You look really exhausted, and you'll be no good for the young hooligan when he comes home.'

I want to argue but Johnny is right, I am exhausted. A short sit down and a hot cup of tea and I'll be fine again. I just wish James would come home. Everything was going so well and now I feel it is all ruined.

Roger immediately contacts his superiors who act quickly; they already have photos of the two boys on file so they are able to release the pictures to the local police force. The searchers also notice a couple of helicopters circling above.

When I arrive home Daisy makes me sit down and gives me a hot tea.

'They'll soon be found, Rose, you know what boys are like, and they always have to push the boundaries.'

'I know you're right but I just have this awful feeling inside.'

The shrill ringing of the phone startles us. I go to answer it but Daisy gets there first.

'Who is this? You better not hurt them, there are a lot of people out looking for them and if you hurt them you will be in big trouble.'

My heart beats fast when I hear what Daisy is saying.

'Who is it, Daisy?' I scream frantically, 'Who's got my boys?'

Daisy listens for a couple more seconds and then slowly replaces the phone. Her face is ashen. She gets out her mobile phone and calls Adam.

'Adam, come back here now. Something has happened.'

In the few minutes it takes Adam to return I have completely broken down and Adam enters the room to see Daisy trying to calm me.

'What's happened, Daisy, has Rose found out something?'

'We have just had a phone call from someone who says they have the boys and they are demanding money for their return.'

'I'll get Roger and the others back here.' Adam uses his mobile and then asks, 'Did they say who they were and how much they wanted?'

'They just say they are a liberation force and they want £100,000 before they will let the boys go.'

'That's ridiculous; we don't have that sort of money.'

'I think they know we are in close contact with the government and they know that there are some rich people there.'

'This gets worse, it's all so stupid.'

'It might be stupid,' I shout, 'but I want those boys back here safely, so someone has better get the money!'

'I'm sorry, Rose,' Adam says as he comes over to me, 'we will get them home, don't you worry. Look here's Roger, I'm sure he will have some good news.'

Roger comes in and there is a look of puzzlement on his face.

'Have you found something, Roger?'

'Well yes, Adam. The helicopters have spotted two lads fitting James and Antony's description, but the weird thing is they are playing in a college playground with a lot of students. They seem to be enjoying a game of basketball!'

I cannot believe what I am hearing, is the whole thing a cruel prank?

'The helicopters are going down now to find out what it is all about.'

'I know what it is,' Mark exclaims with a sigh, 'it's charity week at the local college, they are collecting money for cancer research. Silly kids, they have no idea what they have done. When the MOD descends on them they will wish the earth will swallow them up, they are going to be terrified.'

An hour later James and Antony are back in the house and are both getting a rather sharp telling off from me.

'But, Mum, we were bored and we did know them. They play football with us in the park sometimes.'

'You know you should never go out without telling me. I feel as if I've aged twenty years.'

'Sorry, Mum. We won't do it again, promise.'

'I'm really sorry, Rose; we didn't mean to frighten you,' Echoes a timid Antony.

'I think you two should go and have a wash and get ready for bed.'

The two lads skulk out of the room, neither is quite sure what all the fuss is about, but they did enjoy the ride in the helicopter.

Later Roger tells the others that it was a practical joke, the lads from the college are raising money for cancer research, they had no idea that the two boys were other than they seemed. Just two kids that played football with them in the park. Unfortunately the students got the fright of their lives when the helicopter landed in the college grounds and armed men ran towards them shouting. They got a very stiff talking to by the general Commander and that would not have been pleasant.

The next day a group of students arrive at the house with a bouquet of flowers for me, they apologise for all the trouble they had caused.

I feel sorry for them; they were, after all, doing something for a good cause even though it was a stupid prank. I accept the flowers but still give them a good telling off for giving me such a scare, but I knew it was not as bad as the reprimand they have already received from the military

After they have gone Johnny remarks, 'You are a great big softy, Rose; I thought you were going to physically lay into them considering what they had put you through.'

I shrug my shoulders, 'I am just glad to have the boys back safely and maybe the experience has taught them and the students a good lesson.'

'It is a shame their fundraising went wrong though,' Johnny responded wistfully. 'Maybe we can scrape some money together for their charity.'

'And you call me a softy!'

Chapter Twenty-Four

It is the evening before the big party, the marquee is up, the tables are ready and all the food is prepared. The garden looks like a magic grotto with lanterns, flags and banners. The children have been sent to bed early because tomorrow is going to be a long day. We doubt whether any of them will get much sleep as they are far too excited. The weather report promises a dry and sunny day and this evening is pleasantly mild.

There is a knock at the door and I go to answer it. 'Adam,' I shout, 'it's someone for you.'

Adam is pleasantly surprised to see Maddy standing there. 'I thought you had forgotten me.'

'Now could I have done that? Anyway I heard that there was a big party here tomorrow and I could not possibly miss that,' Maddy said with a grin.

We sit in the garden enjoying the calm before the storm, Roger and Sylvia join us. It is a time of reminiscing, so much has happened to us over the last twelve years.

'It's really weird, do you realise that we are living the history that we learned about in our time?'

'Do you know, Mark, I never thought about it in that way. We are actually experiencing things that we were taught in our lessons. Who would have thought that we would have been around for the one hundred year anniversary of the Titanic's sinking? And of course the 60th anniversary of Queen Elizabeth's ascension to the throne. We have been given many privileges by our Elders. The biggest one being our lives, without their foresight we would have joined the fate of our peers.'

'I know what you mean, Adam, but do you ever think about our world, do you ever imagine what our friends are experiencing?'

'I think that is dangerous ground,' Adam interrupts, 'if we start trying to imagine what is happening in our world now it will break us. We must stay positive and try to proceed with the task given to us.'

'Do you think that if you are listened to and countries stop polluting the atmosphere that it will affect what is happening in 3011?'

'I do believe, Roger, that there is always two paths to follow and depending which path is taken the future will follow. If a wrong path is trodden and then corrected in time then the future will alter. So I am hoping that if the World now goes down the correct route then a brighter future will remain for longer.'

Jim has become part of the extended family and he is fascinated by his friends' experience and knowledge, but he also has a deep admiration for Daisy and tonight he has decided to see whether he has a chance to build on their friendship.

'Daisy, can I have a word with you in the kitchen?'

She looks puzzled, 'Is it something to do with the food, Jim?' she replies as she follows him into the house.

Jim is extremely nervous as Daisy enters the kitchen; he is shuffling from one foot to the other.

'What is the matter, Jim, you look like a child who has an awful secret to reveal.'

'Not an awful secret, Daisy, I am wondering if you could possibly consider going out with me?'

Daisy is stunned, she has always liked Jim but has never thought of him as a partner, such thoughts are alien to her. She has watched the others form relationships and is secretly envious. She never thought a chance like that would come her way.

'I think that would be very nice, Jim.'

'Great!' Jim says his eyes sparkle like a child given an unexpected treat. They speak for a little longer and then return to the garden hand in hand. This is noticed by us but not a word is spoken, just a few faint smiles appear.

The conversation has moved on to lighter memories and we are all laughing at the experiences that we had when they first arrived and how we felt in this strange new world.

'Do you remember when we first materialised there were fireworks exploding in the sky, we thought it was a volcano erupting.'

'That's right, Rose, it was quite frightening we thought we had been transported too far back and we expected to see dinosaurs roaming around.'

'That's awful,' Sylvia said, 'you were so young and so brave.'

'We had been specially chosen for the mission, they knew we could cope with most occurrences, but it was frightening.'

'You were lucky to have arrived where you did; I think if you had ended up in the middle of a city it would have been even more challenging.'

'I agree with you, Roger, but our Elders had done a great deal of research and we honour their expertise. It was a perfect place and the people we first met were fantastic.'

'Do you remember that awful winter when you all helped Alf to bring in the sheep?'

'Yes, Rose, that was really bad, the snow was so thick we could hardly walk in it. Alf's favourite sheep dog fell into a frozen pond and Alf refused to leave him. We had terrible trouble helping the poor animal out of the freezing water.'

'I can remember that, Adam, but do you know what was best about that day, going back to the farmhouse where Rose and Martha had been cooking up a hot stew to warm us up. That was the best meal I've ever had!'

Adam agreed with Daniel. The reminiscing went on through the night. Above us is a clear sky with a full moon looking down with stars dotting the blackness.

One by one we start drifting off to their beds. Our heads full of memories and of the celebrations yet to start. Adam stays behind with Mark.

'Did you bring the Mirror with you, Mark?'

'Yes, but I'm not sure what you need it for.'

'I know tomorrow is going to be a big day for all of us but I can't stop thinking about the Summit. It's looming up fast now and I just wondered if we can get some idea of how it will go. You know what they say forewarned is forearmed.'

'We can but try. We won't be able to change things but we can be ready, I suppose, for awkward questions.'

'Exactly. We will wait until everyone has settled down. You know what Roger is like; he keeps popping up just to see what is going on. I know he is only doing his job but on this occasion I want it just between you and me.'

Adam cautiously opens the Mirror, its surface is swirling with an opaque mist. This is not normal; it usually shows a clear reflection of the person looking into it, just like a normal mirror would.

'There's something going on here, Mark, look at this.'

Mark peers over at the mirror. 'What do you think that means, Adam?'

Before Adam can reply an image appears, it is of their world, it shows fire and destruction as we have never witnessed before. We are both horrified at the scene in front of us and we know what it means.

'It looks like we are too late to help the people we have left; our given task has failed them.'

'We know that we could only extend the life of the planet for another five hundred years, Mark, we left nearly one thousand years in the future. We can still give those extra years of normality. No one can halt the process of evolution. Our task is just as important as it always was. The Elders knew that they were doomed that is why they sent us away, to give us a chance. That is also why they sent the last six children. We must honour their decision and commend their bravery in the face of overwhelming catastrophe.'

'It is still hard to face the inevitable destruction waiting for all of us. Do you think we should tell the others what we have seen?'

'We must stay positive, Mark, we are in 2012 and this is our time and life now, not 3011. We have a duty and the knowledge to help and that is exactly what we are going to do. I do not think it will benefit anyone to reveal what we have seen; we all knew that it was inevitable; this is not the time to disclose such awful news.'

'I agree, Adam, this is not the time.'

'Thanks, Mark. Are you ready for the question and answer time?'

'Let's get on with it before anyone starts to wonder what we are doing out here and comes to investigate.'

The first question Adam asks is, 'Will they believe us?'

The Mirror responds, '*No.*'

'How can we convince them?'

'*The memory sticks.*'

'Will that be enough?'

'*No.*'

'What else can we use?'

'*Patience.*'

'Will that be enough?'

'*No.*'

'What else then?'

'*The Children.*'

'Do you mean the innocence of the new arrivals?'

'*Yes.*'

'How can they help?'

'*They know.*'

Adam and Mark look at each other feeling completely baffled. Adam closes the Mirror.

'I think that is enough for now, but I must admit that the only positive answer it gave us is about the new children and I don't understand what it is getting at.'

'That makes two of us. Do you think the children have evolved to a higher level than us or that they hold some sort of secret?'

Adam and Mark talk for a while longer, they realise that they will not be able to solve the mystery of the new children now. They decide to join their partners and get a good night's sleep.

Chapter Twenty-Five

All the children are up at the crack of dawn, blaming the sunshine streaming in the windows. It is of course the excitement of the day's coming events that has them bubbling over with the urge to get everyone out of bed and moving.

'What's the time?' Daniel asks scratching his head as he enters the living room, he looks at the clock, 'It's only half past five, what is this noise all about?'

'The party is today!' Jenny shouts as she jumps up and down.

'I know, I know,' says a frustrated Daniel, 'but it doesn't start until midday. Can't you all go back to bed for a while?'

A sea of young faces turn to him in complete shock. Did he really think they can go back to bed?

'Okay, okay I give up. Who wants breakfast?'

By the time Daniel has sorted the food the other adults start to appear from their rooms.

Johnny and I are first. 'How kind, Daniel, to feed all the children, it's a bit early though, isn't it?'

Daniel shot me a black look, 'I didn't have any choice, they did not think my suggestion of going back to bed was a very good one.'

I laughed and join in to help.

By seven everyone is up and getting ready for the day ahead. Most of the preparations have been done so it does not take long to put in the finishing touches. Becky and Daisy decide to cook up pancakes for elevenses which, actually, would be ready at nine considering how early we got up.

Thankfully the children settle down for a while after they have eaten. Adam and Mark thought they would have a talk with Steven and Antony to see whether they can shed any light on the confusing message the Mirror has given them. They make an excuse that they want the boys to help them with something special.

They tell them they want to surprise the women that have done so much to get ready for today. So they are off to the florists to buy some flowers.

It is a beautiful day so they go through the park, and as it is still early it is deserted, they sit down by the lake.

'Steven, before you were transported here did the Elders give you any special instructions?'

Steven looks at Antony and it is quite obvious to Adam and Mark that they are hiding something.

'Have you something to say, Steven?'

'It's very awkward, we were told not to reveal anything unless it is an emergency, but how did you know?'

'The Elders sent us something that we can use to help with our task. So I am presuming that whatever they told you they wanted us to know.'

'I don't know what to do.'

'You know what our task is; surely if you have anything that will help us to fulfil our objectives it is important that you tell us.'

The boys are getting uncomfortable; they keep fidgeting and looking around.

'Look, no one can overhear us here, just tell us and we will decide if it is important enough for us to use. If we do not think it will help us we will forget you ever told us.'

'Is this a trick?'

Mark is getting exasperated, 'You are one of us, we are not the enemy, we must stick together.'

'Shall we, Antony?'

'Go on, Steven, tell them.'

Steven starts to speak and the more he reveals the more Mark and Adam are astounded. They have never heard anything like it before, they were right in thinking that these children have evolved far beyond themselves. They are amazed that these young children have had such responsibility laid on them. When Steven finishes he looks quite pale.

'Are you all right, Steven?'

'Yes, can we go now?'

'Just one question, do the others have the same qualities as you two?'

'Yes.'

'Come on then let's move, we have a party to go to!'

The boys get up and run across the park as if nothing has happened.

'What do you make of that, Adam?'

'I really don't know, Mark, but for now we will keep it between the two of us, agreed?'

'Agreed.'

They follow the boys across the park in to town to get the bouquets, each lost in their own thoughts.

The Jubilee celebrations start at midday and a stream of friends and neighbours join us and our ever-growing family in the house and gardens. The atmosphere is electric with excitement, children are running around waving flags and adults are enjoying the good food, good wine and good company.

It seems that on this special day there is to be a silent agreement that all troubles, worries and differences are to be forgotten.

We watched the big screen showing the royal barge with its entourage of boats from all over Britain even some from the distant shores of the Commonwealth travel up the River Thames. It is a shame that it is raining in London but that did not stop the Queen from smiling, she looks so proud of her family and her country.

'We are lucky to be blessed with good weather,' remarks Daisy, 'goodness knows how they are managing with street parties in London with all that rain.'

'I don't think that will spoil their day, it's remarkable how resilient Londoners can be,' laughs Roger.

In the middle of the afternoon it is decided to hand out the commemorative coins and mugs to the children. Much to Sylvia's surprise we have all secretly agreed that she will be queen for the day to do the honours.

'Sylvia, will you come over here for a minute?' asks Adam.

'What's all this about?' she asks as she sees the crimson cloak and the magnificent crown.

'You have been voted our Queen for the day and your duty will be to hand out the gifts to the children.'

'Wow, what an honour,' she exclaims as the cloak is put round her shoulders and Adam ceremonially places the crown on her head.

We all agree that she looks quite regal and is the perfect choice for such an important job. The children are lined up and each child curtsies or bows as they receive their gift. Cameras are flashing like crazy as proud parents eagerly record the special event.

The local group start to play, they have thought very carefully about the type of music people will like to hear, they start with popular music from the early fifties and then follow with the sixties and an hour later seventies classics can be heard. They carry on in this way until they reach the present day favourite tunes, but are also continually playing requests from everyone.

'That group is very good, what are they called?' Roger asked Mark.

'Believe it or not, Roger, they are called "The New World," and they are local lads.'

'Very apt, Mark, and am I right in believing they come from Jim's café.'

'Yes, they are close friends of Daniels; they want to become more involved in our quest. They are good lads, very intelligent and there is something different, even unique, about them that I can't quite put my finger on.'

'Intriguing, I wonder what their background is.'

'Roger, you have that look in your eyes, you're not going to start digging into their origins are you?'

'Who me?' Roger replies smiling as he turns and walks away.

In the early evening things quieten down and we sit around chatting, the children have worn themselves out for now, the smaller ones have fallen asleep and the parents take advantage of the brief lull. The next big event are the fireworks but they will not start until 10:30, so some adults help with the never-ending washing up while others put out fresh snacks on to the tables.

Adam feels this will be the right time to present the bouquets to the ladies. Becky, Mary, Daisy and Sylvia and I are the recipients of the flowers and even though we say it was our pleasure to help we receive our gifts proudly.

A little later Mark goes to find Adam; he wants to tell him about his conversation with Roger.

'I shouldn't worry too much; Roger has an inquiring mind, that's what he is trained for.'

'Do you know much about the group, Adam?'

'Not really, but I agree with what you said there is something unique about them. Maybe Daniel knows more. Let's see whether we can find him.'

They eventually find Daniel in the house, he looks exhausted, but then he has been keeping the children amused for hours.

Mark and Adam sit down with him.

'Can I get you anything, Daniel, a cup of tea, coffee?'

Daniel looks at his friends suspiciously. He smiles.

'Okay give, what are you two after?'

'Nothing much really, just some information.'

'I see, well if it's going to be like that, I will have coffee with one sugar and milk.'

Adam does the honours and when he comes back Mark asks, 'Daniel, that group out there, you know them pretty well.'

'Correct, they have been coming into the café for a few years. They're a nice bunch of people. Why do you ask?'

'You must have noticed that they are different. I can't quite put my finger on it, but there is definitely something unusual about them.'

Daniel sighs, 'I suppose I should have realised you would notice one day. You are right they are different, but basically they are just like any other young adults. Their main obvious talent is their music but they are tied together by something that happened on their birth.'

'I'm intrigued tell us more.'

'They all come from different areas of the country and they were all born on 9th December 1992 at 23:45, during a total lunar eclipse.'

'You're joking they were all born at exactly the same time!'

'That's right, Mark, miles away from each other, but their lives have always been running in parallel. They all ended up at the same university and it is there that realised they had some kind of special bond. Those three boys and the girl have the power to see into the future, not only see it but to experience the emotions felt in the future.'

'That's weird, how come you know so much about them?'

'Well you see, Adam, they recognised me straight away, they had seen our lives in the future. By talking to me they automatically linked to our world.'

'That must have scared them. They must have thought we were some kind of aliens.'

'Not quite, but they asked to see me at their lodgings and when I went there they gave me the third degree.'

Daniel explains that in one way they are the same as us but they are also people of their own time. They made Daniel promise to keep their secret and in return they will do as much as they can to help in the completion of the task.

'I have never heard of such a phenomena happening before, but I suppose there are many strange things happening in time and space that we never hear about.'

'You are probably right, Mark, but will you both agree to keep their secret?'

'Of course we will, and we must hope that Roger's curiosity doesn't uncover anything.'

It is getting dark outside and soon it will be time for the big finale, the fireworks. They go outside to join everyone else; Johnny and Jim are preparing a safe space for the display to begin. All the children are equally tired and excited and so the fireworks are started.

The display is greeted by clapping and lots of wows as we all watch the rockets shoot into the night sky before they explode into hundreds of multi-coloured stars. On the ground golden rain shoots up into the sky followed by red, blue and silver balls.

It really is quite spectacular and the finishing touch is a large screen of fireworks spelling out 'Diamond Jubilee 2012 Elizabeth II'.

As the fireworks die down people start to leave, sleeping children in parent's arms, definitely ready for their beds, it has been a long day.

Soon there are just us and our partners left and the group packing up their instruments.

Mark goes over to the group, 'You were fantastic, thanks a lot for coming, I hope we see more of you. Our door is always open.'

They look at him a bit puzzled but realise that he may know more than they think.

'Thanks, Mark, we'll keep that in mind.' Then they leave.

After clearing up in the garden and getting the youngsters settled in bed, we collapse in the sitting room. We need to wind down before taking to our beds.

'That was a great day. Who would have thought that we would have had the chance to be part of history?'

'It was good, Daisy, wasn't it? We have been given so many fantastic opportunities by the Elders; I hope we can live up to their expectations,' Mark says as he cuddles his pregnant wife. They are so looking forward to the arrival of their twins.

'We have a hurdle to jump in a couple of weeks, if we are successful that will be our thanks to those we left behind, but for now I suggest we focus on the here and now and revel in the fact that we have had a fantastic day.'

'Here, here, Adam,' we chorused.

The evening continues with us pointing out our own highlights of the day and the funny moments until at last we succumb to overwhelming fatigue and go to bed.

Much to Adams disappointment Maddy has to leave the next day. She promises that she will be at the Summit to give them all her support.

Chapter Twenty-Six

The next few weeks is spent preparing for the Summit, Roger and Sylvia attend a number of meetings with their superiors and report back to us instructions and suggestions they are given.

We are getting nervous, especially the younger children.

Mark and Adam have kept the secret Antony and Steven has revealed to them as promised, but the time has come for that to change. It is only right that everyone should know the powers that the young ones possess. However, they feel it is not their place to reveal the facts; they want the children to come forward with the information.

A special meeting is called so that we can all be involved in forming some kind of structure to the forth coming revelation to the world's leaders as to exactly who we are and why we are here. We decide that it will be better to have it without Roger and Sylvia so they chose a time when they have both been called away for a couple of days.

It is to be at this meeting that cards are to be laid on the table so that all secrets and confidences are to be made known to everyone. It is going to be difficult because a number of us have kept things to ourselves mostly for very good reasons and a few for personal reasons.

The air is heavy as we congregate in the large lounge, each one of us wishing they were somewhere else, we know how important the next few weeks are going to be and how carefully we will have to be in what we say and do.

Mark and Adam start with their admission that they have been using the Mirror to try to get some guidance. It told them to use the Memory sticks and to be patient with their audience as they are going to be very sceptical of the things they are seeing and hearing. The Mirror told them that the information we give may not be enough but it revealed that the younger children could help.

We look at the children quizzically.

Steven stands up, 'You said you wouldn't tell anyone, Adam.'

'I haven't but I would like you to tell them. I think it's time, don't you?'

Steven, Antony, Laura, Violet and Julia huddle together for a while talking softly.

'All right, we will tell you but you must remember that we were told only to reveal our secret in an emergency.'

'I think that this might be the appropriate time, Steven, it is our only chance to fulfil our task. If they don't believe us once we are exposed they will not give us a second chance. They will treat us as freaks or even worse, as a danger to mankind.'

Steven hesitates and then starts to explain.

'We are able to project images and sounds from back home. Everything we have seen, heard and done is stored in our brain and we can transform that data on to a blank screen.'

There is a gasp of incredulity.

'However do you achieve that, Steven?'

He turns to Daisy, 'We can focus our brains to project thoughts through our eyes. You will see beams of light coming from our irises and when they hit the screen images appear. A few seconds later the sounds start.'

'Does it hurt you?' Daisy asks, she is concerned of the damage it can do to them.

'Not at the time, but if we do it for too long we get a bad headache.'

There is silence once again. We can't quite believe what we are hearing, and if we can't believe it how can they expect the conference to understand. Then Antony stands up. 'Do you want me to show you?'

Daniel, still completely amazed by what we have just been told, asked, 'Is it just random images or are you able to focus on particular occurrences?'

'We can focus on anything that is in our memory. Is there something special you would like me to project?'

There are hundreds of things that Daniel would like to see, his curiosity is running wild, but he says, 'How about showing us our home where everything is happy and normal. Can you do that, Antony?'

'I can show you everyone going about their normal routine, laughing, playing and working, but remember, Daniel, you left a number of years before us so you might see a difference in behaviour. It may not seem as laid-back as you are used to because things had deteriorated dramatically.'

'Point taken, Antony, please continue.'

Antony turns to face a bare wall, it looks as if he has gone into a trance and then shafts of light appear from his eyes and as they hit the wall images form. The images are in colour and moving, soon everyone can make out people talking and working, going about their normal day-to-day business. After about five minutes the sound of laughing and chatting is heard.

There is a collective sharp intake of breath from the room; we cannot believe what we are witnessing. Everything is so clear it is like being in the same room as the scene unravelling in front of us. It is surreal, Daisy feels she can stretch out to touch the people and the objects; she wants to talk to her friends that she has left so long ago and who are now adults like herself and are there in front of her. Then suddenly the scene vanishes, Antony has closed his eyes. He has seen the effect it is having on his friends young and old. Antony thinks it best to limit their exposure on this first occasion.

The silence is broken by an explosion of questions.

'Wait, wait. We can't answer all your questions at once. Just one at a time!' pleads Steven.

So the next hour or so is filled with exchanges of information that only we will understand.

It transpires that not only did the younger children have photographic memories but they have evolved the capability to transfer their memories into living images. They are the only ones that had this gift and the Elders did not understand how it had occurred but they knew it would help us to complete their task. Isaac is too young to be tested but he was sent with them because he had been the very last baby to be born. They wanted to give him the chance of a proper life.

Adam closes the meeting, we have covered enough ground and the rest of his companions look exhausted. We all decide that the information that has been uncovered is best left between us and not revealed to Roger and Sylvia. It will be our bonus card at the Summit, our last chance to convince the world that now is the time to make a better future for everyone, before it is too late.

Roger and Sylvia return unexpectedly that night and they are puzzled by their friends' strange mood.

'Has anything happened that we should know about?' Roger asks. 'You all seem very quiet and withdrawn.'

'No everything is fine, Roger,' Daisy replies with a smile, 'I think we are all suffering with the after effects of the jubilee celebrations. We were so busy preparing for it and then the day itself was great and now everything seems a bit flat.'

'I know what you mean, especially as the next thing we have to prepare for is the Summit and that won't be so enjoyable. They are driving us mad at head office, what with all their questions and instructions. Sylvia and I don't know whether we are coming or going.'

The conference is now just a week away, the venue has been arranged, it is going to be held at The Sage in Gateshead where the theatre can comfortably hold up to 1700 delegates. The Sage conforms to a strict environmental code and therefore is an ideal choice, especially as it will take delegates to the north of England rather than having everything concentrated in the capital.

There will be plenty of room for the world's media as it is deemed to be as important to cater for them as it is for the world's leaders. It is imperative that when this conference takes place everyone receives information first hand. The British government are handling the whole thing as if they have a live bomb in their hands. It is vital that everything is dealt with in an open book policy. One wrong move and it can all explode with disastrous consequences.

The format of the conference is going to be as simple as possible; we will be seated on the stage. Behind us will be a large screen.

There will not be any long speeches just a short explanation as to why delegates are there; that the information they are about to see and hear will benefit the whole world, present and future. With assurances that questions will be answered at the end of the presentation. They will then go straight into showing selected contents of all four memory sticks, after which we will identify ourselves and try to answer questions.

It depends on how this last section progresses as to whether Adam feels it necessary to play his trump card. He does not want Steven or Antony exposed unnecessarily.

It is also decided that our partners and children will go to the Sage but will watch the proceedings on an internal link in a private room. There are quite a few arguments about this as they obviously want to give support to us but it is finally agreed as a prudent safeguard.

The evening before the conference the children are sent to bed early. It will be an early start in the morning, a coach will arrive for us all at 7am to take us across to Gateshead.

We sit in the lounge accompanied by Roger and Sylvia, talk is intermittent as we are nervous of the consequences that our revelation can have.

About nine o'clock Adam turns to Roger, 'I wonder, Roger, if you and Sylvia wouldn't mind leaving us for the rest of the evening.'

Roger looks shocked, 'You've never excluded us before, what are you up to, Adam?'

'We're up to nothing, Roger, you must trust us. We five came here to fulfil a task and in that we are one unit. Tomorrow is our chance to make our Elders proud of us, so tonight we want it to be just us, so that we can relive our past and remember the friends we left behind.'

'But we promised not to leave you alone.'

'Don't be stubborn, Roger, these are our friends they are not going to do anything to upset the proceedings,'

Sylvia scolds her husband, 'come on, we can do with an early night ourselves.'

Sylvia practically drags Roger out of the room.

Adam stands in the silent room and solemnly starts to speak, 'I think tonight needs to be marked as a milestone in our lives, we five were sent here on a mission and tomorrow is going to show whether we have failed or succeeded in our task.'

He pauses and then continues, 'I think it will be fitting if we have our "last supper", to eat and talk together as we did in the beginning. This may be the last chance we get, we have been through a lot together and we know we have all tried to live up to the trust put on us.'

'Hear, hear, Adam, let's toast the future and whatever it deems to throw at us.'

'Well said, Mark,' Daisy replies as she goes to the kitchen and I follow her. We are going to retrieve the secret stock of food we had prepared earlier.

We eat and chat long into the night and just before we go to bed we consult the Magic Mirror one more time.

Mark takes it from his pocket and asks, 'Is there any more we can do?'

We all stare into the looking glass, there is a long silence and then it answers,

'*PRAY.*'

Mark slowly closes the mirror and returns it to his pocket. 'There's our answer, let's hope our prayers will be answered. Good night, everyone.' He then gets up and leaves the room.

We follow suit and soon the room is empty.

Chapter Twenty-Seven

The following day sees a noisy house at an unearthly time in the morning; everyone is rushing around to be ready for when the coach arrives. Dead on 7 o'clock there is a knock on the door. When Daisy opens it she sees a black coach escorted by four black cars and every window of each vehicle is blacked out. It looks more like a funeral procession than an outing. It did not pass her attention either that every man and woman she sees standing by the vehicles is armed.

Adam joins her at the door and when he sees their escorts he takes a deep breath and comments, 'That's scary. I hope it does not frighten the children.'

Johnny has arrived early from the farm; he has left James with some friends in the village. Becky has been staying with some army friends in Yorkshire and has left her three children with them as she wanted to be with Daniel at the Summit. Mary arrived with her that morning so that she can be near Mark on this very important day.

We are soon all on the coach, which although looks horrible from the outside, is quite comfortable inside. We have an attendant to see to our every need, there is a toilet and shower and a small galley on board. We even have televisions on the back of the seats where we can watch DVDs or play computer games. The children are in their element.

We are so busy exploring all the perks we have that it is only Adam and Mark who notice the escorting cars, two at the front of the coach and two at the rear, and to complete the set a black helicopter hovering above.

Adam and Mark look at each other, 'Good luck, Mark.'

'Thanks, Adam, good luck to you as well.'

The journey goes without a hitch, which isn't surprising when Adam realises they are travelling on empty roads.

'Mark, have you noticed that there is not a single vehicle on the road except us. It's been like that since we left home.'

Mark turns to look out of the window. 'You're right, Adam, and I think I know why. We have just past a junction and there are police holding back the traffic.'

'You're kidding,' Adam says as he turns round to look. 'Why for goodness sake are they doing that?'

'Who knows how their minds work, I suppose it is their way of protecting us, but to my way of thinking it is only making us more obvious.'

Adam sighs, 'I will be so glad when this day is over. I never thought I would wish precious time away but I have to admit I am very nervous of the outcome of this conference.'

'I feel the same, Adam, but we must put on a strong front for the others; if they see we are getting jumpy it will not improve their nerves, we all need to feel positive and that will reflect in our presentation. It is our only chance to get the right reaction from the world's delegates.'

We arrive in Gateshead just after eleven and we are all looking out of the windows.

'What's that river, Daisy?'

'It's the Tyne, Violet.'

'Wow it's big, and look at all those different bridges. That one looks new, has it got a name?'

'Yes, Antony, that's the Millennium Bridge but it is also called the "blinking eye" because when a large ship goes under it the bridge rotates upwards and it looks like a closing eye.'

'That's clever,' states Steven.

'What is that great silver building over there, Adam; it looks like a giant armadillo?'

'That is The Sage, Julia, and that is where the conference is going to be.'

'Cool.'

Everyone laughs at Julia's choice of words; she is obviously acclimatising to the modern day language.

Our convoy makes its way to the rear of the building, which pleases us as there is so much activity at the front. The world's media are clamouring to get pictures and interviews from all the important people that are attending the conference.

We are ushered into a room laid out with food and drink. Adam is delighted to see Maddy waiting for them. 'I told you I would be here. I know how important this is for all of you.'

'I've missed you, Maddy. I wish you wouldn't keep disappearing.' Adam kissed her on her cheek.

'I promise that I won't disappear again.'

Adam smiled and took Maddy by the hand. 'I will make sure you don't.'

One of their escorts explains that everyone will have lunch before the conference begins at one precisely. We are shown facilities for freshening up and then asked if there is anything else we need. When we say no, the escorts leave and we hear the door locked after them.

'Well, they are rather abrupt and why did they lock us in. They either don't trust us or they're frightened someone might try to get to us before the meeting starts.'

'It is rather strange, Daniel, but at least we will get some peace for the next couple of hours.'

'I suppose so, we might as well start on the food, I have to say it does look rather nice and we did have breakfast really early.'

Adam laughs as we all dive into the banquet left for us. 'Anyone would have thought you lot hadn't eaten for weeks!'

He is pleased though that we have not shown any hint of nerves about the coming events.

'This is a lovely place isn't, Adam, what is it used for?'

'It was built mainly for concerts, Rose, they seem very proud of the acoustics in the main hall. I believe it is used for conferences as well and even weddings, but I think this is the most important meeting they have ever hosted. I get the feeling they are revelling in the fact they were chosen as a venue rather than somewhere in London.'

'Do you know the itinerary for this meeting, Adam?'

'As far as I know, there will be a short welcome and then an explanation as to why they have all been invited. This will consist of concerns regarding the changing weather patterns and the people's part in accelerating the affects. Then they will drop the bombshell and tell everyone who we are and why we are here.'

'That is going to cause bedlam.'

'Yes, Rose, it will, but the speaker is going to keep order and placate everyone hopefully by saying questions and explanations will be at the end of the presentation. They will show all four memory sticks and then we will be introduced properly.'

'Will all of us be expected to answer questions?'

'Probably but I will try to be main spokesperson.'

'What will happen if they don't believe what they see, or even worse they think we are part of some British plot to cause panic?'

'We have the younger disciples. Even the British government don't know what powers these children have. They will be our last hope in trying to convince people that we are here to try and save our planet for as long as possible from destruction.'

I am in deep thought and then say, 'Adam, what do you think our chances are of succeeding?'

'I really don't know, Rose. All we can do is try our best, what happens after that, well, I can't even begin to speculate.'

I shrug my shoulders and go to join the others at the food table.

Adam watches me go, he has a good idea of what I am thinking, it will be the same as everyone else. Will our lives be completely ruined once our secret is made public?'

The two hours pass quickly; we have all freshened up after eating our fill. There has been a great deal of chatting and laughing mainly caused by nervous energy. Then there is a knock at the door and we hear the key turn. It is a pleasant surprise to see Roger and Sylvia enter the room.

'Hello, everyone, we have been sent to take you to your seats, are you all ready?'

'I think so, Roger. It's nice to see you both again. We need friendly faces; I have to admit we are getting a bit nervous now.'

'It'll be fine, Adam, just follow us. You will be seated in the auditorium before they open the doors for the delegates and the media.'

Our partners are taken to a separate viewing room and then we are led down a corridor, no one speaks. Each one of us is caught up with our own thoughts. Eventually we reach the door that will lead us on to the vast stage.

'Here we are now, are we all ready?' asks Roger brightly.

He is greeted by a sea of dismal faces.

'Come on, it's not as bad as all that. This is your chance to complete your task. I would never have thought in a thousand years that you would have had the opportunity of a platform as extensive as this. You have all the world's leaders here and the media; I have never known anyone that has been given such freedom of speech as you all have now.'

'You're right, Roger; we needed a pep talk, thank you. Come on, gang, let's give them hell, because if they don't listen to us that's exactly what they will get.'

After Adam's short speech we brighten up and prepare ourselves for battle as we file onto the stage and into our seats.

The arena in front of us is huge and thankfully empty for now, behind us is a large screen where the Elders recordings will be shown. Our seats are at the left-hand side of the stage and on the right is a single podium where it is assumed the person opening the conference will stand. The whole auditorium is lit like daylight. We can see that the seats in the hall are marked with people's names and country.

We all hold our breath when we notice the doors open at the back of the hall, there is no rush, people are guided to their appointed seats. We are aware that our presence is causing a great deal of curiosity.

'Just take a deep breath and stay positive,' Adam whispers to us, 'remember we have the upper hand, we know why we are here.'

After about twenty minutes everyone is seated, the world's media are positioned at strategic places around the vast auditorium, it is important that they are able to relay accurately the course of the conference as it will be broadcast live to the four corners of the globe.

The hall falls silent when a very authoritative-looking man strides up to the podium, his demeanour left no doubt that the serious business is to start.

'Your Royal Highnesses, Ladies and Gentlemen, I would first like to thank you on behalf of the British Government for agreeing to attend this conference. What you about to see and hear is going to be incredibly hard to believe or understand but I assure you that it is all bona fide information. Because of its contents I would like to ask you to hold all questions until after the four short films have been seen.

'We have all experienced unusual weather patterns in the last few years, some of them causing catastrophic damage to countries and a great loss of lives. We have had many explanations, some feasible, some completely insane but we have never had suggestions of how we can control what is happening to our planet.'

At this point the auditorium becomes noisy with fidgeting, sighing and even vocal outbursts. People did not expect to be called to a lecture on green issues so close to the Olympic Games. This is not what they had come for, and for a while the whole conference looks as if it is collapsing; the speaker however takes control again.

'Please, please all we ask is for a few hours of your time. The people on my left are adequately informed to answer all your questions at the end of the films.'

The auditorium becomes hushed again and the speaker gives the signal for the lights to be lowered and the first film to start.

They run through the films taken from the Elders memory sticks one after the other and then the lights come back up.

There is a minute of silence before the barrage of questions start.

The American representative begins, 'Yeah, very good, but I didn't know we were brought here to watch a sci-fi movie.'

The speaker replies, 'They are not a film, they are fact.'

'Are you trying to tell us that those films come from the future, how gullible do you think we are?'

The speaker turns to Adam, 'Adam, will you like to reply.'

Adam stands up to face a hostile audience; he takes a deep breath, 'Good afternoon, my name is Adam and sitting behind me are my colleagues. We wish to explain why we are here and the content of the films you have just been watching. We shouldn't really be living in your time because myself and four of those with me belong to the year 2999.'

There is an audible noise of disbelief from the audience.

'How stupid do you think we are?' is shouted from the back of the auditorium.

'Will you just give me the chance to explain? Those films you have just seen, they are not fiction, they are of my home and my friends. I had to watch yet again my world being destroyed and you sit there ridiculing me and my home. What will it take for you to realise that what you saw is Earth in a thousand years. Your planet, this planet becoming a burning wilderness with air so acrid that everything, yes absolutely everything is dying!'

The media is broadcasting live around the world and the chaos it is causing is jamming every form of communication. People are asking for confirmation that this is not some kind of stunt to magnify the impact of the Olympic Games just to make sure that all eyes are on Britain.

Questions rain down on us and we try to keep calm and answer clearly and simply.

'What about the ones you call the new disciples, what are their roles in your so-called quest to save the planet?'

'That is a simple question to answer,' replies Daisy, 'they were sent back in time to save them from imminent death.'

The hall goes silent. It seems that the information that is being given is too much to take in, or maybe it is because what is being told is too horrible to actually believe. It is much easier to ridicule the facts than to accept them.

Adam knows they are going round in circles, they have their trump card yet to play. He is hoping it will not be necessary but there did not seem to be any positive signs of understanding the Armageddon that is approaching the planet.

The speaker comes forward and raises his arms to silence the crescendo of voices rising in a never-ending barrage of questions.

When it quietens down he addresses the hall, 'I think now is a good time for a break, to allow us to collect our thoughts and refresh our bodies. The meeting will convene in an hour; refreshments are laid out for you in the restaurant. We will start again at 4pm. Thank you.'

We are ushered off the stage and we are guided back to our private room, where we too have refreshments waiting. We all know that we now have to use our trump card. If that does not produce the right response then there is nothing more we can do.

Steven and Antony are talking quietly in the corner, Adam has noticed their separation from the rest of us and knows what they are discussing. He makes his way across the room to join them.

'You both look very serious, how do you think it's going?'

'Complete rubbish, Adam. They just seem intent on proving that everything they have seen and heard is a gigantic hoax. We find it completely humiliating, they have watched their planet dying, our friends dying. In fact absolutely everything they know and treasure was being horrifically destroyed in front of their eyes and still they want more proof. Steven and I have decided that we will have to show them from our perspective in the only way we can. I will go first but if the strain on my body proves too much for me then Steven will continue.'

Adam sighs, he had really hoped it would not come to this and he realises how dangerous it is for the boys to have to show the world through their eyes.

'You are both very brave and no one will have blamed you if you had refused to take the stage today.'

'There is nothing more we can do, Adam, bravery does not come into it, bravery is what the people in our time have shown in their dying moments. We have no other choice but to salute those we have left and try to our last breath to make these idiots realise what they are doing to our planet.'

'Well said, Simon.' We clap our approval.

Adam, Simon and Antony are so wrapped in their conversation that they had not known that the rest of us had stopped talking and are listening to them.

There is a knock at the door and we realise it is time to face the opposition. We are led back to the stage, it is an empty arena in front of us and we thought everyone had left, and then the big doors at the back open and people start to come in to take to their seats once more.

It is nearly ten minutes before everyone is settled and then the hush is deafening, every single person is wondering what is going to happen next. Delegates etc. have obviously been discussing what has been seen and heard while they were on their break. However, it does not take a mind reader to work out that prognosis fell into the usual different camps, those who believe. Those who think it is a trick. Those who are too frightened to believe. Those who wonder how they can make some kind of profit from the information. Those who think it is divine recompense and those who would just like to live in blissful ignorance because it wouldn't affect their lives now would it!

The Speaker approaches his podium and looks at the sea of faces watching him expectantly; he turns to Adam hoping that he will be able to magically produce something that will sway the conference to a positive to conclusion. However, he knows that everything has been shown and spoken about already and all of that hasn't seemed enough for the audience in front of him.

Adam stands up and smiles at the Speaker, who then sits down admiring the persistence and stamina of these strange young people.

'Good afternoon, everyone. You must be weary of my voice and confused by all that you have seen. We have opened our lives bare to you, but we sense there is still doubt in many of your minds. There is not much more we can do to convince you but we were all sent here from the future by our Elders to fulfil a task. We are going to lay our lives on the line with just one more revelation. The Elders gave us a chance to live while everyone else knew that they were going to die eminently, we want to give you and your future generations the opportunity to live and enjoy life on Earth for as long as possible. So two of our youngest members have agreed to show you just one more proof that we have been revealing nothing but the truth.'

The Government officials backstage and in the auditorium look bewildered; they thought they knew everything that there is to know about these young people. It seems though; they have kept something from them. The officials are now feeling apprehensive, is this a trick or something that will threaten the dignitaries. They just hope they haven't made a very big mistake.

'Antony, Steven, please come and join me.'

The boys stand either side of Adam.

'Are you sure you want to do this?' he whispers to them.

'There is no alternative, Adam,' Antony quietly replies.

Adam lifts his head to face the audience.

'These boys left their home at least a decade after us therefore they have different, how can I describe it, let's just say they are able to do things that we cannot. When we original travellers arrived back to your time we found that our IQ was much higher than children here of the same age. These younger members have gone a step further in the evolution chain. I hope you will remember that they are still children though. Antony, would you like to begin?'

Antony steps forward and looks at the mass of faces in front of him.

'Hello, everyone. I hope I can help you to believe that we are telling the truth and our only aim is to prolong the life of this planet. What I am about to do will drain my energy so there is a limit to the time I can continue the experiment. There is nothing weird about me, like all humans my brain stores everything I have seen and heard. The only difference is I can show you what my brain has absorbed.'

There is an immediate amount of whispering coming from the four corners of the auditorium. People cannot believe what they have just heard.

The Speaker stands up. 'Please, please let the child continue.'

'Antony, is there anything you need to show us this new revelation?'

Antony turns to the Speaker, 'Yes, please. Can I have the screen at the back of the stage put back in place? Then I would like all lights turned off and any other form of electrical equipment.'

Adam is proud of Antony, he is commanding the stage without a shred of nerves.

'Why do you want everything turned off, Antony?'

'Because, sir, if there is no electric our honoured guests will not be able to think that there is some form of trickery going on. I hope that they will realise that we are telling the truth.'

The Speaker turns to his superiors at the side of the stage and they nod their heads.

'We will do as you ask, Antony. How long will this last?'

'For as long as my strength holds out, sir.'

The screen appears at the back of the stage and one by one the lights go out. The auditorium is in complete darkness Antony can still be seen, but only barely, as far above him is a skylight letting in the waning afternoon light.

There is a deathly hush and then Antony's eyes become brighter, he turns to face the screen, as he does this rays of light project from his eyes onto the screen. Within a few seconds images can be seen, children playing, adults working and birds flying around. As the images become 3D the sound starts.

Antony plays back his memories of his old life; he even shows the views outside the glass domes, the destruction, and the hell on Earth that he has witnessed. He relays the deaths of his friends, the animals and the vegetation. Antony continues his recollection of his old life for twenty minutes, the hall remains silent.

We are getting worried, we wonder how much longer Antony can continue to over exert his body and mind.

Suddenly Antony collapses to the floor, the lights come on and medics run to his aid. He has stopped breathing.

Antony is rushed away in an ambulance.

Adam faces the stunned audience, he is so angry.

'You've got what you came for. Sensationalism, are you happy now. That young lad could well have given his life for what he believes in, for what he is trying to convince you all to believe in. He wants to help you give this planet another five hundred years before the destruction begins. It is up to you now, Earth needs Global Co-operation, what are you going to do? Will you continue to fight over territory, money, religion and any other petty arguments you have? All those things will mean absolutely nothing when the planet reacts to the damage you are constantly raining down on it.'

At that point, we are escorted from the stage. The audience sits still for a few minutes and then start to leave the auditorium in total silence. Each representative from every civilisation of the world lost in their own thoughts.

But what are they thinking?

It is now up to everyone on our planet to put the protection mode ON.